"I want to get out of here."

Jane kept the scissors pointed at the stranger. He claimed he didn't know her, but she had learned people hardly ever told the truth.

With her free hand she tested the doorknob behind her. It wouldn't budge. She was trapped in the isolated cabin. Somehow she found her voice. "W-who are you?"

Before he could reply, they heard the crunch of tires on the snow outside, and then footsteps on the porch. The man's eyes widened. "Hush," he mouthed.

"No!" Jane wanted to scream, but before she could, the man grasped the wrist of her hand holding the scissors and tossed them away. His other hand he clamped over her mouth. When she heard the sound of footsteps by the cellar door, she tried to jerk free.

"Oh, no, you don't," he whispered, his hot breath feathering her face. He removed his hand from her mouth and pulled her against his powerful body, rendering her scream nothing more than a muted squeak. "I said be quiet."

Fear vanquished her confusion. She didn't care who he was, or why her body seemed to know him. She gulped another lungful of air, determined that this scream would tear out his eardrums. But before she could let loose, his strong mouth and soft lips came down on hers.

ABOUT THE AUTHOR

When asked about why she wanted to write romance fiction, Adrianne Lee had this to say: "I wanted to be Doris Day when I grew up. You know, singing my way through one wonderful romance after another. And I did. I fell in love with and married my high school sweetheart and became the mother of three beautiful daughters. Family and love are very important to me and I hope you enjoy the way I weave them through my stories. I love hearing from readers." If you want a response or an autographed bookmark from Adrianne Lee, please send a SASE to P.O. Box 3835, Sequim, WA 98382.

Books by Adrianne Lee

HARLEQUIN INTRIGUE
296—SOMETHING BORROWED, SOMETHING BLUE
354—MIDNIGHT COWBOY
383—EDEN'S BABY

Don't miss any of our special offers. Write to us at the following address for information on our newest releases.

Harlequin Reader Service
U.S.: 3010 Walden Ave., P.O. Box 1325, Buffalo, NY 14269
Canada: P.O. Box 609, Fort Erie, Ont. L2A 5X3

Little Girl Lost
Adrianne Lee

Harlequin Books

TORONTO • NEW YORK • LONDON
AMSTERDAM • PARIS • SYDNEY • HAMBURG
STOCKHOLM • ATHENS • TOKYO • MILAN
MADRID • WARSAW • BUDAPEST • AUCKLAND

For—Betty Daus, Barbara Smith and Kayleen Marlow,
whose enthusiasm and unswerving support
bolster me in the hard times.

And Kris J. Sundberg, one terrific attorney
and an even better friend.

ISBN 0-373-22438-9

LITTLE GIRL LOST

Copyright © 1997 by Adrianne Lee Undsderfer

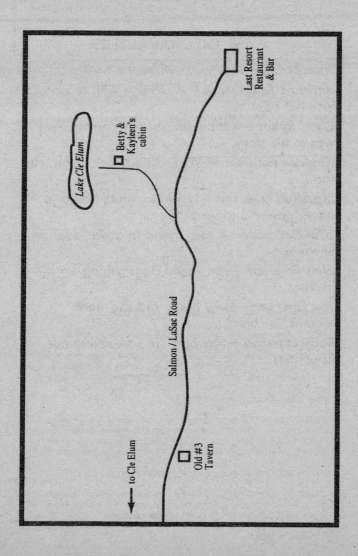

CAST OF CHARACTERS

Jane Dolan—A woman without a past.

Barbara Jo Dawson—A woman with reason to fear her past.

Chad Ryker—A man whose only commitment was to his story.

Kayleen Emerson—When things got tough, she ran.

Marshall Emerson—How far would he go to attain power and wealth?

Edie Harcourt—A real friend in a world full of enemies.

Elvis Emerson—He would do anything for his brother.

Joy Emerson—How badly did she want Marshall's child?

Betty Dawson—Her only sin was loving her daughters.

Chapter One

Two more women had been murdered. Strangers to her. Just names on the radio. At least that was what Jane had thought until four hours ago. Her head still pounded from the shock, her hands still trembled. The Cle Elum *Gazette* lay on the truck seat beside her. The murdered women's pictures were blazoned on the front page, photographs that had jarred loose the first memory she'd had of her past life since the crack-up on Interstate 90 five years ago.

Just thinking of the catastrophic accident brought the acrid stench of burning metal and flesh into her nostrils, the horrendous sights into her mind's eye. All she remembered of it was walking down the freeway, clutching her baby to her chest. Carnage had lain behind her—a tangle of intertwined buses, semitrailers and cars, jammed together like logs on a giant campfire.

Miraculously, she and Missy had escaped without serious injury; Missy with a tiny contusion on one cheek, herself with most of her hair singed off and a lump on her temple that had stolen her memory. The emergency-room doctor, a true optimist, had claimed that her memory might return any time.

She'd also assured Jane that someone would come to identify them.

Jane had never understood why, but that assurance had terrified her more than her nightmares of the burning bus. She'd heeded that self-protective instinct and had managed to survive for the past five years without needing to know who she'd been, or what her life had been like before the freeway pileup.

Why was she starting to remember now?

Why was it suddenly important to remember now?

And why did the prospect of remembering still terrify her?

She stepped on the gas, increasing the pickup's speed as she left the town of Ronald, Washington, behind. Black clouds hung low, obscuring the snowcapped mountains. It would soon be dark. The road wound through the woods, leading her toward her destination, but her mind lingered on the events of the day.

Jane stole another glance at the *Gazette.* She hadn't actually recognized the two women from these photographs, but some instinct, some indefinable sense, had told her they were connected to the part of her life that she feared recalling. The feeling was so strong she'd gone to the Cle Elum funeral home where the Kittitas County coroner had had the bodies taken.

Their images, still too vivid, sprang into her head. Her stomach churned. Sweat broke across her upper lip and fear gripped her heart. As she'd looked on the lifeless faces of the two women, she'd been struck again with an overwhelming sense of recognition. With a blood-chilling dread. But even the unnamed terror hadn't kept the words *mother* and *sister* from screaming through her brain.

Bile climbed into the back of her throat. She forced it down with a hard swallow. If those two women were her mother and sister, if they had also survived the multiple vehicle crash, been living less than an hour from her for the past five years, why hadn't they come looking for her? For Missy?

It seemed too far-fetched to imagine that they had also lost their memories. What then? But as she tried to remember, panic closed her throat. Even as she gulped for air, Jane wondered if that was it. Fear. Had her mother and sister been frightened by the same nameless terror that haunted her now?

The thought preoccupied her, and Jane drove another mile before realizing she'd passed the lane she sought. She maneuvered a U-turn, tires squealing like the keening inside her head. If only she could tap into the source of her fear.

At length she found the right driveway and pulled into it. The woods were denser, pressing close, blocking out the ominous clouds that threatened momentarily to unleash a predicted snowstorm.

Her tires crunched on the frozen, unpaved ground, and the pickup bounced from one pothole to another, jostling Jane, sending her purse to the floorboards. Slowing the truck helped little. She passed an A-frame log cabin that appeared deserted. Although it was a Wednesday afternoon, nearing most people's dinner hour, the next two dwellings were also dark. Many of the residences around here, she knew, were weekend and summer homes owned by people in the Seattle area.

The murdered women's cabin hugged the edge of Lake Cle Elum and should be just ahead. Panic stirred within her. She struggled to stay calm. She had to do this.

She thought again of her encounter at the funeral home with the deputy sheriff in charge of the case. He'd seemed a bit too curious as to why she'd wanted this address, and her explanation had only caused his hard eyes to narrow with increased suspicion. She hadn't stuck around to pur-

sue the subject with him, getting the address instead from
a local vendor only too eager to discuss the grisly murders
with her.

The road ended abruptly. Through the woods beyond,
she could see the shallow, frozen expanse of Lake Cle
Elum. She braked. Her gaze brushed over the rustic, sin-
gle-story cabin, which looked to be about a thousand
square feet in size.

A glaring band of yellow ribboned the Douglas firs surrounding the small residence—crime-scene tape. It flapped
in the wind, harsh saffron against the bleakness of the win-
ter-bare trees. Jane felt as if someone were winding the
tape around her heart, her head, squeezing ever tighter.

She drew a wobbly breath. Falling apart would not do.
She shifted into Reverse and backed the pickup forty yards
down the road to the nearest house, parking behind the
garage. Getting arrested would not do, either.

Cold nipped her cheeks and nose as she scrambled quietly out of the truck and ducked stealthily through the trees
toward the cabin. Ignoring its no-trespass warning, she
scooted under the police tape and crept toward the porch.
Her heart thudded in her ears. Red evidence tape banded
the front door.

Jane stole up to a picture window. Rubber-lined drapes
concealed the interior, fitting together so tightly there was
not even a crack to peer through. Her frustrated sigh
fogged the air in front of her face. She had to get inside.
The thought scared her as much as it lured her. She fought
the urge to flee. There might be something here that would
help return all of her memory.

Perhaps the women had kept a key hidden outside. She
bent to lift the rubber mat. As her eyes came level with
the doorknob, she froze. Just where the solid red band
pressed against door and frame, the tape was slit—cleanly,

as if by a sharp knife or razor blade. A shiver tracked her spine. Someone had been here before her.

Might be here still.

She jerked around, rapidly scanning the perimeter. The whole area appeared deserted. That didn't mean there wasn't someone inside the cabin. Her stomach pinched. Maybe she should call this off. Forget the whole thing. *And go on wondering forever who I really am?*

No. Now that the memories had started, there was no turning back, no more running. She had to brave this. But not without a weapon. She hefted a short, club-size hunk of wood from the pile stacked beside the door and reached for the knob.

Panic rushed her again, and sweat flushed her body. Maybe she should call the deputy and report the violation of the crime scene. She saw again his hard eyes and knew she would have her own explaining to do if he found her here. Either she did this now, or not at all. An impulse like none she'd ever felt wrapped her gloved hand around the doorknob.

It twisted easily. She shoved the door inward. It emitted a minute creak. Her mouth dried. Her pulse skittered. She gripped the split log until her knuckles ached. Stepping cautiously inside, Jane called out, "Is anyone here?"

No one answered, but a squeak like someone stepping on a loose floorboard vibrated from within the depths of the cabin. Her pulse leaped higher. She called out again. Her voice echoed back to her. The squeak was not repeated. Nor was there any other sound that would indicate the presence of another person. Jane breathed easier. The noise had probably been nothing more than the normal groaning old houses like this were prone to make. That, and her imagination.

She swung the door shut against the weather, unintentionally closing out what little daylight remained. For several heart-thudding moments, she stood stock-still in the darkness listening to the hum of a tired refrigerator motor, detecting the faint scent of dead fire ash, old bacon grease and something indistinguishably distasteful in the icy air.

The moment her eyes adjusted to the dimness, she found a light switch. The sudden illumination revealed a small living room furnished with a potbellied woodstove, an ancient television set, two worn armchairs, and two mismatched end tables sporting gaudily painted ceramic lamps.

Jane took a step forward, but stopped cold as her gaze fell on two large dark stains, like huge pools of spilled ink, on the threadbare carpet. Again, bile rushed up into her throat. She choked it down, bringing her free hand to her aching temple. Somehow, she had to get through this. She glanced at the odd black powdery substance that coated the surfaces of the tables. Soot? Or fingerprint dust?

A shiver ran up her spine. Making herself move, she inspected the house. Two tiny bedrooms opened onto the living room, with a tinier bathroom in between. A fair-size kitchen at the back accessed a cellar that apparently doubled as a laundry room; the washer and dryer looked on their last legs. Indeed, all the furnishings appeared to be garage-sale rejects.

She thought of her own cosy apartment in Ellensburg and her throat constricted. God, to think Kayleen and Mom had lived in this bleak hovel for five years... Jane started as though an unseen hand had reached out of the past and slapped her. Her vision blurred. Her knees wobbled. She bumped against the wall.

Kayleen and Mom. Fear throttled her. She gasped for air. The deputy sheriff had identified the women as Mary and Louise Dickerson. Inexplicably, she had wanted to correct him, but hadn't known how or why the names seemed so wrong.

Because they were wrong.

Kayleen and Mom. Mom... Of course, Betty. Betty and Kayleen...what? She struggled to recall. Pain wrapped her skull tighter. Dickerson? No. She was certain it was something else. But what?

The answer eluded her.

But now she was positive that they had been using aliases, and there was only one reason for that: They *had* been afraid of something. Or someone. Ice water flowed in her veins. *Get what you want and get out of here.*

Quickly, Jane returned to the first bedroom, set her club at her feet and flung open the closet door. A few dresses, slacks, and blouses. Nothing of quality. Nothing like Mom had been used to. This new revelation coming so soon on the heels of the last, again stole her breath. What had her mother been used to?

Something more or better than this. She didn't know why, but she suspected they had once been very well-off. What had driven them to this? How had they ended up in near poverty without a single possession from their former lives?

She turned her attention to the chest of drawers. The black dust was here as well, soiling the scarf that covered the scarred maple top and lightly coating a hefty perfume bottle. She recognized the brand, a fragrance that could be bought by the gallon for pennies; its sweet, cloying aroma lingered in the air, but the scent released no memories for Jane.

She began searching the chest of drawers, realizing that someone had already been here, evidenced by the black dust smudging lingerie and sweaters. In a bottom dresser drawer, she came across a cheap jewelry box. She sat on the bed, settled the box on her lap and lifted the lid. Inside were several pairs of earrings—inexpensive, faddish, nothing dating back more than a couple of years; nothing old enough to merit her remembering it.

Impotent fury and disappointment got the better of her. She swept the box from her lap. It tumbled to the floor, the worthless jewelry scattering. The clatter returned her senses. This was a crime scene. She wasn't supposed to be here. She sure as hell didn't want to leave evidence of her presence.

Cursing under her breath, Jane leaned over to gather the pieces. A flash of gold among the brass caught her eye. It belonged to a good-size, heart-shaped locket. Even from where she sat, Jane could see it was old.

She reached for it, discovering that it was not only old, but of genuine quality. The scrollwork was detailed, intricate, and somehow familiar. Her headache thumped harder and the precious metal felt as if it were burning her hand. Both convinced Jane that she was right about the piece. Hope and excitement battled her fear of remembering, but try as she might, she couldn't make a connection.

With her fingernail, she nudged the small lever at the side of the locket. The heart sprang open. Each half held a photo of a young girl, probably ten and twelve years of age. One of the girls had hair the same white blond as Kayleen's had been; the other girl had braids the same dark mahogany as her own hair. Had features very like her own. Excitement squeezed her chest. It had to be. This had to be a photograph of herself. The other girl, then, would be Kayleen.

Jane glanced at her reflection in the full-length mirror nailed to the closet door, then gazed again at the photo, seeking remembrance of the time when she had looked this young.

The migraine won out. Discouraged, she snapped the locket shut. The tiny *click* seemed to echo in her ears, and a name wavered just beyond her grasp; not Jane Dolan—the name given her by the emergency-room doctor—but her real name.

She clutched the locket to her thudding heart, her eyes squeezed shut as she strained for the memory. Nothing, not even something as simple as her name, could penetrate the wall of fear that hid her past from her. And the two people who could have told her had yesterday been brutally slain in the other room.

No. She would not dwell on that. Could not think on it without falling apart completely. Shoving the thought away, she could not avoid another: The person who had crossed the tape before her might very well have been the murderer. The house chose that moment to let loose another eerie creak—as though someone were in the kitchen. Alarm spurted through Jane.

She shoved the locket into her coat pocket and lurched off the bed, gathering the jewelry back into its box. Had the murderer come back? Had he been here all along? With her pulse galloping, she returned the box to the bottom dresser drawer, reclaimed her crude club and hurried into the living room.

It was deserted.

She didn't waste time in relief. She doused the light, started opening the door a crack. The crunch of tires outside paralyzed her. She mustn't be caught. Not by the police...or anyone else.

Jane moved like a blind person in unfamiliar surroundings through the dark house until she reached the cellar door. She gained the top of the stairs, her heart thumping like a hammer. Cautiously, she pulled the door shut just as the front one opened. Her breath huffed out of her in quick, short spurts.

The cellar had two tiny, ceiling-high windows that offered a modicum of light. Stepping gingerly, she descended the wooden staircase to the cellar's shadowy depths. The air was cold and smelled of laundry detergent and stored apples. As soon as the soles of her cowboy boots touched solid concrete, she groped her way to the corner where she'd seen the washer and dryer. Overhead, she heard heavy footfalls.

Was it the police? Or someone more dangerous?

The footsteps reached the kitchen. Jane ducked down beside the washing machine just as the door banged open. Light flooded the cellar. With her length of wood at the ready, she jammed herself against the cold appliance. She held her breath and listened hard. A man muttered something unintelligible, but she heard enough to realize that if she knew this voice she didn't recognize it.

She had to see him.

With her pulse drumming in her ears, she peered around the washer. A bear of a man filled the doorway. A Mariners baseball cap reposed atop his greasy black hair and an ugly scar slashed his left cheek. It was a face she wouldn't soon forget, but one she did not recollect.

He descended the first step. Jane flinched and pressed herself lower between the concrete wall and the edge of the washing machine. The man pounded down the stairs, his footfalls as heavy as the thudding of her heart. He moved across the cellar to within inches of where she hid. The stench of his flowery aftershave, combined with the acid taste of her own fear, sickened her.

A second passed.

Jane gripped her club tighter.

Afraid to breathe, she cowered just out of sight.

Seconds were soon a minute.

She felt light-headed from lack of air.

Scarface muttered, "Told the boss this was a waste of time. Ain't no kiddy stuff down here, neither."

No kiddy stuff? As she risked taking a short breath, Jane pondered that. Were these two people looking for a child? She thought of Missy, glad that she was safe in Ellensburg with her sitter, Mrs. Ferguson. She wouldn't want her little girl in the hands of a man like this.

Again shoe leather slapped the wooden stairs, this time going up. The light blinked off. Jane chanced another peek at the man. He stood in the open doorway, dialing a cell phone. He pressed it to his ear. "It's me. He didn't lie, boss. Don't know why you thought there'd be any kid's stuff here."

He listened, starting through the door, still talking. "I'm leavin' now."

The door banged shut. When she heard Scarface moving toward the living room, Jane let her breath out in a whoosh. Her heart was not as easily brought back to normal. Why had he and his "boss" expected to find a child's things at Mom and Kayleen's house? What child? An unthinkable possibility flashed into her mind. Surely not *her* child? Not Missy? The prospect washed her with terror.

The voice overhead silenced. The front door slammed. Then all was quiet. She waited where she was for five minutes, swearing she could hear more than her own breathing in the semidarkness of the cellar.

Rats?

That thought sent her rushing up the stairs. At the landing she groped for the door handle. It wouldn't budge. "Oh, no, he locked me in."

She gave the knob another twist, harder this time. It resisted. She swung her club at it. The clank of wood against metal rang out and the recoil from the impact sent pain jarring up her arm to her shoulder. Jane swore and tossed the piece of log to the cellar floor.

Exasperated with herself and the situation, she spun around and gaped at the two dinky windows set high in the back wall. Snow floated against their grungy panes. Already the ground was layered an inch deep, and the earlier duskiness of the day had given way to a reflective full-moon brightness, alleviating the inky darkness of the cellar.

Consternation raced through her. If she didn't get home soon, Mrs. Ferguson would be frantic. Would probably think she'd had an accident. "Damn!"

How was she going to get out? Even if she could reach the windows and knock out the glass, she could never squeeze through. Of course, she could scream for help and hope someone would hear—a possibility as remote as her winning the state lotto.

What she needed was something to jimmy the door latch. Hadn't she seen a tool chest? She groped for the light switch. As the illumination chased away the shadows, she released the breath she hadn't realized she'd been holding, and started down the stairs.

Her mind swung back to the man who'd just left. Who was Scarface? Who was the "he" Scarface had referred to? The murderer? Her knees felt like wet sponges as that idea took hold, raising myriad other questions. Had "boss" hired someone to kill Kayleen and Mom? Was "boss" someone they knew?

Someone she might also know? Someone she didn't remember? The pain in her head sent a flash of white before her eyes and she shook herself.

She needed to get out of here. Spotting the tool chest,

she knelt and flipped open the lid. Inside were paintbrushes and a pair of sharp-pointed scissors.

Behind her, boxes tumbled.

Jane's pulse skipped. She grasped the scissors and lurched around, expecting to see a mammoth rat.

Her heart stopped completely as a man, rising like a cobra to the music of a flute, heaved himself up from among the tumbled boxes.

A scream jump-started her heart. Shrieking, she lunged up the stairs.

"Hey!" The man sprinted after her.

She wheeled around, brandishing the scissors's sharp points at him. He stopped two steps below her, and Jane found herself staring into the grayest blue eyes she had ever seen, a jaw so lean and chiseled it could cut steel, a nose bold with generations of character, and blond brows so furrowed they must be giving him a headache to rival her own.

His tawny hair was long and wild, and he exuded a startling raw sensuality that tickled something deeply feminine in her. That paralyzed her. Her breath clogged in her throat.

Dear God, he was drop-dead gorgeous, but if he was the killer returned to the scene of the crime, she would be the one dropping dead.

The salty taste of fear flushed Jane's senses and restored her nerve. At work, she'd been manhandled by the occasional drunk and had given as good as she'd gotten. Without a deadly weapon. She waved the scissors at him. "Stay away from me or I swear I'll gut you like a deer."

"Whoa." A wry grin quirked his mouth as he pulled back, his hands raised in a gesture that was at once disarming and little-boyish. "I've had women threaten me for sins I've admittedly committed, but, lady, I've never laid eyes on you before. Trust me, I won't hurt you."

"If I've never laid eyes on you before now, why would I *trust* you?" Was he lying? Did she know him? She lifted the scissors higher.

He replied, "All I want is what you want—to get out of here."

Keeping the scissors pointed at his midsection, Jane studied his face anew, trying to ignore the heady pull of his aftershave. He claimed he didn't know her. Truth or lie? It unsettled her to think she would feel this drawn to him if she didn't know him.

She delved the aching chasm of her mind for the answer while extending her free hand behind her back to test the knob again. She had no memory of this man, and the damned knob wouldn't budge. Her mouth dried. She was trapped. Somehow she found her voice. "Who are you?"

From outside came the crunch of tires on snow, then of footsteps on the porch. The man's eyes widened. "Hush."

He rose another step. Jane reared back, bumping the door, lifting the scissors.

"Quiet," he growled. With one swift, lithe movement he joined her on the landing and grasped the wrist of the hand holding the scissors.

"No." Jane started to scream. Cursing, the man clamped his free hand over her mouth, then twisted her arm behind her back, wrenched the scissors from her grip and tossed them toward the cardboard boxes. They landed with a soft thud.

Beyond the cellar door, from somewhere inside the house, came the sound of footsteps again. Hope flared in Jane. She jerked her wrist free, levered her palms against his chest, bunching her arm muscles, lifting a knee.

"Oh, no, you don't," he whispered, his hot breath feathering her face, shooting fear and confusion through her. He raised his hand from her mouth and grabbed her wrists, pulling her against his powerful body in a vise grip that eclipsed all her struggles as effectively as any passionate embrace, bumping the wind from her lungs and rendering her second attempt to scream nothing more than a muted squeak.

"I said, be quiet," he ground out in a clenched whisper.

Fear vanquished her confusion. She didn't care who he was, or why her body seemed to know him. She gulped another lungful of air. This scream would tear out his eardrums.

His mouth landed on hers.

CHAD RYKER KNEW HE WAS over the top on this. Dangerously so. But pushing the envelope was as natural to him as the crooked pinkie finger on his left hand. Besides, ignoring conventions had paid off too many times for him to question or alter what some felt was his greatest personality flaw.

Even so, scaring women was definitely not his style; however, this damned female didn't seem to appreciate the peril they faced if they were discovered.

He was acutely aware of her soft curves pressed taut against him; acutely aware that it had been too long since he'd enjoyed a woman's touch. But he liked his women to enjoy the experience, too, and there was no mistaking how much this one was hating it. He understood her terror, but he didn't dare lift his mouth from her supple lips and explain. Not the way she was squirming. She would scream the roof down.

That could get them tossed in jail.

Or killed.

Over the pulse thundering in his ears, he strained to hear

any sound coming through the cellar door. A loud bang could have been the front door being slammed.

JANE BIT THE MAN'S lower lip. He let her go with a yelp, and she drove a knee into his groin with every ounce of her will to live.

"Ughhh!" He dropped to his knees, groaning.

Jane charged, ramming the heels of her hands into his shoulders. His head jerked up. As she shoved him off the landing, she saw pain and surprise in his stunning gray-blue eyes. He shot backward, then ground to a stop half-way down the stairs, his boot heels hooked on a riser, his whole body bent forward at the waist. He sounded like he was dying.

Screaming for help, Jane jerked around and grabbed the doorknob. It resisted—then, to her surprised relief, popped loose and the door sprang open. It hadn't been locked. Just stuck. She darted through it. No one was in the house. Or outside. All that remained of whoever had just been there was one set of footprints in the snow, leading to a pair of tire tracks.

With her heart thundering and her feet slipping, Jane ran hell-bent for her pickup. She had just yanked the door open when she heard the man call out, "Stop or I'll shoot!"

Fear twanged down her spine. Did he have a gun? Not that she'd felt one while she'd been pressed to every inch of him, but she wasn't waiting to find out.

Bracing for a bullet in the back, she landed in the cab of her truck and had the engine started before she saw him coming, staggering through the trees. She slammed the pickup into gear and seconds later fishtailed onto the main road.

"Dammit!" Hurting like hell, Chad grabbed a tree and

caught his breath, staring after the truck, his reporter's brain automatically recording the license number.

A hint of her delicate perfume lingered on his coat. Who was she? What connection did she have to his story? He was damned well going to find out. "Go ahead and run, hellion. You can't hide from me."

Chapter Two

In her Ellensburg apartment, some thirty miles east of Cle Elum, Jane's doorbell rang. The second she saw her best friend Edie Harcourt standing there, she had to resist the urge to throw herself into her arms. "I didn't mean for you to run over."

"Like I could run in this snow." Edie, the emergency-room doctor who had first attended to Jane and Missy after the interstate accident five years ago, looked every day of her thirty-six years tonight. "My legs feel like I'm wearing concrete boots. One emergency after another since five this morning."

Contrition flashed through Jane. She'd been so wrapped up in herself, she hadn't considered that this weather would likely have caused Edie as brutal a day as her own. "Want to talk about it?"

"Heavens no. I'm not up to a replay." Edie shrugged out of her damp coat and hat and hooked them on the hall tree next to Jane's and Missy's parkas, slipped out of her boots and ran a hand through her short blond hair without concern that it now stood on end. Her soft blue eyes were awash with worry. "I want to know what's going on with you. You sounded so strange on the phone."

Jane supposed she had sounded strange. She certainly

felt strange, with all the unfamiliar sensations and emotions buzzing through her like a horde of ugly, stinging insects. She rubbed her temples where the headache lingered. "I'll tell you all as soon as Missy is in bed."

"Mommy!" Both women turned at the child's voice issuing from the bathroom. "I'm getting cold!"

"Oops, I was just drying her off when the doorbell rang." Jane managed a smile and pointed Edie toward the kitchen. "There's fresh coffee. Help yourself."

Like the rest of the compact apartment, the kitchen was decorated in shades of gray blue. Jane had often wondered whether she'd always had a penchant for these hues or if the affinity had come on her after the accident. Now it struck her that her favorite colors were very like the eyes of the tawny-haired mystery man at the cabin. She wondered again if she knew him. Knew him intimately?

The question zinged a stab of pain through her skull, roused her fear and sent his disturbing image fleeing.

She hurried to the bathroom. Five-year-old Missy stood on the mat, a huge towel draped around her shoulders like a floor-length cape. Jane dropped to her knees, lifted the towel upward and rubbed the fluffy fabric against her daughter's long, wet, platinum hair, then gently across her chubby body.

Missy gazed at her earnestly. "Mrs. Ferguson and I built a snowman today."

Grinning, Jane rewrapped the towel around her daughter and hugged her. Some of the tension in her muscles dissolved. "I'll bet it's the best one on the block."

Missy peered up with deep-set aqua eyes that were duplicates of her own. "Can I show Auntie Edie and you?"

"Not tonight, sweetie. It's past your bedtime."

"Aw."

"Hurry and get your jammies on and I'll read you a story."

"I want Auntie Edie to read it."

Jane tapped her daughter's button nose. "All right, sweet pea. You may ask her as soon as you're dressed."

"Goody. I'll get dressed real quick."

Missy hurried off to her room, and Jane returned to the kitchen, filled a mug with coffee and joined Edie at the eating bar. Edie was reading the Cle Elum *Gazette*. Jane had forgotten to put it away when she'd arrived home. Maybe it was just as well. It would make what she had to tell her friend a bit easier.

If anything could make this easier.

Edie finished reading and glanced up. "Life is so precarious. But no one should die like these two women did."

Heartbreak jabbed Jane and tears clogged her throat. She'd thought she was ready to talk about this. Maybe not.

"Auntie Edie, you can read me my story now."

Both women turned toward the little girl. Missy wore red pajama tops and green bottoms. Since she'd started kindergarten this past September, she'd insisted she was big enough to dress herself and even though she didn't often select the right color combinations, as now, or always manage to get the right buttons in the right holes, Jane never criticized.

Grateful for the time that Missy's interruption would give her to regain control of her anguish, Jane glanced at Edie. "I volunteered you."

Edie smiled with genuine delight. She loved children, but had never been able to carry one to full term, and Jane knew the heartache it caused her. Edie replied, "I would love to read to my favorite girl in the whole wide world."

Missy beamed. Her cheeks were round and peachy and deeply dimpled.

A warm glow swirled through Jane, melting the innermost layer of chill that had incased her heart since this afternoon. Whatever she might have done wrong in this life, she'd done this one thing absolutely right. She bent down and opened her arms. "I want a big kiss and then you can have your story."

Missy threw her arms around Jane and gave her a noisy smooch, then let go of her and scooted over to Edie, grasping her hand. "I have a new book from the library."

Laughing, Edie allowed herself to be dragged off the barstool and led across the living room.

Twenty minutes later, Missy was tucked in and the two women had regrouped at the eating bar with freshly filled mugs. Jane felt more in control. Ready to talk. Ready for the scrutiny of Edie's professional eye.

The doctor's frown held concern. "Something serious has happened. Tell me."

The moment of truth had arrived and again tears threatened. Fighting them, Jane glanced toward the kitchen window. The miniblinds were closed against the night. Ellensburg was home to Central Washington University, and several students resided in this building. The shrieks of laughter drifting up from two stories below indicated that a group of them were out enjoying the fresh snowfall.

Jane drew a bracing breath and faced her friend. "Those two women in the paper...I believe they're my mother and sister."

"What?" Edie's eyes widened and she reached for her hand.

"No." Jane pulled back. "Don't give me any sympathy right now, Edie. I've got to tell you this or I'll burst, and any compassion will undo me."

Edie nodded. "I understand. Just tell it the way you have to."

Jane clasped her hands together as if she could keep a tight grip on her grief just by stilling them. She started with the sudden flash of memory and where it had led her. She saw Edie struggle to control both her shock and compassion, struggle to listen without reply.

"I had to go to their cabin. It was the only thing I could think of that might jar loose more memories." Jane told her everything, including her narrow escape from the man in the locked cellar and her treacherous drive home through the blinding storm. "Mrs. Ferguson was frantic when I arrived. I probably looked a fright. Anyway, it took nearly fifteen minutes to convince her I was okay before she'd go home to her own apartment."

"Are you sure you *are* okay?" Edie's eyes were huge.

Jane braced herself for questions about her mother and sister. But Edie kept her promise. "The guy had a gun?"

"Well, he *said* he had a gun. I didn't see one." Or feel one. Jane took a drink of coffee and pondered the handsome devil who'd scared ten years off her life—who'd disturbed her on levels she didn't understand. "It could have been a bluff.

"The truth is, he could have hurt me when he took the scissors away, but he'd seemed genuinely more concerned about saving himself from injury—about keeping our presence unknown to whoever had entered the house."

"Why?" Edie tore open a package of artificial sweetener and shook it into her mug.

"Well...there's the obvious." Jane pulled a face, feeling heat spiral into her cheeks. "We entered the cabin illegally. The police had it sealed."

Edie arched a perfect brow. "You risked being arrested?"

"I had to. Wouldn't you have...in my place?"

"Perhaps." Edie didn't seem convinced. "But, my God, Jane, the man might've been the murderer."

As if she hadn't thought of that. "I know. But I don't think he was."

Edie threw her hands up. "How can you know that?"

"I can't." It was totally illogical and yet she felt so certain about this. Why? She thought again of his kiss—there had been nothing threatening about it. Was that her only reason for this conviction? Or did she know the man?

Edie broke into her musing. "Did he give you any explanation for what he was doing there?"

"No, but—" Jane broke off. She couldn't look Edie in the eye. "Our encounter wasn't the kind where talking was a priority."

"What aren't you telling me?" Edie studied her thoughtfully. "Do you think you know him?"

That question again. Jane took a drink of her coffee and glanced around at the cozy home she'd created for Missy and herself over the past five years. Inexplicably, she felt on the brink of losing this safe haven.

"Jane," Edie said again. "Do you think you know this man?"

"He said we'd never met."

"But you can't be certain?"

"No," she admitted, pressing her fingers gingerly to her temple. "Every time I try remembering, my head feels like it will explode." She blew out a frustrated breath. "I hate this. It's like struggling with a thousand-piece jigsaw and having no idea what the whole picture looks like."

"You can't push a river upstream, Jane." Edie's expression softened and her generous mouth tilted up at the corners. "And if it's giving you such headaches, perhaps you shouldn't try."

But how could she not try? "Oh, I nearly forgot—I

found something today." Jane hopped off the stool, went to her parka and dug into the pocket, her fingers curling around the gold locket. It felt singularly familiar in her palm. Tears stung her eyes. Blinking them back, she returned to the counter and handed the open locket to Edie.

"I remember it. It belonged to my mother." Tremulously, she pointed to the pictures inside. "That's Kayleen, and that's me."

Edie studied the photographs. "Missy takes after your sister, doesn't she?"

Jane peered closely at the tiny photo, seeing what she hadn't seen at the cabin. Why, the picture could have been of Missy. Something indefinable slid through her, knotting itself around her chest, giving her a sense that she'd finally found a tangible link with a past she could not recall. "Yes, she does."

Why hadn't she remembered while Kayleen and Mom were still alive? Heartache threatened to overwhelm her. She took several deep breaths, fighting off the tears, fighting her fears of the unknown.

Through watery eyes, she gazed at Edie. "I didn't realize when I visited the funeral home, but driving back from Cle Elum, I remembered something about my m-m-mother."

Jane shuddered and reached for her cup. Edie waited patiently while she swallowed several sips of coffee and could finally continue in a steadier voice. "Mom was very vain about her hair color. Always dyed the gray as fast as it came in. She kept it about the color of mine. Whereas Kayleen had natural honey blond hair. Look at these photographs."

She poked the newspaper. "Mom's hair is completely gray, and Kayleen's, although you can't tell from this black-and-white picture, was dyed a shade Lucille Ball would have loved."

Edie's eyebrows shot up. "My, you really are starting to remember."

"Just enough to scare me." She thought about Scarface, about his search for "kiddy stuff." What had his boss really been looking for? She drained her mug and another face filled her mind. "Edie, why can't I remember Missy's father?"

Edie plowed her hand through her hair again. "You'll remember...when you're ready to."

"Maybe I divorced the jerk. Or maybe we were never married." Jane felt an uncontrollable urge to move. She snatched both coffee mugs and lurched off the barstool, hurrying around and into the kitchen where the coffeemaker stood.

The noisy students outside were quieting, but it gave her no peace. "Maybe we were running away from him. Maybe he's the reason we left our old life-style behind. Maybe my mother and sister were afraid of him. Maybe he's the reason they never came looking for Missy and me. Maybe they were scared if they found us, he might, too."

"Or maybe," Edie interjected, "they were told that you'd both died in the accident. It was such a horrendous pileup of cars and buses and semitrailers. Nothing like it before or since in the state of Washington. So many lives were lost, so many bodies burned beyond recognition. Some only identified by dental records, others by jewelry or bits of surviving clothing. And unlike a plane crash, there was no passenger list, no way to be absolutely certain how many were killed."

Jane shuddered at the images that sprang into her head, the brutal stench of burning twisted metal and seared flesh that forever lingered in her subconscious—the one memory she wished she could forget. "Maybe I should have handled this differently."

"Maybe." Edie sighed. "Maybe I shouldn't have listened when you begged me not to advise the police or newspapers of your amnesia. But you were so upset, so…terrified."

"I was. I still am, but I don't know what I'm terrified of. Or who."

"I've often wondered if I did the right thing by giving in to my sympathy for you, but I'd just miscarried my first baby and I took one look at you and little Missy, and my heart went out to you. Somehow I identified with your fear. But it was wrong not to have reported the facts straightaway to my supervisor. If I had, you might have been reunited immediately with your mother and sister."

"No." Jane reached out to her friend. "Don't think that."

Edie nodded grimly. "On the other hand, in light of what happened to your mother and sister, I think your fears were justified…that perhaps we did do the right thing in not pursuing your true identity."

"But what now?" Fear, as black as the coffee in the glass carafe, swam through her, prodding the ache in her temples. The hand holding her coffee mug trembled. "What if someone from our past murdered Kayleen and Mom? Someone who would kill Missy and me—if he knew we were still alive?"

HE WOULD BE LUCKY to make it to Cle Elum alive, Chad thought, as he pulled out of the parking lot of The Last Resort, a restaurant and bar located less than half a mile from the Dickersons' cabin. Snow blanketed Salmon/La-Sac Road and swirled against his car's windshield with a hypnotic brilliance, making driving a slow, hazardous process.

All through dinner, he'd pondered the afternoon's events at the cabin. Who was the wildcat with the glorious mahogany mane and decidedly kissable lips? Who'd come into the cabin forcing him to silence her in that most unprecedented way? And who was the guy looking for "kiddy stuff"? Not that he didn't have his suspicions. Too bad he hadn't been able to steal a glance at him. Had the brunette? Maybe. She was one gutsy lady.

He decelerated as he drove the half mile through the town of Ronald, famous for the Old No. 3 Bar, then picked up speed slightly, only to slow again minutes later as he entered Roslyn, known to television viewers everywhere as Cicely, Alaska, the town where "Northern Exposure" had been filmed.

It was like driving through a Christmas card, Chad thought, as he wove through the picturesque little town. Home and shop and street lights twinkled in the frosty night, reflecting off the snow, casting old and new building alike with a lacy beauty that might have been brushstroked by Currier and Ives.

A laughing couple darted into the street. Cursing, Chad hit the brake. His car lurched. Skidded. Stopped. The woman had long brown hair like the woman at the cabin. His pulse quickened. She turned to face him. It wasn't her.

Chad sighed. The couple reached the other side of the street, and he lifted his foot from the brake and set the car moving again. He conjured the image of the mysterious brunette, taking a lengthy mental look at her. She'd worn a bright ski jacket, tight jeans and cowboy boots.

Her long, dark mahogany hair fell about her heart-shaped face, natural and lush and silken looking, the kind of hair a man could get lost in; but only now did it occur to him that her deep-set aqua eyes were somehow familiar. Was it possible? Could she be...?

He reached the city limits and pressed his foot harder on the gas pedal. Lights from the town dimmed in his rearview mirror. The darkness gave the heavy snow a blinding quality. He squinted as if against a glare, concentrating to keep the car on the road. He hadn't expected when he'd set out from Seattle this morning that his investigation would lead to a double murder.

That it would lead back to his own past.

The wipers clicked back and forth as fast as his thoughts, as ineffective against the heavy snow as his reasoning power was against emotions he'd thought long buried. "Don't let this investigation get personal," his editor had warned. Vic would have a snit fit if he knew how personal it had gotten in the last few hours.

Chad laughed without humor. "Yeah, it's way too personal now, Vic, old man." The cellular phone in his briefcase chose that moment to ring, startling him out of his reverie. He glared at the briefcase. Probably the paper. Probably Vic. Screw it. He was on his own time. His own expense.

Chad reached inside the briefcase and shut the phone off. He was in no mood to talk to anyone. Especially Vic, who thought the sun rose and set on Dr. Marshall J. Emerson. The doctor had everyone fooled. An old enmity churned in Chad's gut, snaking out of some ancient corner of him, lifting like a vile odor he couldn't shed.

The tires skidded on the compacting snow and Chad automatically let up on the gas. The car came quickly under control. He wished he could regain his own control as easily. But he couldn't. *That* required a stiff drink and a good night's sleep—not a lecture from his boss.

The lights of Cle Elum loomed out of the snowy darkness and sent his mind in another direction. The bodies were at the local funeral home, which was where he would be first thing tomorrow. And all day—if it took that long. He expected someone would show up to claim the bodies of the two women. He suspected he knew who that someone was.

If he was right, his story would rock this state like the second coming of Mount St. Helens.

THE PHONE WOKE JANE. With her eyes closed, she fumbled for the receiver, then balanced it near her ear. "'Llo."

"Have you heard the news?"

"Edie?" Cobwebs crisscrossed Jane's mind. She struggled to open her eyes and discovered she possessed all the symptoms of a major hangover: headache, gritty eyes, achy limbs, unsettled stomach. Impossible. She hadn't imbibed anything stronger than coffee last night. "What news?"

"It's on the radio already."

She managed to lift one eyelid. The room blurred. No light peeked from behind the miniblinds at the window. She shook her head and lifted herself on one elbow. She glanced at the clock radio. Five in the morning. Damn. She yawned. "I have to close the bar tonight. This news of yours had better be—"

"Not my news. Your news. The police have arrested someone." There was a delicate pause. "You know...for the murders."

Jane jerked to a full sitting position, the need for more sleep fleeing with the rapid acceleration of her heart. Her scalp felt too tight for her skull.

"Who?" She tensed, bracing to hear the name—a name that might demolish the walls around her memory.

"A Dean Ray Staples."

Jane repeated the name in her head again and again, but it rang no bells. "It's not a name I recall."

"He grew up in Vantage, drifted from job to job in the Tri-Cities area. Landed in jail for burglary a few years ago and decided to get back into the profession when he was released last month. He's ripped off several of the cabins in the Salmon/LaSac area. Apparently, your mother and sister were unlucky enough to surprise him in the act."

Unlucky. The word slammed into Jane, and she choked down a sob as she pushed her hair up out of her damp eyes. "H-how do you know all this?"

"As soon as I heard someone had been arrested, I called Zoe who works the night shift at the jail. Zoe and I were best friends all through high school."

"H-how can they be sure he's the one?"

"His fingerprints were all over the cabin and the gun they found on him is the one that—"

Edie broke off, but not before she'd given Jane an unwanted visual. Tears streamed unchecked down her face. Impotent rage pinged through her brain. Nothing. They'd died for nothing. The waste. The man had shot them for a cabinful of junk. Her throat clogged and she barely managed to say, "Thanks, Edie...for calling."

"I didn't want you to hear it on the radio."

"I appreciate that."

"I thought it would ease your mind. You know, from thinking that someone from your past had killed them."

Jane was too consumed with grief to absorb this at the moment. She thanked Edie again, and hung up, then buried her head in her pillow and sobbed herself to sleep.

TWO HOURS LATER, Missy woke her. "Mommy, I can't reach the cereal."

Jane pried her swollen eyes open. Missy had donned

pink leggings and a yellow-and-blue sweater. "No cereal for you this morning, sweetie bug. It's cocoa and waffles."

"Mickey Mouse ones?"

"You betcha." She threw back the covers and climbed into her sweats, feeling more energetic than she expected she would. Knowing her mother and sister's murderer was under lock and key, surprisingly did help. Knowing he wasn't someone from their past, someone she couldn't recall, had taken the edge off the startling memories, and lessened her fears of the past.

But only time could ease her heartache at losing her mother and sister before she had found them again.

Trying to hide her distress from Missy, she explained to the child that her outfit didn't match, then let her decide whether she wanted to wear the pink leggings with the coordinating pink-and-black sweater, or the yellow-and-blue sweater with the matching yellow-and-blue leggings. Missy decided on the pink set.

Jane hugged her. "Good choice. The waffles will be ready by the time you're dressed."

In the kitchen, Jane turned on the radio. The morning news affirmed Edie's report about the arrest of Dean Ray Staples—without the details of his past or the facts about the gun and fingerprints. While Missy ate, Jane sipped coffee, thinking. With the murderer under arrest, she could make private arrangements for her mother and sister's funeral.

CHAD PARKED HIS CAR on Harris across the street from the entrance to the funeral home. He shut off the motor and settled in for a long wait. Reaching for the double mocha espresso he'd purchased minutes ago, he glanced at the sky.

Fat, fluffy flakes of snow were starting to fall, fluttering to the ground like a billion paper airplanes gliding on the shifting breeze.

The phone in his briefcase rang. Hoping it was Billy Bonze, his researcher, with the information he'd requested, he snatched it up. "Ryker, here."

"Got it," Billy answered. Billy, an eager cub reporter and computer whiz kid, boasted he could find anyone anywhere. Chad hadn't yet known him to fail.

"Whew. Half hour. You're setting records, Bonze." Chad placed his coffee container in the car's drink holder and started writing. "So, tell me…Kayleen Emerson's sister is a sexy brunette, right?"

Bonze laughed. "No way. I'm looking at her photo right now. Taken at the UW campus. She has a head-huggin' buzz cut of ice blond hair like that 'Stop the Insanity' freak. And no makeup—like some kind of hippie. Brutal, man."

Perplexed, Chad frowned. "What's her name?"

"Barbara Jo Dawson."

Chad wrote the name on his tablet and tapped it with his pencil. He'd felt certain he'd found the connection between the mysterious brunette and the murder victims. But it appeared he was wrong. "How about that pickup license number?"

"A 1980 Chevy four-by-four. And it's registered to one Jane Ann Dolan." Bonze read off her address in Ellensburg.

"Did you find out anything else about this Ms. Dolan?" Chad doubted it, given the length of time his researcher had spent on the project.

"Of course." Bonze surprised him. "What do you want to know—she works nights in a local bar, supporting herself and her little girl."

"No husband?"

"No record of one." Bonze moaned. "Jeez, Ryker, don't tell me you've got me working on company time just so you can add another name to that black book of yours."

"Hey, would I do that?" Chad ignored Bonze's resounding "Yes!" He was too busy pondering the secrets of the mysteriously intriguing Jane Dolan. "See what else you can find out about her. And fax me that photograph of Barbara Jo Dawson."

"Sure. Gimme a fax number."

"I'll have to call you back on that."

"I'll be here."

Ten minutes later, Chad was still mulling over the paltry information on Jane Dolan. He couldn't believe he was wrong about her connection to the murder victims. He needed that fax. But did he dare leave? He checked the time.

Snoqualmie Pass had still been closed when he'd left the motel. If Marshall J. Emerson's emissary hadn't made it over the pass yet, there was plenty of time to arrange for the fax, receive it and get back here to watch.

He started the engine and pulled the shift lever down. A familiar-looking pickup truck turned off First Street and headed straight toward him. Chad froze. Was it her? The windshield wipers swished fat snowflakes across the glass, leaving a smeary wet patch, but through it he made out the face that had haunted his dreams with sensual pleasures throughout the long night. "Hello, Ms. Jane Dolan."

He watched as she continued to the end of the block, turned onto Railroad and disappeared. Chad held his breath. Cle Elum was a small town. If she wasn't coming to the funeral home, he would soon pick up her trail. But a moment later, she walked around the corner. He shut off the motor, climbed out of his car, and watched her coming up the sidewalk, the gentle sway of her rounded hips mesmerizing him.

She was wearing an outfit much like yesterday's: tight jeans, cowboy boots and that brightly colored parka. She was slender, but not in an underfed way like the women he'd dated recently. He found her fuller curves alluring.

Her long hair drifted loose in the breeze, snowflakes settling and melting on it. His breath caught as if dragged away by the wind. But it wasn't the wind. It was this beguiling creature with the very kissable mouth.

God, how he would love the opportunity to kiss her for real.

He scrambled across the street. She had just grasped the door handle to go inside when he caught up with her. "Jane? Ms. Dolan?"

She stiffened, stood stock-still for several pulse beats, then lurched around. Alarm filled her beautiful aqua eyes and she cringed back from him. "You! How did you learn my name?"

"Your license number." Chad held his distance at the bottom of the steps, remembering none too pleasantly that this woman was perfectly able to fend off any unwanted male attention.

She took a defensive stance, reinforcing his assessment of her. Only her voice betrayed any vulnerability. "Who—who are you?"

Why hadn't she also asked what he wanted? It was a natural question—one most people automatically asked when he approached them. And she had more cause than most, after their encounter yesterday. Her eyes were hard, hard and damned lovely. So like *her* eyes. Maybe Jane Dolan already knew or suspected what he wanted. Maybe she even knew who he was. "My name is Chad Ryker."

If she'd heard of him, or connected his name with the

newspaper, it didn't show on her face. She lifted her chin. "Should I know you, Mr. Ryker?"

"Maybe." Impossibly, she seemed more tense than she'd been but a minute before. He decided to play his hole card anyway. "I knew Kayleen."

Chapter Three

Fear flushed hot across Jane's body, stealing the cold from the air immediately around her. Qualms about her unknown past had had her second-guessing her decision to come here, and had left her wrestling with herself over whether or not she should leave the bodies of her mother and sister unclaimed.

Why had she let Edie's call this morning convince her that she could come forward without risk of publicity? Without repercussions? Damn. Why hadn't she let Kayleen and Mom go to their final rest without acknowledgment of any kind? Had her bad judgment placed Missy in jeopardy?

This man—who knew that the woman the police called Mary Dickerson was actually Kayleen—was he capable of resurrecting a past that could destroy what was left of her family? The possibility chilled her, and the chill was like a slap in the face. She mustn't give in to the panic nipping at the edges of her mind, burning her stomach. She had to think. She shook her head at him and shrugged. "Sorry...Mr. Ryker, is it? I don't know who you're talking about."

Before he could respond, and knowing he would follow, she pivoted and escaped through the door, buying thirty seconds of thinking time. The funeral-home lobby was deserted. A scent akin to a rose garden in full bloom—and totally at odds with the wintry weather outside—floated in the air. Muted voices wafted from an inner room somewhere nearby.

But Jane's thoughts held her attention. Chad Ryker had said he knew Kayleen—which meant he knew she'd been using an alias. Did he also know why? She heard the door open behind her, her stomach muscles responding with a twinge. She didn't look around.

"Ms. Dolan?"

Jane flinched. If he knew why Kayleen was using an alias, why was he calling her Ms. Dolan? There was only one reason she could think of: Chad Ryker wasn't sure where she fit into the puzzle. He was fishing. Playing poker—a game she knew a little about from the bar. Her confidence sharpened. He might be holding a pair of aces, but he needed a few more cards to win the pot.

"Ms. Dolan?" His hand landed on her shoulder. She stiffened and spun around, shrugging free of his grasp. Reflexively, she raised her purse as a weapon, and Chad Ryker stepped back out of her reach, probably leery of her after last night's knee to the groin.

She said, "I told you I don't know anyone named Kayleen."

His gray-blue eyes narrowed, and he studied her for a long, tense moment, obviously trying to figure out whether or not she was lying. Finally, he shook his head, and his sensuous mouth tilted in a wry grin. "You know exactly who I'm talking about."

Denial sprang from her. "No, I—"

"Your sister."

A fresh wave of panic swept her. Had she guessed wrong about him? Did he know her, too? Jane jammed her purse against her stomach in an attempt to stem the trembling. "I don't have a sister."

It was a half-truth, a lie that Kayleen would likely have approved of, if it kept Missy and her safe from whatever had set them on the run in the first place.

"If you're not sisters, then what is the relationship?" Chad brushed at his snow-dampened hair in a gesture so casual, he obviously did it often. The tawny waves glistened with moisture. "And don't deny there is one. Your eyes are so like hers that you have to be related."

Then he didn't know it for fact. Might not know her name. Simultaneously, disappointment and relief whirled through her, loosening her grip on her purse and nearly buckling her legs. One part of her longed to pick his brain. Another part warned her that further contact with him and discussion of this topic weren't safe.

Chad couldn't decide if she was telling him the truth or lying through her sweet plump lips. Those glorious aqua eyes with the golden flecks generously sprinkled through the irises betrayed nothing. Was she Barbara Jo Dawson or Jane Ann Dolan? Damn. He needed that fax. And he needed to get her to open up, to trust him. "Why don't we go somewhere and talk?"

"You and I have nothing to talk about."

But the panic that popped instantly into her lovely eyes spoke to his reporter's heart. Fed his curiosity…and roused an odd protective instinct he felt for few women. They had plenty to discuss. Maybe if his offer was more tantalizing… He arched a brow at her. "Wouldn't you like to know what I was doing at the cabin yesterday?"

"No." She answered too quickly, and her tone told him he'd struck a nerve. She wanted to know his motives as badly as he wanted to know hers. On the other hand, whatever had her panicked might just rob her of that inquisitiveness; it had his piqued to the max. "Let me buy you a cup of coffee."

At that moment, a lanky man, dressed in a Western-cut black suit, emerged from the room where Jane had heard the voices. "I'm sorry to have kept you waiting." He ambled up to them without hurry, as though nothing much ruffled him. Jane envied him the trait. He held his hand out to Ryker. "Roger Diggins. How may I help you?"

His gaze shifted to Jane and she saw recognition dawn in his dark eyes. Her nerves leaped. Roger Diggins was not only the funeral director, he was also county coroner. One word out of his mouth about her visit here yesterday and he would put the lie to everything she'd denied to Chad Ryker. Right now, she still had Ryker's doubts as a buffer between his suspicions and the truth. She had to get him out of here.

"Thank you, but we were just leaving." She grasped Chad Ryker by the arm like he was some sort of date and steered him outside, undoubtedly leaving the funeral director staring after them in bewilderment.

Snow fell harder now, small stinging chips of ice. The cold smote her heated cheeks. Chad Ryker grinned down at her and put his gloved hand over the one she had hooked around his lower arm. "I'm glad you changed your mind."

The strength of his grip conveyed a protective force. A possessive one. The comfort it roused in her boosted her annoyance. She tugged her hand free and frowned at him. "My mind is as set as ever."

"Fine, then run away again." He tilted his head toward the funeral home. "I'll just go back in and tell Roger Diggins that there might indeed be something he can help me with."

Jane silently cursed his interference and the lousy judgment she'd used in coming to Cle Elum this day. She squinted against the driven downpour, wondering which course of action to take. Stay and talk. Or get in her truck and go home.

Her gaze slid over the irritating devil beside her. She couldn't deny he was appealing. He was also devious. And strong. Still, she'd held her own against him once and come out okay.

He grinned at her. "One cup of coffee?"

She ground her teeth. She ached to be away from him. But he'd learned her name from her truck license—which likely meant he had her home address, too. If she ran now, it would only be delaying another encounter later. On her home turf. That gave her the shakes. Better to get this over and done with, to get the disturbing Chad Ryker out of her life with as little hoopla as possible. "All right. One cup. The Sunset Café."

THE RESTAURANT WAS redolent with the aromas of breakfast: coffee, bacon, sausage, syrup. Jane's stomach gurgled as they found a clean booth and settled in. Chad ordered, and the waitress returned immediately. She filled their cups from a copper-colored carafe, which she then placed on the table before hurrying off.

Chad unzipped his parka, revealing a sweater beneath. It was a soft blue that heightened the intensity of his eyes. Something warm and sensuous swirled through Jane's belly. He cocked his head to one side—a disarming gesture. Whether it was calculated or not, she couldn't tell. Nor could she tell if he was aware of how enticing it was.

He reached for the pitcher of cream, but his gaze stayed locked with hers. "Since you claim you don't have a sister and don't know anyone named Kayleen, why don't you tell me what you were doing at the cabin yesterday?"

"Why don't you go first?" she countered, tugging off

her wet driving gloves and curling her chilled fingers around her hot coffee cup.

"Because I don't think you want me to tell the police Kayleen's real name."

The cup wobbled in her hand. She warned herself to stay calm, reminded herself that he didn't hold all the trump cards. "I don't think you're in any position to blackmail me, Mr. Ryker." She lifted her cup to her lips. "Besides, I might simply have been at the cabin out of morbid curiosity."

He watched her drink, a devilish glint in his arresting eyes. "Most single mothers wouldn't risk breaching a crime scene for the sake of 'morbid curiosity.'"

"'Single mother'?" Jane stiffened. She dropped her cup on its saucer and lurched to her feet. "You've done more than get my name from the state licensing department. Who the hell are you, Ryker?"

His fingers circled her wrist like a restraining bracelet and he replied in a fierce whisper, "Just a man who wants to know why Kayleen Emerson was using an alias, why she was living in hiding, and whether or not the answers to the first two questions are the reason why someone killed her and her mother."

All thoughts of flight left Jane. This was exactly what she herself wanted to know. But what if this man with the soft eyes and the charming smile was lying? What if Ryker already knew the answers to all these questions and was trying to lure her into some kind of trap? He seemed honest and sincere enough. But she couldn't risk Missy's safety on how someone seemed.

It struck her suddenly that he'd called her sister Kayleen Emerson. She repeated the name in her mind several times and was rewarded with a sharp jab of pain at both temples. She blinked, suddenly feeling light-headed.

Concern cleared the anger from Chad's face. He tugged her wrist, pulling her down in the seat. "You don't look well. Did you have anything to eat this morning?"

"Coffee," she admitted.

He insisted she get something sweet into her; ordered her a huge cinnamon roll, then wouldn't let her talk until she'd consumed three solid bites. As she ate, Jane tried staving off the headache that always accompanied each attempt to remember her former life. It was as if she didn't want to remember. But that couldn't be. Logically, knowledge offered her a solid shield against all her fears of the past.

She took another sip of coffee, then asked, "Why and how did you get so much information on me in such a short time?"

"Why? Natural curiosity after yesterday. That and my certainty that you were related to Kayleen."

"How did you learn so much about me so quickly?"

"I—" He broke off. Damn. He'd nearly said he never revealed his sources. Might as well admit outright that he was a reporter. That would have this gorgeous brunette clamming up fast, running to her pickup even faster. His gaze fell on her inviting mouth, and he had to concentrate hard on what he was saying. "I don't think it's any secret that all of our lives are stored in some computer memory bank somewhere."

She couldn't argue that. The sad fact was, every hour of every day, with every step forward in electronic progress, each one of us relinquished another piece of privacy. She stared at the coffee remaining in her cup. Oddly, its murky black color made her realize her head felt clearer, her reasoning powers restored.

She raised her eyes to Chad Ryker as something occurred to her. If he was involved in whatever had set her family and her on the run, he would know for certain that she was Kayleen's sister. He wouldn't be guessing. And...he would have approached her a lot differently than he had.

However, even if she had no need to fear him in that area, it didn't mean she could trust him. The only things she knew about him instinctively were that he exuded a natural sensuality that spoke to the core of her, that told her he was a man who loved women. Who had likely loved lots of women.

Oh, yeah, Chad Ryker reminded her exactly of the kind of sweet-talking, skirt-chasing cheat she usually attracted. And always avoided. She ignored the sexual tug his heady gaze elicited in her. Despite his faults, he might be able to help her. "If you want me to level with you, Ryker, you're going to have to tell me the whole truth. Starting with how you knew my sister."

Her sister. Chad sank back in the booth, struggling to control the familiar jump of excitement that hit him whenever one of his hunches paid off. So she *was* Barbara Jo Dawson. Why, then, was she calling herself Jane Dolan? The same reason Kayleen had been calling herself Mary Dickerson? Anticipation flared through him. Could she give him the story he'd come to get from her sister?

She was staring at him, waiting. The wary gleam in her eye told him to proceed with caution. A lot was at stake. That jackpot he'd been expecting to score with Kayleen might still pay off. If he tempered his bet. But, damn it, he'd intended playing interrogator, not the other way around.

So what part of the whole truth could he tell her? He wasn't ready to divulge his relationship with Kayleen, nor the fact that he was a reporter. Still, he had to say something. "We were friends."

"Good friends?"

Chad flinched inwardly. Lying came easily enough in his profession. Not on the page; but sometimes to get the story in the first place, he'd been forced to tell a tall tale or stretch the facts. Why was it bothering him now? Maybe it was the leery innocence in this lovely woman's face. She was an intriguing puzzle. One of the puzzles was why Kayleen had never told him about her. "Good enough friends not to believe that story her husband told about her running off five years ago with her lover."

"Her husband...?" Jane's hand flew to the side of her head as pain and panic collided within. Why did every snippet of new information cause such physical distress?

"Marshall J. Emerson," Chad said.

She closed her eyes and drew a deep breath, riding the wave of pain until it leveled out. She gazed earnestly at Chad. "I...I don't know that name."

"Don't know—? He was your brother-in-law for four years. For—" Chad broke off, abject confusion in his frown, his tawny brows dipping like twin blades over his gray-blue eyes. "What am I missing? What's going on?"

Jane drew another breath, this one wobbly, self-conscious. She glanced across the restaurant, not seeing the roomful of diners, not hearing the murmur of colliding conversations, the clank of silver against china. Slowly, she returned her gaze to his. Could she trust this man? That remained to be seen, but right now, she felt oddly compelled to tell him everything. "I don't know my own name, either. Not my real name. Jane Dolan is the name the doctor at the hospital gave me."

Chad's eyes opened wider. For the length of five heartbeats, he studied her, then leaned forward, planted his elbows on the table and tugged at the pinkie finger of his left hand, the gesture absent, nervous. "Amnesia?"

"Yes," Jane spoke softly. She told him she'd been involved in the Interstate 90 crash, and was relieved that he recalled it, that she didn't have to elaborate. "I took a pretty good bump to the head. It stunned me. Wiped out all my memory of anything beyond five years back."

Chad felt his jackpot dwindling, slipping away altogether in his unexpected compassion for his star news source. For Kayleen's sister. "If you don't know who you are, then how do you know about Kayleen?"

"That's just it. I don't know about her. Very little, that is. Every time I try to remember, my head feels as if an anvil landed on it."

Chad frowned again, sympathy and confusion clouding his reasoning powers. "I don't understand. Then what brought you to the cabin?"

Jane rolled her neck and sighed. "I saw Betty's and Kayleen's pictures in the paper and my reaction nearly sent me to a hospital emergency room. I knew I knew them, but I didn't know how or why. I told Diggins I was family and asked to view the bodies. He let me." She shuddered uncontrollably. "It didn't knock loose any real memory or recognition, only raised more questions. More confusion. So, I went to the cabin hoping I'd find something out about them."

"Did you?"

She hesitated, wondering if sharing her first solid memory with this virtual stranger would somehow strip the preciousness of it, render it something less. She glanced out the window at her side, and realized the thought was as fanciful and light as the flakes of snow drifting from the dark sky.

She glanced back at Chad. What was she really frightened of? She'd already told him all the hard stuff. What was the point of concealing the one memento she'd found?

She opened her jacket to reveal the gold locket that she wore hanging around her neck. "This...with Kayleen's and my pictures in it. It belonged to our mother. Betty..." She trailed off sadly, the last name still eluding her.

"Dawson," Chad said softly. "Her name was Betty Dawson."

Jane blinked at him. "Betty Dawson."

Yes. It was right. Pain, black and searing, rammed through her skull with blinding ferocity. She released the locket and grasped her head in both hands, her elbows propped on the table. As though from a great distance, she heard Chad Ryker's voice. She tried to lift her head, tried to assure him that she was okay, but couldn't seem to move or talk.

Her vision blurred, and she felt something wet and hot on her cheeks. Tears, she realized with a jolt. Horrified that she was creating a scene, she ducked her face lower. She couldn't bear to draw unwanted attention, couldn't stand seeing pity in strangers' eyes. It brought back all the emotional pain of the emergency room five years ago. She'd had to endure it then. Not now. Please, God, not now.

"Jane, Jane." Chad leaned across the table, speaking softly, alarm shooting through him. She shrugged him off. At a loss, he pulled back. His first instinct was to sweep her out of here, as quickly and as inconspicuously as possible. But something about the way she'd huddled into herself told him it was important to her to get through, in her own way, whatever it was that had her in its grip.

He resisted the impulse to scoot around the booth and pull her into his arms. Yet, he couldn't help asking, "Is there anything I can do?"

"No." The word was a whisper.

It curled around Chad's heart like a banner, denying her

neediness, attesting to her strength. But he needed more than strength from her. He needed her memories. He was sure she held the key to nailing Marshall Emerson. Disappointment and frustration assailed him. He'd made provisions for all kinds of setbacks, from plan A to plan Z. None of his contingencies covered amnesia. Where did that leave his story? His investigation?

Deliberately keeping his gaze from her, knowing instinctively that too much attention would add to her distress, he poured himself another cup of coffee and added a large dollop of cream. He could come forward, identify Kayleen and Betty, write a few stories on their living under assumed names, living in hiding. He could blow Emerson's claims that Kayleen had left him for another man, could get the good doctor some court hassles over committing bigamy, but in the end, the slimy bastard would come out unscathed.

Kayleen and Betty would still be dead.

Maybe he was barking up the wrong tree. Maybe Dean Ray Staples actually had murdered them. He dragged his spoon through his cup until the liquid was a soft camel color. Would Vic even run a story on Emerson based only on supposition and innuendo? Highly unlikely. He did look at Jane now. Saw she was starting to rouse.

The pain in Jane's head had subsided, lowered to a level where she could open her eyes without wincing. She scrubbed her damp cheeks with her napkin, embarrassed that her nose was probably red, that this man likely thought her on the verge of a nervous breakdown.

Chad wondered if she would ever remember the past. He didn't know much about amnesia. If a bump on the head had wiped out her memory, would another bump return it? He couldn't bear the thought of such a thing happening to her ever. Not once. And certainly not twice.

She shoved her hair up and lifted her gaze to him.

Jane saw sympathy in Chad Ryker's eyes and heat flushed through her. She didn't want pity, but she didn't want his sympathy, either. She hiked her chin high. He mustn't think her vulnerable. Mustn't think he had the upper hand.

"Sorry. It's just a lot to take in." She couldn't understand her mind's resistance to remembering, wouldn't even try to explain it to a stranger. She glanced behind him, her gaze falling on a portly man just exiting a neighboring booth. He seemed to be studying them. Jane stifled the urge to stare back at him, and the more habitual urge to ask herself if this was someone else who knew her.

Chad touched her hand, and the warmth it conveyed was disconcerting and seemed to come straight from his heart. "I'm sure it's tough…not remembering."

Maybe he was one of the good guys, after all. Jane gave him a weak smile. Then, knowing she was probably risking another blast of pain, she asked, "Do—do you know my name?"

Before he could answer, the portly man who'd been staring at them stopped beside their table. He clapped a hand on Chad's shoulder. Chad lurched around and looked up. Don Brickman, a reporter from a rival newspaper. Chad's heart nose-dived.

"Well, well. Small world, Ryker." Brickman beamed. "Don't tell me the *Courier* has you covering the Staples arraignment, too?"

"Excuse me?" Jane reared back, her gaze darting from Chad to the fleshy-faced man standing above them. Staples. The *Courier*. Her heart tripped. Her throat tightened. She gaped at Chad. "You're a reporter with the *Northwest Courier?*"

Chad blanched. "I—"

"Danged right, he is. Their star investigative reporter."
Brickman slapped Chad's shoulder again. "Mark my
word, if Ryker's here, there's more to this double homicide
story than meets the eye."

As though someone had punctured a hole in her soul,
the heat drained from Jane's body. A reporter. Investigating the double homicide. Dear God. She'd told everything
to a reporter. Been taken in by those damned gray-blue
eyes and a disarming grin. She wrenched two one-dollar
bills from the bottom of her purse and tossed them on the
table, gathered her belongings and slid from the booth.

Chad was right behind her when she reached the entrance. "Jane, don't go."

She spun around, more to stop him from making a scene
than to listen to anything else he had to say. "Leave me
alone."

He reached for her, thought better of it. "I'm not here
for the newspaper."

It was a blatant lie, but Chad decided this was no time
to split hairs.

A pleading echoed from her eyes. "Please, pretend we
never met."

He could see she was riding on jagged nerves, that she'd
had enough for one morning. He nodded and let her walk
away. He knew where to find her. And he would. Later.

She hurried to the double doors and collided with a man
coming through them, the impact so fierce, Jane landed on
her bottom. Chad started toward them, but the man was
apologizing, helping her to her feet, and Chad knew his
interference would only embarrass her more.

The man smiled at Jane, studying her face, apparently
appreciating the fact that she was a beauty. She thanked
him, then brushed past him and out the door.

The man stood where he was for a full minute staring

after Jane, then he turned as Chad started past him, giving Chad a clear look at his face. Cold flowed through Chad's veins, clenched his muscles.

The man was medium height, his body husky from daily hours at the gym, his hair long and brown, his eyes such a dull blue they appeared lifeless. But Chad knew a sharp intelligence lived behind those eyes. Elvis Emerson, Marshall's kid brother.

Had Jane recognized him?

Chad hurried outside and into the parking lot. She was sitting in her pickup, the engine idling. Probably warming the heater.

Had Elvis recognized Jane?

His heart thudded against his chest, and he willed her to hurry and leave—before Elvis figured out why she looked familiar. She backed out of the parking space.

Footsteps crunched on the snowy ground behind him. Alarm sent his pulse skipping as Chad glanced around. Elvis Emerson was also staring at Jane's truck. The excited glint in his pale blue eyes confirmed Chad's worst fear. He had recognized her.

Chapter Four

"On the board of the Fred Hutchinson Cancer Center."
Dr. Marshall J. Emerson paced the oak floor of his home
office, scowling as though this appointment to the FHCC
board weren't something he'd striven for for the past ten
years. "My big promotion and Kayleen has to pop up.
Damn near spoiled it."

"Really, Marsh." Joy Emerson, who looked a good
eight years younger than she was, shook the letter opener
at him. "Don't let people hear you say that or they'll think
you killed those women."

Marshall rammed a hand through his short brown hair
and glared at his pretty wife. His foul temper made controlling a fleeting guilty look impossible. "Are you sug-
gesting...?

"Certainly not." She strode across to him and touched
his cheek tenderly. "Don't be angry, tiger."

"I'm sorry. There's just so much at stake."

"Your new appointment? You said it wouldn't be any
big deal if someone found out about the bigamy. Has
something happened to change your mind?"

His gut clenched at the mention of *that* predicament.
"No, I don't think that's going to happen. As far as the
world is concerned, those two women were Mary and Lou-

ise Dickerson. No reason to think anyone will connect them with my long-dead wife and mother-in-law.''

She nodded. ''Even if they did, you can't be held accountable. How were you supposed to know Kayleen hadn't died in that fiery freeway crash? The authorities were the ones who found her wedding ring and declared hers one of the bodies whose ashes were retrieved from that carnage. You thought you were a widower.''

That was true. If it came out that Kayleen had been alive at the time he'd married Joy, there would likely be a hassle, but he doubted it would affect his new position on the board of the FHCC—not after he'd donated a new wing to the center.

''Marsh, does this mean we aren't legally married?''

''I'm not sure, but just in case, we'll go to Idaho next weekend and have another ceremony. If it gets out, we'll say we were just renewing our vows.''

''Oh, that will be romantic. Guess I shouldn't have been so worried Kayleen could come back and hurt us.''

The old fear swept Marshall. What had his gut churning was something more devastating than bigamy. If Kayleen and her mother had survived that freeway pileup five years ago, had those incriminating papers she'd stolen also survived?

Joy murmured, ''We really ought to thank Dean Ray Staples.''

''Who? Oh, yeah.'' He recalled the name of the man arrested for the murders. ''I'd like to shake the guy's hand.''

She pressed herself close to her husband in an obvious attempt to get his mind on other matters. ''Marsh, about the next in vitro...''

He reared back and glared down at her, shaking his head. ''No, Joy. I'm not going through that hell again.

Three tries is enough. If you want a baby so damned bad, we'll adopt one.''

She frowned. Her mouth puckered, giving her the look of a petulant child whose father had decided he'd spoiled her for the last time. "I don't want just any baby, Marsh. I want to be a mother to *your* baby. I want *your* child.''

The determination on her face left no doubt that she would move mountains, if necessary, to accomplish this.

"Well, that doesn't seem to be in the cards for us. I can't stand another round of this, Joy. Two years is too much. Either we adopt, or we remain childless. You decide. But those are the only two options I'll consider from here on.''

Unshed tears glistened in her eyes. "Do you think it's been a picnic for me?''

"I know it hasn't.'' He kissed her forehead. "That's why it must end.''

She moved against him again. "But I just know this time will take....''

Marshall wrapped his arms around her. It was what she'd said every time. He loved that she wanted his child, but the powers that be deemed otherwise. No sense denying facts. False hopes were for fools.

"You're so tense, tiger.'' Joy ran her tiny hands up and down the small of his back, leaving hot spots everywhere she touched. Marshall felt the tension in his body giving way to desire. Joy ground her hips against his. He groaned and crushed her to him.

He didn't want her getting pregnant, had privately hoped none of the procedures would work. Stretch marks, weight problems forever afterward. No thanks. Joy's body was centerfold perfection. He wanted it to stay that way. He nuzzled her neck, drawing in the heavy fragrance she always wore. Joy. She joked that Jean Patou had created it and named it for her.

She certainly inspired *his* creative side.

He couldn't say the same for Kayleen. She'd considered sex an obligation, not the adventure that it could be. She'd preferred evenings at home to going out. She'd called his friends snobs, his attempts to increase their social standing a joke. But the hellcat in his arms now was as ambitious as he was.

The telephone interrupted the thought, immediately cooling his ardor. Was this the call he'd been expecting since yesterday?

"Someone has really poor timing," Joy cooed.

"I have to get this." Disregarding her protestation, he scooted her out of the room, closed the door, and grabbed the phone receiver before the third ring started. "Hello."

"Sound a little anxious, bro. Maybe you should prescribe yourself some of that Valium you're always doling out to those rich Bellevue housewives."

Elvis. It *was* the call. He ignored his brother's wiseass comment. "You find anything at the cabin?"

Marshall held his breath.

"Nothing of interest to us."

"Nothing?" The breath left his lungs with a huff. Relief sloughed through him. "Good. Then this business is done and behind us."

"Maybe not."

Marshall felt his pulse hitch. "What the hell is that supposed to mean?"

"Well, you aren't going to believe this—hell, I hardly believe it myself—but I think I literally ran into B.J."

"B.J." was Elvis's nickname for Kayleen's sister. Marshall's heart plunged to his toes with the speed of a descending roller coaster. "Barbara Jo is alive, too?"

"I can't say for sure. She doesn't look the same, but I got a real good look at her face and I think it's her."

Marshall sank to the edge of the desk, overwhelmed by this news. Barbara had survived the crash? Did that mean…could it mean…? He was afraid to explore the possibility his mind had leaped at. "You have to find out for sure."

"A friend got me the woman's name from her pickup plate. She's calling herself Jane Dolan."

Marsh grabbed a pen and tablet from the drawer and wrote the name Jane Dolan in bold letters across the top sheet. "What's the address?"

Elvis told him and Marsh added it below the name. Elvis said, "I'm on my way to Ellensburg now."

"Call me back right after you talk to her." His pulse skipped through his veins, his palms dampened and fear ripped along nerves already frayed. "Maybe she knows…maybe she has—"

He broke off as Joy's whisper penetrated his shock. "What is going on, tiger? You're as white as my old uniforms."

Joy had stolen back into the room as quiet as a ghost and was staring at the name and address he'd written on the tablet. He flipped the tablet over and covered the receiver with his hand. "I'll explain in a minute."

But he didn't want to tell her this latest development. Not until, and if, he had to.

"Don't worry, bro," Elvis said. "I know what to do. If she has what we're after, I'll get it back."

"Good. I'll be waiting for your call." Marsh hung up the telephone.

"Marsh, what did he say? What's the matter?"

His laugh held no humor. "For the first time in my life, I have money, prestige and power. I'm on top of the heap.

King of my own realm. Everything should be smooth sailing. No more worries. But damned if complications don't keep popping up like zits on a teenager.''

"I thought Elvis was going to see to it that Betty and Kayleen were laid quietly to rest as Mary and Louise Dickerson."

"He is."

"Then what are you worried about? Who is this 'she' I heard you discussing? This...Jane Dolan?''

He didn't answer. His head ached with anxiety. What if this woman Elvis had bumped into today really was Barbara Jo? What if she had the pages Kayleen had stolen from his personal journal five years ago? The pages that hadn't been found in Kayleen and Betty's cabin.

"Sometimes I wish I'd never made friends with Kayleen in college." Joy's voice rang with hatred. "The only favor she ever did me was leaving you. But then, I should have had you from the beginning. Not her."

He had to get those papers back...before they landed in the wrong hands. Before they landed him in jail.

"Marsh?" Joy snuggled up to him.

But Marshall was as far away as Ellensburg. His mind on the past, not the present. If Barbara Jo was alive and she didn't have the papers, would she know what had happened to them?

"Marsh, if you're out of the mood," Joy sighed and stepped away from him, "I'll take a shower. I'm going skiing with some of the gals at Snoqualmie Pass this afternoon, at Hyak."

Lost in his own thoughts, he didn't see the hard glint in Joy's eyes that would have told him skiing might not be the real reason she'd decided to drive over to the pass. He just nodded absently and the second she closed the door, flipped the tablet over again. The name "Jane Dolan" glared up at him.

All the bad possibilities.

And one good one.

A pinch of hope tweaked his heart. If this woman *was* Barbara Jo, was there a snowball's chance that Melissa had also survived?

He stared at the phone, trying to decide a course of action.

THE MAN WITH GREASY black hair and a nasty scar slicing the left side of his face answered the telephone on the third ring. "Boss, didn't expect to hear from you again so soon. What's up?"

He bent over, lacing on leather boots—one, then the other—as he listened in silence, grunted where appropriate, then straightened. "Sure thing, boss. I understand. If I get right on it, I should be able to eliminate this problem as easily as the other two."

Chapter Five

The afternoon deteriorated faster than the morning for Jane. With fury lashing every nerve, she'd driven from Cle Elum to Ellensburg as recklessly as a drunken divorcée. To her further annoyance, the dark morning shaded patches of ice along the freeway a gray blue, the same hue as Chad Ryker's eyes. His face kept flashing clear and bold into her mind, his grin teasing her with sensual suggestion and hinting at knowledge of a past that she could not remember.

Knowledge that she both craved and feared.

Upon arrival at home, she'd hurried immediately inside and begun throwing Missy's and her clothes into their three pitiful sports bags. But the hollow rattle the last drawer in her daughter's bureau made as she shoved it back into place, stopped her cold. What was she doing? Where was she going?

Anywhere! her brain screamed.

Recognizing the panic in that answer, Jane sank to the floor and buried her head in her hands. What had she told Chad Ryker that could be so serious she needed to uproot a little girl from the only home, the only world, she'd ever known? She forced herself to take several calming breaths, then slowly, mentally walked through her conversations with the reporter. Nothing. She'd told him nothing that justified this frantic upheaval of Missy's life.

Then what *had* caused her panic? She considered and eventually recalled his saying he wanted to know why Kayleen Emerson was using an alias, why she was living in hiding, and whether or not the answers to the first two questions were why someone had killed her and her mother. A chill swept through Jane. His questions were too close to her own, and, she realized with a start, they meant that neither of them really believed the police had the culprit in custody.

She knew why she didn't believe it: her overall uncertainty about everything during the past two days. But what was his excuse? She shoved herself to her feet, swearing. She suspected why Chad Ryker wasn't satisfied: He wanted a scandal—juicy headline material. The story of a couple of women killed after interrupting a burglary wasn't the kind of exciting stuff that won Pulitzer prizes.

The hell with Chad Ryker. He was a jerk. A real friend of Kayleen's would never use her death to further his career. But as sure as cowboys loved the Ellensburg Rodeo, Ryker would print such a story. Only his would be more detailed than most. Thanks in part to her.

She growled and barely stopped herself from slamming Missy's door. What good would breaking the door do? It wouldn't prevent Ryker from meeting his deadline. Nothing could do that. Let the traitor run his story. What harm could come from it?

The question brought on a blinding headache.

HOURS LATER, JANE'S headache lingered, a dull pain at her temples, aggravated by the thumping beat of the jukebox and the smoky air in the Buckin' Bronc where she tended bar.

The lounge sported photos of past Ellensburg Rodeos displayed in red frames to match the upholstered booths and barstools. Recent renovations had updated the rustic appeal of the place, a popular hangout of locals and legal-age college students.

Jane plunked another six glasses into the dishwasher, then straightened to find Edie standing across the counter from her—the first welcome sight she'd encountered all day.

"You look as whipped as I feel." Edie plopped her purse on the bar and gave Jane a shake of her blond head. Dark smudges underscored each of her blue eyes and the lines around her mouth seemed more noticeable than usual. "I could use a giant margarita. Pronto."

Jane complied, making the strawberry drink the way her friend preferred, and setting the frothy pink concoction in front of her moments later. Edie took an immediate gulp and glanced around the lounge. Two couples with fresh drinks occupied the first two booths. "At least you're not too busy tonight."

"Actually, we've been slammed—until about ten minutes ago. Suited me fine. I needed the diversion. I'm tired of dwelling on my problems."

"Tough day, huh? Me, too, kiddo. I've been going to call you since noon, see how the morning went, but I haven't had a minute to catch my breath since those three semis decided to go ice-skating on I-90. Luckily no one was critical."

Jane stifled a shudder at how close she'd come to being in the accident that had tied up the interstate for the past eight hours. If Chad Ryker had detained her any longer... This time the shudder would not be suppressed. "I must have gotten out of Cle Elum minutes ahead of them."

Edie's face went bright red. "Well, that was pretty insensitive of me."

"No, it wasn't. Accidents are your business. I don't expect you not to talk about them." But occasionally, like today, the subject made her queasy. "I heard they've only just reopened the freeway."

Edie nodded, and managed a smirk. "Took them two hours to get all the people in and six more to clear away all the spilled hay and tires and computer parts."

Edie swallowed another sip, then looked questioningly at Jane, her expression querulous. "So, how did your morning go?"

Jane pressed her lips together, drew in a deep breath, then exhaled slowly. "I didn't claim the bodies."

Edie froze with the glass halfway to her mouth. "Why not?"

"Remember the handsome devil I told you about from the cabin? Well, he was waiting for me at the funeral home. Turns out he's a former friend of my sister's."

"Really?" Edie's tone sounded cautious. "Was he able to fill in some of the blanks for you?"

It seemed to Jane that her friend was as anxious on this subject as she was. "He told me my mother's last name. And that Kayleen was married to a Dr. Marshall Emerson. I'm assuming his practice is in the Seattle area. Have you ever heard of him?"

"No." Her lips drew into a thin line as she considered. "Can't say I have, but mine is a huge profession. Is he a GP or a specialist?"

"We didn't get that far. I tell you, Edie, every time I try to remember it feels like my head will explode with pain. Doesn't make the process enticing in any way."

Edie scowled at this. "That's odd. The kind of amnesia

you have shouldn't cause that reaction to remembering. That's a symptom of fugue.''

Jane gaped at her. "What—oog?"

"Fugue. Commonly called hysterical amnesia. A person suffers memory loss brought on by a psychological trauma. In other words, the precipitating event is so horrible the person's psyche can't assimilate it, so it represses it. Any time the person gets close to the memory of that event, they are traumatized again. That's the psyche's way of protecting the individual. Ergo, fear or awful anxiety, blurring vision, terrible headaches, sweating, nausea, disorientation.''

Jane blanched. "That's exactly the kind of reaction I've had the past few days to every flash of returning memory.''

Edie frowned thoughtfully. "I suppose you could have both retrograde and fugue.''

Jane knew the term "retrograde." Edie had used it when she'd first diagnosed her condition after the accident. Said it was caused by the bump she'd taken to her head. "It's possible to have both?"

"Yes..." Edie fell silent, but her scowl deepened and the worried look in her eyes seemed to build as she sipped her drink.

Jane scanned the customers in the bar, decided no one needed immediate attention, then leaned toward Edie. "Is it worse for me that I have both kinds of amnesia?"

"Worse?" Edie tilted her head. "I wouldn't say worse. Just different.''

"In what ways?"

Edie pushed her hand through her hair, mussing it unconsciously. "While there's no guarantee you'll remember any memory lost to retrograde, the other is lost to repression. It may or may not come back. But since you're starting to remember, it seems inevitable that it will.''

Jane's muscles ached with tension as she swiped the counter with the bar rag. "Could the accident have caused both amnesias?"

Edie shrugged. "That's the only trauma in your life that I know of. It would have been enough. But there may be something else. I'm sorely afraid, Jane, that only you know what triggered the fugue."

Fear clawed the corners of Jane's mind. "I'm not so sure I want to know."

"Of course not. Like I said, that's symptomatic of the condition."

Symptomatic. The tightness in Jane's chest eased as she considered this. "Are you saying once I've recalled whatever caused the trauma, this awful fear and anxiety will disappear?"

"That's my understanding." Edie sighed as if in sympathy. "But getting to that point will become increasingly more difficult."

"Great," Jane said without enthusiasm. But pleasant or not, she now wanted to remember. She wanted her history restored—even if it meant facing whatever had set her family on the run. Whatever had kept Kayleen and her mom in hiding. Doubt dampened her palms—doubt that her fear was only symptomatic.

The thought was disrupted by one of the remaining couples calling, "Good night." The other couple, she realized, were signaling for another round. Jane mixed the drinks, delivered them and cleaned off the vacated table, then returned to Edie. "Want another?"

"Oh, all right. It's Dirk's turn to fix dinner and tomorrow is my day off."

"How are you and Dirk doing?" Jane asked, in reference to Edie's recent marital distress.

"Better. He's finally ready to try for another baby."

Edie shoved the glass toward her. "Hey, you didn't tell me how the handsome, former friend of your sister's stopped you from your morning's mission."

"Some friend." Jane mixed the cocktail ingredients in the blender, then poured them into a clean glass. "Turns out he's an investigative reporter for the *Northwest Courier*—after a story for the paper."

"Good God."

As Edie downed the second margarita, Jane apprised her of the meeting with Chad Ryker and all that she'd done upon arriving home, including her panic to run away and finally her decision to stay.

"Well, I'm glad you didn't just take off." Edie shoved her empty glass aside and reached for her purse. "But if things drive you to that point again, before you actually leave...talk to me first? Promise?"

Something in her tone sent a chill through Jane, but she promised.

"Guess I'd better get home before Dirk sends out a posse. If you remember anything else—I'll be home all night and tomorrow."

Jane nodded. "Drive carefully. Those roads are getting slicker by the hour."

As Edie left the bar, a man brushed past her. He glanced around for a moment, then strode to a back booth. Jane arrived seconds later. "What can I get you?"

"A menu and a tall Jack Daniel's and Coke."

Jane felt there was something vaguely familiar about the dull blue eyes beneath the mop of brown hair, but no name bounded instantly to mind, no connection of place or time, no mental point of reference she could explore.

But since nothing about him revived her headache, she guessed that however or wherever she'd known this man, it was likely sometime within the past five years. Not knowing for certain, however, hardened her resolve to regain her memory. She fixed his drink and returned to his table. She laid the menu down and informed him of the night's specials.

All the while the man stared at her as if he knew her, too. But unless he broached the subject, she decided not to pursue it. Most likely, he merely reminded her of someone. God knew, there were hundreds of strangers in this bar each week, customers who pulled off the freeway to wet their whistles, or stopped in after visiting their college kids. "I'll give you a few minutes to decide. Signal when you're ready."

But when she glanced at him again a few seconds later, he didn't seem to be studying the menu at all. Instead, his pale eyes followed her, making her feel as though he were touching her. Studying her. Her stomach pinched. She took her time returning to his table. "Are you ready?"

"As I'll ever be." His tone suggested he was ready for more than food.

She sighed in exasperation, realizing his interest in her was plain old lust. Just another dog looking to satisfy an itch. His expression altered, became more smug as though he had a secret he might or might not share with her. Her tolerance thinned to snapping, but she held her temper. "What?"

"Steak," he said. "Medium, baked potato with the works and salad, ranch."

"Sure thing." She spun away from him, stuffing her anger. He wasn't the first unpleasant man she'd encountered. Hell, he wasn't even the first one of the day.

That one, she realized with a jolt, was walking toward her now.

Jane froze. Ever since she'd left Cle Elum, ever since she'd seen Chad Ryker in her rearview mirror as she backed out of the parking lot of the Sunset Café, she'd had the urge to pack up Missy and disappear. One look at that handsome face, those haunting gray-blue eyes, and the feeling returned to slam her gut.

If she could walk out this moment and go home and repack, she would. But she was the only one on duty for another half hour. She retreated behind the bar. A moment later he hitched onto one of the stools. She glared at him. "What do you want?"

"I want to talk to you."

"What do you want to drink?"

He half grinned at her. "Irish coffee, please."

She mixed the drink and shoved the cup across the counter, recalling she hadn't turned in the other man's order. She hurried to the kitchen, then lingered as long as she dared. She hoped Ryker would be done with his Irish coffee when she returned. But his cup remained full as he dragged a spoon around and around in tiny circles. She began unloading the dishwasher, feeling the eyes of the man in the back booth on her; feeling Ryker's eyes on her.

"I would have been here sooner," Ryker said, stopping her cold. "But I got stranded in Cle Elum."

She glanced sideways at him. "Too bad you weren't stranded there permanently."

He let that go unanswered for four heartbeats, then said softly enough that only she could hear, "I thought you wanted to know your name...."

Jane dropped the glass she held. It shattered on the hard floor. She swore, started to pick up the broken pieces, but tears sprang to her eyes and pain rammed into her head. Flustered, she railed at Ryker in a fierce whisper, "I can't deal with this. Not here. Not now."

She scooted out from behind the bar and made a beeline for the back exit, passing the man with the pale eyes at a wind-stirring clip. She shoved outside, into the freezing air. Her body, flushed with fear, welcomed the cold. She crossed her arms over her chest. If she could just hold on until Vesta arrived. Just a few minutes more.

The door opened behind her. She glanced over her shoulder. Chad Ryker stood there, concern etched on his face. That his traitorous heart held any compassion amazed her. He asked, "Are you all right?"

She laughed without humor, unable to recall the last time she'd felt "all right" or normal or like her old self— whatever, whoever that was. Frustration fisted like a band around her heart, and she knew then that it didn't matter how terrified she was, she had to know. "Tell me...."

The second the words left her mouth, panic grabbed her breath. She closed her eyes and fought it.

Chad stepped up beside her, then gently gripped her upper arms. He'd seen her collapse once today. He didn't know what to expect, but she was trembling beneath his grip and he wasn't sure the cold had caused it. He shrugged out of his coat and pulled it around her shoulders.

While he'd been stranded in Cle Elum, he'd been too busy covering the Interstate story for the late edition to do any research on amnesia. But he had Bonze looking up and E-mailing him some articles on the subject.

She turned pleading, pain-filled eyes up at him. "What is my name?"

"Barbara Jo Dawson," he said softly, his breath puffing in the frigid air.

If his breath had been a block of ice striking her head, the pain would have been equal. She bumped against his solid chest and he wrapped his arms around her. He held her like that for several long minutes, enjoying the way she fit against him, thinking he should drag her back inside where it was warm, worrying that her shock would be deepened by the cold.

Behind them, a man said, "Hey, is everything okay out here? You've got some new customers and I'm sure my steak must be done by now."

Chad glanced around and suffered a shock of his own. Elvis Emerson. What was he doing here? His steak? He'd been in the bar? Damn. How had Chad missed seeing him? Jane squirmed from his embrace and shoved his coat at him. Chad automatically gathered his jacket, his gaze riveted on Elvis. How long had he been standing there in the doorway, listening? How much had he heard?

Jane hurried up to Elvis, offered a quick apology, but showed no signs of recognizing her sister's former brother-in-law. "I'll get your dinner immediately."

Inside the lounge, Jane breathed a sigh of relief. Vesta had arrived and with her usual brusque friendliness was handling the new customers. Jane delivered the man's dinner, then joined Vesta behind the bar, where she was eyeing the half-emptied dishwasher and the abandoned broken glass. She studied Jane a moment with sharp green eyes. "Something happen here I should know about?"

Vesta, her boss, was nearing fifty, looked forty, and had a heart the size of Grand Coulee Dam.

Jane sighed. "I'm not feeling well. Do you suppose you could handle this shift alone tonight?"

Curiosity flicked across Vesta's eyes, and Jane knew she didn't believe the lame excuse for ducking out, but she touched a hand to her carefully arranged red hair. "Sure. I don't expect we'll get too much busier with the temperature dropping. Go home."

"Thanks." Jane gave her a grateful smile, knowing she would have to sit down soon and tell this woman she'd started remembering and that there might be other hard days ahead—days when she might not be able to do her job. Vesta would be kind, sympathetic, but she needed reliable employees. It might mean her job. Jane was starting to accept that that couldn't be helped.

With her headache hovering like a stalking insect, she rang out her tab, then headed for the door. She glanced once around the lounge for Chad Ryker, thinking only now to wonder why he hadn't followed her back inside, yet feeling grateful he hadn't.

But when he wasn't in the parking lot, either, she frowned. She would swear on her sister's grave that he wasn't done with her, with his quest for a better story. So why had he vanished?

As she climbed into her pickup she had the eerie feeling someone was watching her. Ryker? Someone else? Or was she just being paranoid? Not Ryker, she decided. He would have no reason to hold back from her now. He would figure she owed him. Then someone else? She started the engine, but by the time she felt the heater kicking out warm air, she hadn't thought of a soul who would be spying on her. And yet the feeling persisted.

She shifted into gear and stepped on the gas, wondering if paranoia was also symptomatic of her amnesia. Headlights glared in her rearview mirror and she saw that one or two other vehicles were also exiting the parking lot. Her anxiety increased. She tried shaking off the absurd thought that she was being followed, but her nerves were raw, her limbs shaky from holding in the tension she'd felt since Ryker had told her *that* name.

She'd shoved the name out of her mind. Refused to dwell on it. To think of it. Without warning it slammed into her head with a blinding force that canceled every other thought. She swerved, bounced off the curb and hit the brake. Gasping, she laid her throbbing head on the steering wheel and caught her breath.

Just a few more blocks. She couldn't think about this until she was alone—in her own small domain. Several minutes passed before she felt strong enough to start out again. At the apartment complex, she skidded into an empty spot and hurried inside, hustling a zealous, well-meaning Mrs. Ferguson away.

Jane locked the door behind the baby-sitter, turned off the Debbie Reynolds movie she'd been watching on TV, then headed straight to her daughter's room.

Missy was fast asleep, her platinum hair spread like spun silk across the cartoon design on her pillow. More than anything else had, the sheer normalcy of this sight, sent Jane reeling. Her vision blurred. She thrust out of the room and managed to shut the door gently before her knees buckled and she sank to the floor.

"Barbara Jo Dawson." The name whispered from her again and again as though she had to try it on as she would a hat before buying it. Fighting the ache in her head and swallowing the bile that kept climbing into her throat, she persisted and discovered that her mind did not reject the name.

In fact, she realized it was there, staining the corners of her memory like an inscription in an aged family album: the impression written in a spidery hand, smudged, faded, but definitely there, definitely readable.

Tears filled her eyes, spilled hot down her cheeks. "Barbara Jo Dawson." Her name. Something that everyone in the world took for granted; however, it was as precious to her as Missy. She hugged herself, rocking back and forth until her breathing returned to normal and the pain in her head had subsided to a dull ache.

The knock at her door was as unwelcome as the falling

temperatures outside. She considered pretending she wasn't home, but anyone who knew her truck would realize otherwise. She peered through the peephole. Chad Ryker's arresting face filled her vision.

Chapter Six

Barbara Jo Dawson, her emotions tender as a fresh bruise, swiped a hand across her wet face and released a shaky breath. Her feelings for Chad Ryker were as confused and complex as the puzzle of her past life.

Was he friend or foe?

On the surface, he was a great-looking guy whose raw sexuality sped up her pulse, but he wasn't the first man who'd stirred her lust, and likely he wouldn't be the last. However, never in recent memory had a man made her feel secure, the way she'd felt in his embrace. Why?

He knocked again as though sensing she stood there, watching him. She hesitated, figuring she would be better off not answering. She didn't want to talk to him, but she owed him a huge thank-you. Determined that was all he would get from her, she opened the door a crack.

He leaned down. Barbara shoved her tousled hair out of her eyes, resisting the inexplicable urge to do the same to the lock of tawny hair that slid across his forehead, giving him the innocent, appealing look of a small boy.

The grin that had haunted her drive from Cle Elum that morning flickered over his firm mouth. "I—I wanted to make sure you made it home okay. That you're okay. Are you?"

He sounded self-conscious, ill at ease, and she suspected this was a rare occurrence for the cocky Chad Ryker, guessed that little rattled him. Her dislike of him slipped a quarter of a notch.

But, she reminded herself, even the most domesticated rat had teeth. He'd disappeared right after telling her her name. Hadn't bothered to wait in the parking lot and express his concern about her ability to drive after knowing how upset she'd been. There was only one reason for his being here now. His story. "As you can see, I made it home in one piece."

"But you've been crying."

Heat climbed her neck, and she yanked her chin up. "That's really not your concern."

He winced as if she'd punched him. "It is, if I made you cry."

Despite her resolve not to let him affect her, the tenderness in his voice grabbed her heart and twisted. She fought a fresh onslaught of tears, knowing their origin was self-pity and nothing more. She didn't want this man's sympathy. Couldn't handle it in her vulnerable condition. She prepared to shut the door. "Thank you for telling me my name."

He grasped the edge of the door and bent toward her. His breath smelled minty and slightly of Irish whiskey. "Then you believe your name is Barbara?"

She swallowed over her ragged pulse. "Yes. It's just taking a bit of getting used to."

"I have something that might make the transition easier."

Interest sprang inside her like a steel trap. Did he? Or was this just a trick to get her to open up to him again? "What is it?"

He glanced over his shoulder, then back at her. "I'd rather not do this here in the hall."

"Why not?" She arched a suspicious brow, hiking her guard up at the same time.

He leaned impossibly closer, his voice a feather stroke across her face. "Because you seem to get a bit emotional whenever I—"

He broke off, straightening as one of her neighbors walked down the hall, making, she realized, his point all too clear. As much as she hated admitting it, Ryker was right. She didn't want everyone in the building gossiping about her. Mrs. Ferguson might hear about it and become more protective than ever. Or worse, might not baby-sit anymore.

Begrudgingly, she invited him inside, led him to her compact living room and motioned for him to have a seat. He chose the sofa, settling at one end. He dominated the room as though he were the centermost point, as though sound waves vibrated from him. Or was it the sexual thread that tugged at her whenever he was near? She strove to ignore *that*.

What she couldn't ignore was how his eyes reflected the warmth she'd always found in this safe haven, or the sharp sense his presence here roused—that this world she'd built for Missy and herself verged on collapse.

She sat in the chair opposite him and clasped her hands together to still their trembling, uncertain of the precise cause of her anxiety. She was deadly certain of only one thing. Squaring her shoulders, she told him, "If you have information that helps me and you're willing to share it, then I'll gladly accept it, but it's only fair to warn you ahead of time that I'm not returning the favor. I won't feed you another thing for your story."

Chad studied her. Beneath the flash of anger in her intriguing aqua eyes, he could see she was frightened. Eager to learn something new about her past. Yet leery as hell. Compassion boiled inside him, and it was all he could do to keep from dragging her off that chair and into his arms.

He schooled the impulse and the desire that spurred it. No doubt she was having a tough time of it. He'd seen others handle tragedy and trauma in all manner of ways. He admired her courage. Hoped it would last. For she would need that courage if he was right about Marshall Emerson. "What makes you think I'm only after a story?"

She laughed. "Are you serious? Can you deny—with a straight face—that you're not?"

He couldn't. No matter who or what, a part of him always thought "story" first—another trait some saw as a character flaw, but that was so inbred in him, he couldn't have changed if he wanted to. He didn't want to. He won acclaim and garnered prizes because he cared about the subjects of his stories, got involved in their lives, their tragedies, their heartaches, and somehow managed to turn them into compelling copy.

But this time the story touched him in ways this woman could never guess. Nor would he tell her. Silently he appreciated the soft shifting of her mahogany hair around her lovely face. "I won't deny that I'll be writing a story about this, but my story won't cause you or your child any harm."

At the mention of her child, Barbara cringed inwardly. "How do you know that? Mentioning me in your story could bring God-knows-what down on us."

Although she seemed unaware of it, his story was the least of her worries. Elvis Emerson was the one who would bring trouble. But, if her reaction to less disturbing memories was any measure, blurting that out at this point would be cruel. It was a tale better told in small installments.

"Then, I won't mention you. I'll refer to you as 'a source close to the case.'"

He watched her consider this and decided he could help her make her mind up. "Before you reject the suggestion out of hand, I think you should know two women murdered in Cle Elum wouldn't usually be my bailiwick. The reason I'm here at all was because Kayleen called me the night before she died."

He saw her tense, then her lovely brows dipped low in a frown. "Why?"

"She said she was tired of living in hiding and wanted to give me an exclusive."

Barbara's breath left her lungs in a whoosh. Her pulse kicked up. She clenched her hands tighter, bracing for the onslaught of symptoms that had plagued her for the past few days. "Then you know why she was in hiding?"

"No." He lurched to his feet, shrugged off his jacket and dropped it to the floor. Then he rounded the sofa, stood behind it, and levered himself against the back of it, his gaze steady on her. "No, and that's the hell of it. She called from a pay phone—did you notice they didn't even have a phone in that stinking cabin?"

He didn't wait for an answer, but plunged on. "She sounded rushed, breathless, as though she was afraid someone would come upon her using the phone, and cause her to run off in fear again. I tried to find out why, but she said she'd explain when I arrived, and hung up."

Barbara held herself as stiffly as a steel rod. Her voice was flat. "And you arrived too late."

He scowled with all the regret in his heart. "I've kicked myself ever since for not acting on my instincts, for not dropping everything and heading across the pass straight-away. But deadlines won't be put off." The biggest ob-stacle, however, had been his boss. He'd had to finagle the time off to do this on his own. Vic wouldn't listen to disparaging remarks about his champion, Dr. Marshall Emerson.

"Is that why you risked crossing the police tape at the cabin?"

He dragged a hand through his hair. "Yes and no. The first time I arrived at the cabin, I hadn't connected the radio news story of the break-in and murders with Kayleen. She hadn't told me the name she'd been using. It was a shock arriving and finding that yellow tape strung around the cabin.

"I contacted the paper and learned the cops considered the murders a simple burglary-homicide. I knew they were wrong."

"But they have the suspect in custody. His fingerprints are all over the weapon."

"They hadn't caught him when I went back to the cabin."

"Why *did* you go back?" She shifted in the chair. "Or is breaking the law okay if you can get your story?"

He stiffened as if she'd slapped his strong, square jaw. "I'm every bit as law-abiding as you. Kayleen is, was, more to me than just a story."

Barbara's eyebrows twitched with curiosity. But the cold set of his icy eyes told her he'd said all he intended to on the subject. Her curiosity deepened. How close had her married sister and this man been? "Why did you slit the tape sealing the front door?"

"I hoped I'd find something the police missed in their investigation of the cabin."

Hope pulled her forward in her chair and brought an instant ache fluttering through her skull. "Did you?"

"No." His voice was frustrated. He leaned over the sofa. "You arrived right after me and I hid in the cellar.

I did search after you left, but if Kayleen had any physical proof to back up her accusations, I couldn't find it.''

Once again, hope and pain danced through her head. She dug her short nails into her palms. "What accusations?"

"Mommy?" Missy's tear-filled voice interrupted. Barbara jerked around and saw her daughter standing outside her open door, pajamas askew, eyelashes damp. Her platinum hair was tousled about her narrow shoulders.

"Sweetie, what's the matter?" Barbara was on her feet and at her daughter's side in a heartbeat, scooping her into her arms.

"I had another bad dream," Missy sniffled.

Guilt swathed Barbara. The poor child had probably picked up on the distress she exuded like a cheap perfume. She'd tried hiding it from her, but children were too good at sensing mood swings in their parents and immediately taking them on as their own. "I'm so sorry, sweet pea."

Missy saw Chad and frowned. "Who are you?"

Barbara noticed the odd way Chad was staring at her daughter—as if he'd seen her somewhere before. "This is Mr. Ryker, Missy."

"Hello, Missy," he said. "You can call me Chad. You can call me Chad, too, Jane."

Barbara's stomach pinched, and she gave him a wobbly smile. It was kind of him not to call her Barbara in front of Missy; she needed time to prepare the child for the name change.

Missy returned Chad's greeting with a shy hello she reserved for those she liked instantly. Barbara couldn't suppress a grin. There was no denying, the man had a way with females—of all ages.

She'd picked up on his charms immediately herself, but Missy's fancy wouldn't be tickled in the same way hers was. She didn't take easily to strangers and when she did,

Barbara trusted her instincts. Missy hadn't misled her yet. Maybe she'd judged Chad Ryker too harshly. She smiled at him.

He said, "She's very like Kayleen."

Her smile fell. This was the second time in two days someone had said that to her, the second time the observation had discomfited her. Why? Children inherited family features. It was expected. Desired. Was it because she had always wished Missy looked more like her, had always feared she looked like her daddy, a man Barbara still could not remember?

She shifted the child's weight to the other hip. Did Chad Ryker know her husband? She would ask him once Missy was back in bed. "I think a cup of hot chocolate is called for."

"With marshmallows?" Missy asked hopefully.

"With marshmallows."

"Can Chad have some, too?"

"If he'd like." Barbara questioned him with a look.

"I'd like."

She lowered Missy to the floor, and they retreated to the kitchen. Chad started to lift Missy onto one of the stools at the eating bar, but Barbara interceded with the speed of a mother bird patrolling her young.

Her overprotective attitude reminded him of his own mother, and deep-seated resentment shuddered through him. But he couldn't judge her like his mother. Their situations were similar, but different.

He stole occasional glances at her as she prepared the hot chocolate. He found himself highly intrigued by Barbara Jo Dawson, attracted by the vulnerability he was seeing now—a guilelessness that was so at odds with the gutsiness he'd encountered yesterday at the cabin. It was obvious Missy adored her and kids had great instincts about people.

As she warmed the milk, Barbara listened to Missy telling Chad about the snowman she'd built the day before. He asked pertinent questions and made the little girl laugh—a sound that went straight to her heart. Missy liked him and that raised her own opinion of him. She disliked him a tiny bit less. If only he wasn't so good-looking, so cocksure of himself.

The thought stopped her cold. Was that why she disliked him? Because he was handsome? Self-assured? Sounded more like she envied the self-confidence he had about who he was—because her own was crumbling by the second.

She placed the full, frothy-topped cups before them. Missy licked at the marshmallow cream, but Chad took a drink, smearing the sticky stuff over his upper lip. Missy giggled and pointed. Chad grinned, and Barbara found herself fascinated by his mouth, imagining what it would be like to be kissed by him in earnest. A real kiss, not an attempt to silence her.

Something warm and delicious tingled through her, surprised her. She didn't usually think about men and romance. Had never encouraged anyone's interest in all the five years she'd lived in Ellensburg, fearing she might still be married. But she wondered now if that was all there was to it. Had she had a bad experience with a man in her past? Missy's father? The question didn't aggravate her headache, or bring an inkling of memory.

The sound of Missy slurping the dregs of her cup broke through her reverie. She grinned at her daughter. "Time for you to be tucked back in, sweets."

"Aww," Missy protested. "Will you read me a short story?"

"A really short one." Barbara swept her up and carried her back to bed.

When Missy was soundly asleep, she returned to the kitchen. Chad had gathered the cups and the pan and put them into the dishwasher. He seemed oddly at home in her apartment.

She didn't want him feeling at home here. "I don't expect guests to clean up."

He raised an eyebrow at her, but kept his expression even. "You're welcome."

Heat filtered into her cheeks as she returned his stare. She caught a gleam of sexual interest in his eyes that spoke to her body in a language that required no words. Desire heated her blood as she argued with herself. Physical love was for other women. Until she recalled who she was and why she'd run from her old life, she couldn't risk involving herself romantically with any man. For all she knew, she was still married to Missy's father.

But, oh, it would be so easy to let this man comfort her, on this night when comfort would be most welcome from any source. She deliberately broke the moment. "Do you know Missy's father? My husband?"

Chad blinked. He wasn't sure how to answer that. Finally, he decided to be honest. "I didn't know Kayleen had a sister. I don't know why she didn't mention you, but she didn't."

Barbara didn't know whether to be relieved or disappointed. All she felt was more curious. Absently, she clasped hold of the locket. Why hadn't Kayleen told him about her? What had their relationship been? "Then you don't know if I'm still married?"

"Sorry." He had Bonze checking into her background, but hadn't heard back yet. "I don't really know anything about you."

She shut her eyes and tried forcing the memory herself. Pain rammed into her skull and sent her reeling against Chad. He grabbed her and held her. She huddled against him and let the secure sensation of his embrace drop over her like a comforter. He helped her back to the sofa. "Maybe you shouldn't try to deal with any more tonight."

"I have to. I have to remember." Her expression touched his heart. "Edie says I don't want to remember. But I do. I swear, I do."

"Edie?"

"My doctor. My friend. Please, help me remember?"

He bent to the floor, retrieved his jacket and pulled the fax Bonze had sent him from an inside pocket. It was a head shot of Barbara Jo Dawson—the one Bonze had said was taken on the UW campus. "Maybe this will help jar loose a few memories. This is what you looked like when you left Seattle five years ago."

With trembling hands, Barbara smoothed the paper over her legs. The picture was grainy, but she recognized her nose, her eyes, her full mouth. "What is up with the bleached-blond crew cut? And no makeup? I look like some sort of major rebel."

"Doesn't it bring back any memories?"

"Not really." She turned pleading eyes on him again. "Tell me something more."

"I don't know anything more about you."

"But you must." She shook the picture at him. "What about this? Where did this come from if you didn't have someone checking into my background?"

"I had my assistant checking Kayleen's background, not yours. He came up with this." Chad shifted on the seat. "But I can have him look into anything you'd like. Tomorrow."

She couldn't wait until tomorrow. "I want to try now. Ask me some questions. Maybe that will work."

He was silent for such a long time, Barbara wondered if he would refuse to help her. She was about to ask him again, when he started gently probing her about Missy's father. Fear rallied with new energy. The ache in her head doubled. She bent over.

Chad hugged her shoulders. "What is it?"

"Just symptoms," she managed. Strengthened by his support, she fought the headache. "Tell me about my sister."

Chad hesitated. "Okay, but we'll stop anytime you say."

She nodded. He blew out a breath. "What do you remember about Kayleen and Marshall Emerson? Anything yet?"

"He was a doctor, right?" she said, repeating what she'd been told.

"He's still a doctor."

She nodded and immediately regretted it, but a memory was surfacing, climbing to the top of the dark abyss inside her head. "They hadn't been married long."

He said, "About four years, I think."

Another memory scaled the edges of that bleak cavity, scooting toward the light of recall. She couldn't quite grasp it. "Did she love him?"

Chad's face paled. "She had his child."

Barbara felt her fear rising. The questions must be getting too close to the trauma. Striving to outride it, she clenched her hands together. "I—I don't remember."

Chad fell silent. She wanted him to continue, needed him to. With sweat flushing her body, she swallowed hard and asked, "D-did something happen to the child?"

He ignored her question, tugged at the pinkie finger of

his left hand. It was crooked, she realized, as though it had once been broken and never properly set. He asked, "Do you recall that Kayleen and Marshall had a baby six weeks before Kayleen disappeared?"

Sudden, fierce panic closed her throat. Every desire she had to reestablish her history flew off on the beating wings of pain. She didn't want to hear this. But she couldn't say the words, couldn't lift a hand to signal him to stop. Her chest felt as if it would collapse from lack of oxygen.

"The baby was a girl." Chad paused, then straightened and grasped her shaking hands in his. His gray-blue eyes brimmed with compassion and sympathy. And some sort of pain she couldn't name. "The baby was named Melissa."

Chapter Seven

"What?" Disbelief rippled through Barbara's laugh, the edges tipped with hysteria. Had he gone too far too quickly? She shook her head, denial written all over her lovely face. "You made that up."

"It's true," he insisted, deciding there was no going back now. He kept his voice deliberately flat. "The child would be five years old."

Anger flared in her eyes. She jerked her hands free from his and sprang to her feet. "I think you'd better leave, Mr. Ryker. Now."

"Barbara, please." Chad stood, keeping his movements easy and calm, his tone soothing. "I didn't mean to upset you, but I'm telling you the truth."

"No. You're making it up as you go—so that your story will be more sensational. Or do you have some other motive?"

"I don't have any motives—"

"I don't believe you." An awful chill grabbed her heart. Had this man ever known her sister? Or had he also made that up? Been given the details of Kayleen's life by someone? The chill deepened to icy apprehension. By Kayleen's husband? She frowned at Chad. "Who sent you?"

"No one, I—"

A dull roar blared in her ears, squelching his words. She grabbed her head and winced in pain as a horrendous thought vibrated to life. Chad Ryker was here as the emissary of her brother-in-law. They were going to claim Missy was Kayleen and Marshall's daughter. They were going to try to take Missy from her. Terror shot through her. She pointed an accusing finger at Chad. "Marshall Emerson sent you, didn't he?"

Chad reared back in surprise. "What? No!" The thought was so ludicrous, he laughed.

Her cheeks burned. "Get out."

"Barbara, you have to listen to me. To believe me."

She threw his jacket at him. "Get out."

"I don't have anything but contempt for Marshall Emerson."

"Liar." Despite his superior strength, she shoved him toward the door. "If you don't stay out of my life, I'll call the police."

"You—"

A deathly eerie scream rolled from Missy's room. Chad stopped. Jerked around. Barbara did the same, her eyes wide with alarm. She ran for the little girl's room. Chad raced after her.

Barbara shoved the partially open door inward. It banged against the wall. She hit the light switch. Dim illumination shattered the darkness. The room was small and neat, gaily decorated in the latest Disney cartoon print.

Chad's gaze flew to the bed. His breath caught. It was empty, the covers tossed back. His heart pounded so fiercely that he remained oblivious to the odd cold for three long seconds. Then it struck him that the temperature in the room rivaled the icy interior of a meat locker. He glanced at the lone window.

The building was old, built when state codes were less

child-safety minded. The window was wood-framed, wide and tall, set in the wall no more than a foot above the floor. The bottom sash hung open to the night like a trap-door into hell.

Barbara let out a sharp cry. "The screen's gone."

Chad's pulse tripped. Awful images filled his head. He beat Barbara to the window, blocked her view and leaned out. His gaze went immediately to the old-fashioned fire escape three feet below and to the left of the wide window ledge. As he glanced down, he saw the ledge was covered with a thin layer of frost, its smooth veneer scored with black smudges as though someone had stood there.

With dread climbing his throat, he lowered his gaze. On the frozen earth, two stories below, a body lay sprawled beneath the streetlight. His heart hitched. A man's body. He'd landed on what appeared to have been a snowman. Missy's snowman? A baseball cap lay beside him, its logo indistinguishable from here. His neck was twisted at an unnatural angle. His eyes stared eerily. Chad had seen dead bodies before and this guy definitely looked dead.

"What? What!" Barbara shoved Chad over, poked her head out the window and gasped.

Chad caught her by the shoulders and pulled her back inside, sorry that he hadn't been quick enough to spare her. She shivered. He said, "It's not Missy."

She nodded, her hand over her mouth. "It's Scarface."

"Who?"

"The man from the cabin," she answered, her eyes darting about the room, her expression preoccupied, terrified. "Where's Missy?"

"I'm right here." The child appeared in the doorway.

He heard Barbara's breath catch as his own left him in a relieved rush.

"Are you mad at Chad, Mommy? I heard you yelling at him."

"No, sweetie, I'm not mad at Chad." Barbara struggled to control her tumbling emotions—the fear, the relief, the quaking in her hands, her knees. At the same time, she curbed the urge to rush to her child, knowing she wouldn't understand, would quickly realize her mother was shaking and ask questions that were better left for another time. Right now all she could do was grin stupidly at the child.

Chad rescued her. "We just had a difference of opinion, sweetheart, and I guess we didn't realize our voices were so loud. I'm sorry we woke you."

"You didn't wake me up. I had to go potty." She ducked toward her bed, shivering. "Mommy, how come you opened my window? It's cold."

Barbara bit back a hysterical laugh and forced a smile. "Silly me, huh?" She stumbled to the bed and scooped the child up into a hug that reassured her the small person in her arms was as well and safe as she appeared.

"Too tight, Mommy." Missy shoved against Barbara's chest.

She loosened her hold and sat back on the bed. "I'll tell you what—since your room is as cold as a Popsicle, you can sleep in my room tonight."

"And Mr. Bear, too?" Mr. Bear was Missy's favorite toy and always slept with her.

"Of course."

"I'm going outside," Chad said.

Barbara nodded, then gathered a blanket around the little girl, who clutched Mr. Bear in her arms. She carried her into the larger bedroom and tucked her into the bed.

Missy's eyes were half closed as she nestled beneath the double bedcovers. "Can I have another story?"

Barbara reached a hand to stroke her daughter's hair,

but she was trembling with cold and shock. Her hand a dead giveaway, she drew it back quickly. Missy hadn't noticed, but if she lingered much longer the little girl would detect her distress. "You've had enough stories for one night."

So have I, Barbara thought, her head throbbing.

Missy yawned and rolled to one side. Within seconds she was asleep. Barbara wished she could put the images out of her head as easily, but she kept seeing the body sprawled on top of Missy's snowman. She shuddered again. What had Scarface been doing at their apartment building?

The long, harrowing day just kept getting longer and more nerve-racking. She cast one last glance at her daughter and said a silent prayer of thanks that the man had not touched her in any way.

COLD SMACKED CHAD'S cheeks as he ran outside and across the frosty snow to where a couple of college students—sophomores, he guessed—now knelt beside the fallen man.

The girl, a baby-faced natural blonde, looked up as he crunched to a stop beside them.

She said, "We can't find a pulse."

"Let me try," Chad insisted, brushing them aside.

The boy, a solidly built redhead who was likely a phys-ed major, rose reluctantly to his feet. "Are you a doctor?"

Chad ignored the question. "I hope one of you called an ambulance."

The girl said, "We were just passing by."

"He screamed loud enough someone probably did," the boy added in their defense.

"Well, just in case." Chad pointed to the building. "Go

on inside and knock on the first door. Have whoever answers call one...and the cops, too.''

"Maybe I should stay here with you," the boy volunteered.

"Jason, come with me," the girl pleaded, her eyes wide with apprehension.

"Go ahead," Chad encouraged, shrugging out of his down jacket. "And bring back a blanket."

Frigid air penetrated Chad's wool sweater, sending a shudder through him. Under the guise of keeping the man warm, he tucked the jacket beneath his chin and did a quick, thorough search of the corpse's pockets—coming up empty-handed. The man had no ID on him. Not so much as a driver's license.

He glanced at the glassy eyes. "Who the hell sent you, bud?"

In the distance he heard a siren. Nearer, came the sounds of the curious finally venturing out into the bleak night for a glimpse of whatever had caused the excitement. The boy and girl returned with a blanket. He took it from them, retrieved his jacket, then covered the dead man's head with the green coverlet.

He told the couple his name, then said, "Stay here and tell the police what you know. I'll be in apartment 2C." He pointed toward the building again, then hurried inside as a squad car pulled to the curb.

CHAD WAS IN THE LIVING room, pacing. He stopped and glanced at her, concern heating his cool eyes. "Is Missy okay?"

"Yes, thanks to you." In that instant all her fury at him was lost in the memory of how he'd quieted Missy's qualms about their argument. "Was he...?"

Chad nodded, his expression grim.

"Who was he?"

"That remains a mystery. He didn't have any ID on him at all."

"What was he doing here?"

Chad grimaced. "I can only guess."

She didn't want him guessing. All guesses would only lead to something bad involving Missy. "Are the police coming?"

"They're here. Outside. They'll be coming up soon."

She shuddered, and he was by her side in an instant, snatching her hands into his. "Don't worry, I'll be right here."

Gratitude filled her heart and altered her perception of him. Somewhere beneath that appealing face, that sexy male magnetism, beat a human heart—with a soft spot for damsels in distress.

This damsel, she realized, longed to huddle in his arms, to find that safe haven she'd felt twice before within his embrace. But she hadn't forgotten the other side of him. Nor that he was a fairly famous reporter. Anxiety stirred anew.

Chad said, "Why don't you sit down before you collapse?"

"Do I look that awful?" She yanked her hand through her loose hair.

His pulse skittered. She looked done in, but despite that, there was something about her that was so damned appealing it surprised him. Women in distress didn't usually awaken his desire. But this woman did, every time he glanced at her.

Curtailing the need, he released her hands and gently gripped her upper arms. "You look shaken. But I'd say that was understandable. Come on, sit down."

He guided her to the sofa and they sat side by side,

turned toward each other. He wanted to take her hands in his again, but settled for stroking a finger over her clenched knuckles.

She didn't pull away from him, or insist that he stop touching her, but panic shone in her eyes and he knew a portion of that fear was his doing. He'd scared her with his story about Marshall and Kayleen; and right now, she had little or no reason to trust anything he said to her.

"What are we going to tell the police?" Her voice quavered.

"As little as possible." He brushed her hair back from her eyes, gingerly caressing her temple. "Just answer their questions honestly, and don't volunteer anything. All we know about this man is that he was apparently a prowler who tried to break in and fell to his death."

"He tried breaking in?"

"Yes, he jimmied the window and his boots scarred the sill."

Again she wanted to ask why. Why this man had come to her apartment, to her daughter's bedroom window. But she didn't want to hear Chad's conjectures. "What if the police ask if we know who he is?"

Chad looked hopeful. "Do you know who he is?"

"I told you." She made a face and waved her hands. "He was the man at the cabin."

"But do you know who he is?" he asked again and his meaning finally sank in.

She thought for a moment, then shook her head. "No."

"Exactly."

She nodded in understanding. "And telling the police I've seen him once before would mean explaining where and when."

"And—" Chad grinned wryly "—would land your shapely rear in the can."

"Yours, too."

"I didn't realize you'd noticed my rear." His grin widened as a small smile toyed with her luscious mouth and pink tinted her cheeks. "So, we'll deny knowing him, ever seeing him, and so on."

She grimaced. "I'm a lousy liar."

"Just stick to the facts. I was leaving when we heard a scream in your daughter's room and went to investigate."

The thought of that man invading her daughter's room churned her stomach. "Will the police believe us?"

Chad rubbed his crooked pinkie. "No doubt of that. Forensics will match his boots with the marks on the sill. Perverts these days are everywhere. The papers are full of stories about them. There shouldn't be too much fuss that one of them fell to his much-deserved death."

Barbara shuddered at the images that his words roused in her mind, and once again she struggled with her returning distrust of Chad. Would there be much fuss? From reporters? Would he use this for another story? Somehow find a way to use this in Marshall Emerson's favor?

A knock sounded at the door.

"Don't worry." Chad patted her arm and lowered his voice. "This should be pretty routine. Oh, and remember your name is still Jane Dolan. All your identification says so. It will simplify things."

As if anything could simplify things, Barbara thought, bracing for the onslaught ahead. But it wasn't as bad as she'd anticipated. The police were efficient, sympathetic, and kept their voices low while investigating the evidence in Missy's room. The worst offenders in the noise department were her neighbors, who, disturbed by and curious about the sirens, had gathered in the hallway and hovered in small groups, gossiping.

The embarrassment unsettled Barbara all the more. But

rattled nerves were entirely appropriate for the circumstances; even she could see they lent credibility to the story she and Chad had told.

Chad, on the other hand, was as cool and smooth as one of the icicles dangling from the eaves outside, obviously a veteran of police investigations. What was his life like on a daily basis? she wondered, watching him hover at the edges of Missy's room as the forensics people gathered their evidence.

His expression was solemn as if he were weighing a heavy problem. Was he pondering which angle he would take on this story? Or some new method to use against her in Marshall Emerson's name?

Disappointment wove its way through her heart. She carried her coffee cup to the kitchen and dumped the remains into the sink. Why was she so attracted to a man who was bent on destroying her?

"Ms. Dolan?" The officer in charge of the investigation, a lanky, former cowboy with sunken cheeks and a big nose, stood in her living room.

Barbara gathered the dish towel from the refrigerator handle, then joined the policeman in time to see the forensics team leaving.

Chad strode to her side.

The officer said, "It appears the frost on the window ledge caused the man's fall. His body's been removed and we'll be getting out of your way now. I just had one more question."

She twisted the towel through her hands. "What?"

From inside his jacket, the cop produced an evidence bag and held it between thumb and forefinger. It contained a silver flask, the kind used to carry liquor. "Does this belong to either of you?"

"It's not mine," Chad said, leaning to peer at it.

Barbara stepped closer for a better look and caught a whiff of something pungent and familiar. The initials W.T.B. were etched in the shiny metal. She shook her head. "I've never seen it before."

"Did it belong to *him?*" Chad asked.

"Most likely." The cop raised his wiry eyebrows. "We'll know more when we find out who he was."

"Where'd you find it?" Chad narrowed his eyes.

"In the little girl's room. Under the chest of drawers." Chad wrinkled his nose and pointed to the flask. "What's in it? Smells like gasoline."

The cop was silent for a moment. "That's purely speculation on your part, Mr. Ryker. The lab would have to confirm that, and even then it might not be for publication."

"What would he be doing with gasoline?" The butterflies in Barbara's stomach took flight, colliding into one another until she thought she would be ill.

The look the men exchanged was all the answer she needed. "Arson?" She choked on the word, twisted the towel tighter. "He was an arsonist?"

"They don't know that," Chad cautioned. "You don't want to jump to that conclusion."

"Why not?" she railed at him, feeling smothered by the protective vibes issuing from both men. "Isn't that the conclusion you jumped to?"

"Ma'am, there's no telling what that man was up to. But you no longer have anything to fear from him."

Barbara shuddered, hugging herself.

Chad put his arm around her shoulders and pulled her to his side. She swayed against him like one wind-whipped tree pressing against another—unintentionally, unavoidably. Her anxiety, her fears, scattered and dissipated in his support, his succor.

Oddly, it set off an ache deep in her core that she could neither specify nor name.

Chad asked, "Is that all you need from us, Officer?"

"Well, you'll have to come in and sign your statements tomorrow, but I expect that will be the end of your involvement."

They thanked the man and he left.

As the door closed behind him, Barbara felt as if the air had been let out of her. Every muscle and bone melted like so much slushy snow. If Chad hadn't been holding her up, she would have dropped to the floor. He led her back to the sofa. "You need to sleep."

She didn't argue, just stretched out full length on the cushions, and even as he covered her with the comforter Edie had crocheted for her last Christmas, she was falling into a lethargy so heavy and deep, she couldn't fight it. It seized her consciousness, spun her around and around—as if she'd fallen into a whirlpool—and sucked her into black oblivion.

BEFORE HER, AN OLD BRICK building loomed out of the dark abyss. She stood still, silent, the ground beneath her feet solid. The sounds of heavy traffic filled her ears. The air reeked of harbor smells, creosote and salt water. It was a place she knew, but did not know.

The door of the building opened, beckoning her. Fear sliced through Barbara. Her pulse skittered and her eyes blurred. She wanted to run in the opposite direction, but her legs disobeyed her pleas, propelling her forward and across the threshold.

A thick haze enveloped the interior. She could see nothing. But the rank smells of unwashed bodies, unwashed clothing rushed over her. Repulsed, she stumbled back. The haze lightened and through the semi-fog, she saw that the room was filled with cots, lined up like headstones in a graveyard. On every cot, a body lay. Were all these people dead? She shrank farther back into the doorway. Was this some gigantic morgue?

As she watched in horror, the corpses rose, first one, then another and another, stretching their hands out to her, reaching for her as if to touch her. Recoiling, she tried to turn and run, but her limbs ignored her screamed commands.

A lone figure stepped from the crowd. Her ripe smell burned Barbara's nasal passages as she moved ever closer. Her tattered coat of indiscriminate color hung open over a stained, garish-pink sweater and orange-striped wool skirt. Grungy men's slacks peeked from beneath the skirt like cuffed bloomers, and grazed the tops of her army boots.

She stretched a bony finger toward Barbara and spoke in an eerie voice. "Help me. Only you can help me, B.J."

Barbara shook her head, her heart clambering against her chest, bile climbing into her throat. "I can't. I don't know how."

"You do." The woman's toothless mouth twisted. Without warning, she collapsed onto her back and stared up at Barbara with dead, accusing eyes.

Barbara turned and ran back through the door, but it no longer led outside.

She was in the lounge of the Buckin' Bronc and she was serving the man with the pale blue eyes. He grinned his nasty, secret smile and called her name. Not Jane. Not Barbara. But...B.J. Like the dead woman.

Barbara jerked awake. Cold sweat flushed her body. The room was pitch-dark. Where was she? This wasn't her bedroom. Soft snores punctured the darkness. She reared back and realized she was on her own sofa. Her chest heaved, and she drew several deep breaths before she was breathing normally again. She switched on the table lamp.

The light flowed over Chad. He startled awake. The second he focused on her, his eyes flew wide open. "What?"

"Elvis," she said. "Elvis Emerson was in the Buckin' Bronc tonight."

"I know." Chad stretched and ran his hand through his mussed hair, then sat straighter. "Hey, you remembered."

Her blood felt icy. "He knew who I was."

Chad nodded. "That's why I took off."

Barbara considered this. Elvis hadn't acted as though he'd known who Chad was. It slowly occurred to her exactly what that meant. If Chad were working with Marshall, Elvis would have known him, would have kept away from him. "He doesn't know you?"

"Most people don't recognize me from the photo the paper runs next to my column."

"You're not working with Marshall?"

"Never." A look of distaste entered his gray-blue eyes, as though even the thought of working with Marshall made him ill. "Kayleen had something on the man, something she thought could ruin him."

If he was speaking the truth, then there was only one reason he kept turning up on her doorstep. "And you think I know what it was."

"That's the size of it."

She shuddered at the possibility that he might be right. "Do you think he sent Scarface?"

"Not Elvis, but I wouldn't put it past Marshall to send them both, just to hedge his bets."

"He's after Missy, isn't he?"

Chad studied her for a long moment, then nodded. "I'd say that was a sound conclusion."

Barbara didn't say another word. She rose, went to the coat closet and pulled Missy's and her gym bags out. Then she headed into her daughter's room and began tossing Missy's things into the first bag.

Chapter Eight

Chad hurried after Barbara, but stopped as he reached the child's doorway. The sight of her throwing Missy's clothes into the bag pitched him back in time to a chilly winter night when he was seven years old. Like this room now, his bedroom had been filled with glaring artificial light as he'd watched his mother cramming his belongings into a similar bag—shushing his questions, warning him to keep quiet, to hurry and dress.

An old dread dragged Chad's heart into his stomach. He stepped into the room and asked Barbara the question he'd asked his mother all those years ago. "What are you doing?"

Barbara continued packing. "I'm taking my daughter away. Right now. As far and as fast as I can."

"No," he said—the one word he hadn't been able to say to his mother.

"No." He went over to Barbara and caught her arm. "I can't let you do that."

She shook him off. "You can't stop me, Ryker."

"I can and I will. Don't make me."

"Why would you?" She glared at him. "You despise Marshall Emerson. I saw it in your eyes. Why would you help him take my child from me?"

Tonight had roused memories of events he hadn't known he'd witnessed all those years ago. They were as vivid now as if he'd seen them as an adult. His mother had also been afraid when she'd packed, but her fear had been for herself. Barbara's fear was for her child, so why did he feel he had to stop her?

Because Kayleen hadn't run away from just Marshall when she'd left; she'd also run from Chad and the life he'd wanted to build with her. Was he afraid that Barbara's taking Missy away would be like Kayleen leaving him again? That Missy was all he had left of Kayleen?

Or was it simply that Missy deserved to know and form her own opinions of her father—a privilege Chad's mother had denied him? He couldn't sort it out, nor could he shake the conviction that running away was wrong. "No child deserves to have a parent snatched away from her."

Barbara's body tensed, reminding him of a mama jaguar poised for attack. "Marshall Emerson isn't Missy's parent. I am."

"You can't be certain of that."

"I *am* certain of that." She shook a fistful of cotton socks at him. "Where is this coming from, Ryker?"

"It's Chad. And it's coming straight from my heart. Look, I don't want to destroy your life. Even if Missy is your daughter—"

"She is!" Barbara growled.

Chad raised his hands as though wanting a truce. "That doesn't give you the right to keep her from knowing her father." As his mother had denied him knowing his father.

"I haven't kept her from knowing her father on purpose, you know." Or had she? A flush of guilt heated her cheeks.

He seemed not to notice. "I'm not saying you did it on

purpose, but if you run away now, that's exactly what you'll be doing."

She sank onto the bed, the socks pressed to her rapidly beating heart. Frustration welled inside her. Why couldn't she remember the man who'd fathered Missy? There had to be some way to resolve this issue. Fear rose at the edges of her mind, warning her off the subject. She fought against it, asking herself a hard question: Which would be worse—remembering, or spending the rest of her life as a criminal on the run?

Her ascending gaze collided with Chad's. He was expecting some response, but she couldn't promise she wouldn't take off at another time. Once all the facts were in. "If I promise to stay for now, would you have that assistant of yours do some checking into my background this morning? Find out who I married, and whatever he can about my husband?"

"Of course." Chad ran his hand through his hair and his body relaxed as if he'd won something more important than a moral victory.

Wondering why, she lurched off the bed and put the socks back in the drawer. Chad watched as, for the second time in less than twenty-four hours, she unpacked. She peered up from her chore. "Why are you so protective of the rights of a father Missy has never known?"

Color climbed his neck. His eyes evaded hers. She thought he looked taken aback and disconcerted and uncomfortable—as if she'd invaded some private sanctuary and were about to steal his most prized possession. "Nothing, I—"

He stuffed his hands into the front pockets of his jeans.

She would have sworn nothing rattled this man, and yet he was rattled. Offering him a gentle smile, she kept her tone light. "Don't go all uptight on me, Ryker. I've bared my soul to you. What's the matter, your wife run off with your kids?''

He jerked, feeling as if she'd touched an exposed nerve. Marriage. Ha. He'd only come close once. With Kayleen. In one short week, she'd changed his life. Made him long to settle down and raise a family. Then, abruptly and without explanation, she'd returned to her marriage, leaving him angry and bewildered, his heart filleted like the catch of the day. ''Never been married.''

Exasperated by his evasiveness, she sighed. ''Significant other, then?''

''Nope. I like living alone.'' Regret swam through his eyes. Regret and something sadder. ''No kids, either.''

He stepped closer to her. His aftershave teased her senses. Her mouth dried. ''The love-'em-and-leave-'em type, huh?''

''That's right.'' He directed a smoldering gaze slowly over her face. ''A good old-fashioned confirmed bachelor.''

She backed up and bumped against the wall. Trapped. She tilted her head, willing her thudding heart to slow, wishing she could hide the desire he had to see in her eyes. ''So many women, so little time?''

He levered his palms on the wall on either side of her head. ''Something like that.''

A few hours ago, that was exactly how she would have sized him up. But she knew him better now. Beneath his playful attitude, a deep-seated hurt endured. She lifted her hair off her neck. ''What's the real reason?''

''That is the real reason. I like women too well to settle for just one.'' His gaze fell to her mouth. ''Even one as tempting as you. So rein in that 'Kiss me' pout unless you're willing to finish what you start.''

The air between them shimmered with raw sensuality.

Barbara swallowed over the need in her throat. "I never start something I can't finish."

"Good," his voice rasped. He reached a hand to caress her cheek, then leaned in to kiss it. "Because I really want you, too."

She nuzzled against the warmth of his mouth as he rained kisses down her neck. The thought that all he was interested in was mindless sex thrilled her. Terrified her. If she'd ever considered sex a contact sport, she was blissfully unaware of it. Was that what she wanted now? No. And yet, she'd invited it.

How would she discourage it now? She shoved a hand against his chest. He pressed her tighter to the wall and took possession of her mouth as though it belonged to him and only him. Her senses betrayed her intentions. She parted her lips, inviting the sensuous exploration of his tongue; dived into passion's pool with him and swam to the edge of abandon, every cell in her body alive with want, damp with need.

Slowly, he lifted away from her, smiling a lopsided irresistible smile. She gathered a shuddery breath and knew she wanted more—more kisses, more caresses, more Chad.

But there would be no stopping at that and she was no longer prepared to finish what she'd started. She shoved him back. Deciding further pursuit of his childhood was a safer course than this, she asked, "Did your parents divorce when you were young? Or stay together and make your home a war zone while you grew up?"

Chad froze, frowned; his tawny brows twitched. The light of desire flickered and died from his eyes like the flame of a guttering candle. He shook his head. "My parents—"

He broke off, muttered something unintelligible and strode to the window.

She stepped toward him. "Why don't you just tell me?"

He pivoted, released a noisy breath. A moment later, he settled on her daughter's bed and pressed his lips together.

She crossed to stand by him. He gazed up at her, a full-grown man with the expression of a wounded little boy. Her heart embraced the child within him. She wished she could help heal his ancient pain, but she could barely deal with her own. She sat next to him.

He scanned the room as if seeing it for the first time. "When I was seven I had a room something like this one. I'd forgotten it until…tonight…when I saw you packing. Then, the memories flooded back."

With his crooked pinkie finger, he smoothed the inch of bedspread separating them. "One night my mother came into my room and packed all my belongings into my overnight bag, the one I used whenever I stayed at my grandparents' house. At first, I thought that was where I was headed. But her actions were strange. Covert. That night, we sneaked out. Left my dad. For good."

Barbara frowned. "Why?"

"At the time I wasn't told, and believe me, I asked. Later, I overheard my mother telling my grandmother— her mother—that Dad had abused her. Slapped her around. I was too young to protest, but old enough to know it was a lie. Dad was a quiet, gentle soul."

"Then, why?"

"Her lover. My first in a long string of stepdads." The only part of his smile that reached his eyes was the bitterness. "I never saw or spoke to or heard from Dad again until I was twenty-three. When I was sixteen, she told me he'd died. God, how I grieved." He broke off, his face darkening. His voice was hoarse when he resumed speaking. "I discovered that was yet another lie when I turned nineteen. It took me four years to find him."

"And?"

Chad's eyes warmed. "He lives in Kirkland. We've been making up for lost time the past six years, but there is so much we can never recapture."

Like me, Barbara thought. Time lost, stayed lost. She put her hand over his. Her gaze told him that she felt his grief, shared his loss.

"Dad remarried a couple of years ago. Nice woman with a disposition that complements his."

Barbara squeezed his hand. She envied Chad that his parents were alive, even if his family had its share of problems. "And your mother?"

"She's still in Florida."

It was obvious he hadn't forgiven her. Perhaps he never would. But she hoped one day he would realize that he ought to, if only for his own peace of mind.

He reached up and traced her jaw with his knuckles. "I don't want Missy to hate you one day."

The warmth of his touch offered solace while his statement disquieted. Why should he care how Missy felt about her in the future? "My circumstances are hardly the same as yours and your mother's."

"I realize that, but you're forgetting the rejection factor."

"What?"

He dropped his hand, his pinkie smoothing the spread again. "A child needs to know both of her parents. No matter how many people around her love her, if one of her parents' affection and attention is withheld from her, she'll feel as if it's her fault somehow. It will shape her whole outlook on the world."

"Hmm." Barbara nodded, staring at his finger. She knew he was talking about himself more than Missy. "You think it will make her distrust all relationships—the way you do?''

He jerked his gaze to hers and suppressed a grin. Damn, she had a way of nailing him right between the eyes. And damned if that didn't appeal to him. He ached to pull her into his arms again, to kiss that saucy mouth of hers. Instead, he finger-combed his hair off his forehead. His libido was too eager to rule his heart.

He'd let another appealing female get to him once. Never again. Barbara could declare his fears of love irrational until doomsday, it wouldn't change them. Or alleviate them. Or his biggest fear—of having a child and never getting to know her; of missing all the years of her life—as his father had missed his childhood.

Barbara arched back, leaning on her arms. Her breasts jutted against her soft golden lambswool sweater, the locket nestled between them.

His mouth watered.

She tipped her head to one side. ''I think you should understand something about me. Missy hasn't had a string of stepdads or 'uncles' to confuse her. In fact, I haven't dated these whole five years.''

His eyes widened. ''Not once?''

She shook her head. ''I was tempted—a couple of times. But how could I encourage a relationship or get involved with someone when I didn't know who I was? Besides, Missy needed stability and I didn't want a man in either of our lives who could also be hurt if and when my memory returned.''

She hadn't been with a man for at least five years? The idea of being the first in that long stretch leaped from his brain right to his groin with a sharp jab of desire. He cleared his throat, forcing his mind away from her long legs in those skintight jeans and back to the subject. ''The return of your memory is going to rock that stable foundation you've built for Missy.''

"Don't you think I know that?" She leaned toward him again. ''That I've dreaded the possibility for five years now?"

As if it had a mind of its own, his finger found the knee of her jeans and traced tiny invisible circles. ''What are you going to tell her?''

"The truth." Barbara's gaze lifted from his hand all the way up his arm like a caress. ''And hope her five-year-old brain can take it in.''

"Children bounce back easier than grown-ups."

"Do they?" Her voice was breathy, an octave lower. She grinned at him. ''A moment ago, you were telling me just the opposite.''

"Well, I—"

The longing in her eyes scattered his reasoning, and all he could think of was wanting her. He reached for her, pulled her unresisting body against his. Hesitantly, reminding himself how new this would be to her, he brushed his mouth across hers, again, and again until he felt her confidence growing, her lips parting.

Then he slowed the kiss, deepened it, lengthened it.

Barbara closed her eyes, fascinated by the new and joyous sensations that flowed through her body in sweet, tingling waves elicited by his hands in her hair, stroking her back, his lips on her face, her neck. At first it was enough just to ride the wave of those sensations, but soon she wanted to participate. She buried her hands in his hair, finding it thick and slightly coarse, with a silken quality not easily detected. Like the man himself.

His neck, corded and strong and warm, pulsed with life. She nuzzled him there, inhaled his scent—a mixture of soap and aftershave and clean male skin—the aroma tantalizing, alluring, like some irresistible potion. Through his sweater she traced the long, hard muscles of his back.

Chad shifted position and lowered her to the mattress, moving his hand inside her sweater, under her bra, his touch like a fire wand on her sensitive flesh. Her nipples hardened against his palm, and her breath rushed from her in tiny moans of pleasure.

Her shyness abating, she gripped his sweater at the hem and sneaked her hands beneath the soft wool to touch his flat belly, his flat breasts, with nipples as hard as her own, and the splattering of coarse hair between them. A torturously honeyed ache twinged the very core of her. She reveled in the feel of him—the firm muscles, the warm male flesh beneath her fingertips—relishing this sensation as though he were the first man she'd ever touched in this way. But deep inside, she knew he wasn't.

Chad moaned and caught her hand, guided it to the fly of his jeans, where his arousal bulged against the fabric. He asked in a ragged breath, "Do you have protection?"

"I—no." Why would she have protection? She hadn't planned on having sex with anyone until she knew if she was still married. She jerked. What was she doing? She shoved herself to a sitting position. "I can't do this."

"What?" Chad looked dumbfounded. "Honey, you're doing it just fine."

"No. That's not what I mean. I can't make love to you."

"Oh, no, it's okay. I wasn't thinking. Of course, you wouldn't have condoms." He stroked her face. "But I have some in my glove box." He kissed her again. "The thought of going out in the cold to get them isn't exactly appealing, but I won't object to starting this over again."

"We can't."

He sat straight up. "Why?"

"Because we're only a few hours away from confirming one way or another whether or not I'm still married. I've waited five years—it seems wrong not to wait a few more hours."

Chad blew out his breath and crammed his hand through his hair. "You've been considered dead for five years. Even if we discover you are still married, it's pretty damned likely your 'husband' has moved on with his life. And that includes sexually."

"I know it sounds dumb." Breathless, she sat up, readjusted her mussed clothing and angled her legs over the edge of the bed. "Under the circumstances, I wouldn't expect him to remain faithful to me, but *I* know I'm alive. If I exchanged vows with someone, I have no excuse for not honoring them."

Sexual frustration furrowed his brow, the cooling embers still glowing in his eyes, but he nodded, a look of understanding on his face as he pulled his sweater over his stomach. "I guess I should leave."

"You can't drive back to Cle Elum now. You're too tired. You'd never make it. And it's too cold to sleep in your car. Take Missy's bed…or the sofa."

Chad stood and distanced himself from her, from the bed. He crossed to the window and threw the sash wide. Frigid air rushed over him, as effective as a cold shower on his remaining passion. But as his blood cooled and control returned, the memory of soft but solid female flesh, hot and yielding to his touch, of equally hungry hands on his own skin, lingered.

"Chad?"

He closed the window, then looked at her. "I'll take the sofa."

"Thank you."

She brought him a pillow and another blanket. He settled down on her sofa, but sleep didn't come immediately. His mind was too busy puzzling over Kayleen's sister. He'd never met a woman with such moral conviction. When her memory fully returned, would he find the true Barbara Jo as virtuous? Or was duplicity a Dawson family trait?

A trickle of self-reproach diluted his anticipation of finding out.

THE ALARM WOKE BARBARA. She opened gritty eyes to the new day and peered sleepily at the offending clock. It was after eight. Missy would be late. For half a second, she considered letting her stay home, then remembered that Chad and she were expected at the police station in a few hours.

Deciding it was best to keep Missy on her schedule today, she leaned over and kissed the little girl awake. "Morning, sweet pea. You've got school. We'd better get dressed quick or you'll miss the bell."

Fifteen minutes later, they discovered Chad still asleep on the sofa. His dark brown lashes lay heavy against his cheeks and his jaw needed shaving. She remembered his heated kisses, his hotter caresses, and desire swelled her throat, dampened her palms. She scooted Missy toward the kitchen, casting one last glance at him. In sleep, the vulnerability he hid so well spread across his face like an open book.

She drew a deep breath, catching his scent mingled with the aroma of freshly brewed coffee, and liked the new fragrance they created. Liked it way too much. She hastened to the kitchen, thanking the gods of invention for adding timers to the new drip-coffee machines. She couldn't remember needing a shot of caffeine as she needed one now.

"Why is Chad sleeping on our couch?" Missy whispered, once they were in the kitchen.

"It was too icy for him to drive back to Cle Elum last night, so I made him sleep here." Barbara made microwave oatmeal, and toast and juice for Missy. "You eat and brush your teeth, then come to my room and get me. I want to call Aunt Edie."

She poured herself a cup of coffee. "Remember, quiet."

Missy nodded, eating with her usual relish.

Barbara retreated to the privacy of her bedroom. She reached for the phone and hesitated. Edie had asked her to call if she remembered anything else. She had remembered. And she wanted to tell her about the aborted break-in before she heard the news on the radio.

But she wasn't sure she wanted to tell Edie everything that had occurred last night. She and Chad... The thought warmed her face. She supposed she could omit that from the conversation. For now. But not forever. She shared everything with Edie. If she started holding back now, policing herself, the relationship would erode.

She swallowed a drink of coffee. But what would be gained by telling Edie she'd nearly run away again last night—without keeping her promise to talk to her first?

She lifted the receiver and dialed. The phone rang once. Twice. Barbara frowned. Hadn't Edie said she would be home all day?

"'Allo." Edie, always an early riser, answered on the third ring, sounding groggy, as if she hadn't slept all night.

Perhaps, Barbara mused, she'd continued hitting the tequila after she'd arrived home and was simply hungover. Maybe she and Dirk weren't getting along as splendidly as she'd said. "Hi, it's me."

"Jane?" Anxious caution replaced the grogginess in

Edie's voice. "Has something happened? Have you remembered more?"

"Yes." She drew a bracing breath. "And the name isn't Jane."

She could have sworn she heard Edie's indrawn breath. "What is it?"

"Barbara Jo Dawson. Formerly of Seattle."

"I see." Edie sighed loudly, sniffed.

Barbara realized with a start that it wasn't grogginess she'd heard in her friend's voice, but distress. "Edie, are you crying?"

"I guess I am." Edie sniffed again.

"Why?" The only time her friend had given in to tears was when she'd miscarried her third baby. She'd feared then that Edie might never stop sobbing, because normally, the doctor wasn't given to weeping. Dread swirled the coffee in Barbara's stomach. Something had to be terribly wrong. "What's the matter?"

Edie paused for a moment, then said, "Self-indulgence. It isn't every day my best friend remembers she's not my best friend."

"What? That's nonsense." Barbara relaxed her tensed shoulder muscles and took another sip of coffee. "You'll always be my best friend. No matter what."

"Oh, I know you mean that now. But let's be honest. Once you've fully recovered your memory, changes are inevitable. Your past is bound to come between us."

"No...I..." But what could she guarantee? She had an awful sinking feeling in her stomach. Why had she thought remembering would be the best thing? It was reaching destructive fingers into too many others' lives—Missy's, Edie's... Who else would she destroy once she overcame the amnesia?

Chapter Nine

Chad opened his eyes, momentarily disoriented in the unfamiliar surroundings. He rolled onto his side and a fragrance as delicate as a spring morning—her fragrance clinging to the blanket covering him—cleared his confusion.

What time was it, anyway? he wondered, kicking off the covers and sitting up. The room was shadowy, but morning peeked from beneath the closed blinds. He groped the floor beside him until he found his watch, then peered at the dial. Nine.

Was Barbara still sleeping? He listened. Silence hung over the apartment. He decided to investigate, wandering barefoot as he yanked his sweater on over his jeans. Missy's door stood open and he checked there first.

Glancing at the mussed bedspread, he thought of the night before, of what hadn't happened between himself and Barbara. And of what had. He couldn't say sex or seduction weren't on his mind when he'd followed her home. But his main objective was helping her unlock her lost memory, finding the key that would solve an old mystery, and bringing a ruthless man to justice.

But from the moment he'd encountered her in that

darned cellar, she'd captivated him in ways both tangible and impalpable.

"Barbara?" He moved to the next room. The door was ajar. The second his knuckles touched the wood, it shoved inward. Her delicate scent issued from within, its fresh aroma seeming to float from the flowered fabrics covering the windows and walls and bed.

His gaze settled on the rumpled bed, provocative images springing into his mind. Of her. With him. His pulse skipped. He wanted this woman as he hadn't wanted any in a very long time, and he had the uncomfortable feeling that once wasn't going to alleviate the need.

But what if she couldn't give herself to him without certain promises—promises he was unwilling to make? The truth was, Barbara deserved a hell of a lot better man than he would ever be. God, how had he let this happen? He needed some caffeine. Now. Surely she had some coffee. He headed toward the kitchen.

Need. It was all about need. If only she didn't need him right now... If only he didn't need her... He would walk out before this path to guaranteed heartache sucked either of them any further along.

The sight of a half-full coffeepot sitting warm and ready buoyed him. He strode to the counter and lifted the waiting mug, dislodging a slip of paper it had been anchoring. A note. He read: "Help yourself. Taking M. to school. Back soon. B."

He filled the cup, then reached for the telephone and contacted his answering service. The fifth message was the one he was hoping for: "Hey, Ryker. Bonze, here. It's midnight and I'm about to hit the feathers. Gathered the info on the Dawson dame—even interviewed a few of her old friends and co-workers. E-mailed it to you a few minutes ago. If you need anything else, leave me a message. I've got this weekend off and I'm unavailable.''

Chad raised the miniblind over the sink and a sense of foreboding as gray as the day descended on him. The next few hours would likely shatter Barbara and Missy's carefully constructed world like a house made of matchsticks. He hated that his efforts to help them would more likely hurt them. But putting off reading Bonze's research would only delay the inevitable.

His laptop was in his car. He donned his boots and jacket and made a quick trip outside. Icy wind whipped against him. Unbidden, his gaze flew across the side lawn, to the smashed snowman, to the yellow police tape and myriad footprints marking the frozen snow—bleak reminders of last night's intruder.

He'd seen enough crime-scene tape in recent days to last him a lifetime. That reminded him—*Scarface* had also been at the cabin. What was it he'd overheard the guy say? Oh, yeah, something about there being no "kiddy stuff." As in Missy? The cold seemed to crawl inside his gut. Who had sent him to search Kayleen and Betty Dawson's home? Who the hell had he called "boss?" Marshall Emerson? Or someone else?

Chad realized he'd jumped to the conclusion that Marshall had killed Kayleen and Betty because their murders had come on the heels of Kayleen's call to him. Of her desire to expose Marshall. He'd reasoned that Marshall or Elvis had somehow learned of Kayleen and Betty's whereabouts. But how? Was he wrong about Marshall? Did the police have the right suspect, after all?

A laughing couple emerged from the apartment building, reminding Chad that he had more immediate concerns. He moved down the sidewalk and across the slick street to his car, unlocked the trunk, and hauled out his travel bag and briefcase.

Barbara had insisted he stay on her sofa last night because she'd thought he still had his things in Cle Elum. He hadn't bothered correcting that assumption. He could have found a motel in Ellensburg, maybe not easily at three in the morning, but he hadn't wanted to leave Missy and her alone. So he'd kept quiet about it.

His protective instincts persisted as he showered, shaved, and dressed in clean clothes. Stowing the bag near the front door when he'd finished, he returned to the kitchen, poured himself another cup of coffee and pulled his laptop from his briefcase.

A moment later he downloaded the E-mail Bonze had sent. Then, with disquiet gnawing his gut, he began reading.

BARBARA KISSED MISSY goodbye, watched her walk into the school, then started toward home through the busy morning traffic. Clouds hung low, as thick and grim as her musings over Edie's predictions about their relationship changing. Would it? She hit the steering wheel. *No, not if I can help it.* She owed Edie too much. Her friendship meant everything. She couldn't have survived without her the past five years.

This day, however, it was the past beyond five years ago that she must face.

The thought sent a stab of pain through her head, a spasm through her stomach. She buckled over the steering wheel. The pickup swerved dangerously close to the vehicle in the opposite lane. The driver honked and shook a fist at Barbara.

The pressure behind her eyes built and a black curtain rose at the edges of her vision. Somehow she managed to pull to the curb and engage the emergency brake. Laying her head in her hands, she fought nausea. Cold sweat broke out over her body and the black curtain rose higher until it wiped out the daylight.

A moment later, the curtain opened and instead of Ellensburg traffic, she saw before her a familiar room. A room in her mother's house in Bellevue. Kayleen was there, too, talking, waving her hands as Barbara fed a squirming infant. Missy.

Kayleen's voice rang out clear and loud with stress. "This will finish him. I can get my divorce with a hefty settlement, and Marsh will lose his medical license and maybe spend the rest of his life in jail. I've mailed a copy of the journal pages to a friend. If anything happens to us, she'll contact another friend and he'll see that an investigation is launched. Meanwhile, we'll be out of Marshall's reach."

The vision disappeared. Barbara blinked and looked around, mentally still in her mother's house. What journal pages? From whose diary? Marshall's? That had to be it, but what had he done that would cost him his medical license and land him in jail for the rest of his life? And why hadn't Kayleen's girlfriend contacted the other friend? Why had no investigation been launched?

Her thoughts resettled on the present, and she realized she was not in Bellevue, but in Ellensburg, parked across from The Palace restaurant. How long had she been lost in a trance, vulnerable to the curious eyes of passing pedestrians? Not only that, Chad would be wondering where she was. Worrying?

Disconcerted, she sat straighter, released the emergency brake and shifted into gear. Preparing to merge with traffic, she glanced into the rearview mirror. Her gaze snagged on two men on the sidewalk. Something about one of them struck a chord of recognition in her. *His mop of brown hair waving in the morning breeze,* she realized. Alarm squeezed her chest. Elvis Emerson.

She swallowed hard and forced her gaze to the man beside him. He was hatless, his short brown hair neatly combed. Where Elvis was husky, this man was lean, and taller by a good three inches. He held himself with great confidence, his looks reminiscent of a movie actor whose name eluded her. But this man's name ricocheted through her brain like an echo in a metal barrel. Dr. Marshall J. Emerson.

A shudder started deep inside her, a mini-earthquake quivering through her body, her limbs, and leaving her rattled and trembling. Marsh's being in Ellensburg boded no good for her. She had to get out of here. Get home.

Recklessly, she hit the gas pedal and bulldozed into the pathway of oncoming traffic. Cars swerved. Tires squealed. Horns blared. She took the corner on two wheels and left the melee behind.

At her building, she darted out of the pickup, raced inside and up the stairs two at a time. She arrived panting, flushed, wide-eyed. Chad sat at her kitchen table, staring at a laptop computer. His head jerked up. She clutched her purse to her thundering heart, trying to catch her breath.

Chad half rose, alarm pulling his brows together. "What is it?"

"He's here," she gasped.

"Who's here?"

"Marsh."

"Marsh?" Understanding dawned in his eyes. "Marshall Emerson?"

Still wide-eyed, she nodded.

"Where?" He scraped the chair back, his gaze darting toward the living room.

"Near The Palace. I just saw him with Elvis."

He crossed to her and took her trembling body into his arms. A lost little girl. But as always before, Barbara felt her fears dissolve in that embrace. Felt her inner strength and determination gather and grow.

"It's all right," Chad said. "I'm here and I'm not going to let him do anything to you."

His assurance that she wouldn't face the past alone, calmed her. She lifted her head and gazed up at him. "What do you think he's doing in Ellensburg?"

"Elvis probably told him he'd found you."

She nodded. "When I saw him, recognized him, it terrified me. I've got to remember why. Have you spoken to your assistant?"

Something flashed through Chad's eyes and his expression, so open moments before, shut down. Her nerves leaped higher. He released her and stepped back, nodding toward the open laptop. "He'd already done some checking on his own. He E-mailed me the information—so you can see it yourself."

Her throat closed. Dear God, this would either save or destroy her. She couldn't stand the suspense. "Just tell me."

Chad tugged his pinkie finger. "About Missy—"

"Oh, Chad," she interrupted. "Missy's whole life is about to take a sharp left turn—straight into God-knows-what. She's about to lose everything."

"Not everything," he said flatly. "She may be gaining a father."

The word sent a twinge of pain through Barbara's head.

"Her father—" she choked. Her face darkened and she grabbed her head as though it might explode. Her eyes rolled back. She swayed. Chad caught her, dragged her into his arms again. This time, she buckled against him as if every bone in her body had turned to mush.

He swept her up, surprised to find she weighed less than he'd imagined. She wrapped her arms around his neck and pressed herself to him, as if she wanted to climb inside him. The thought made him long for something akin to that and desire pooled quick and hard in his groin. It served as a sharp reminder of his yearning for her, and of her need for something very different from him.

He carried her to the sofa, laid her gently on the deep cushions, and covered her with the crocheted comforter. She seemed to be in some sort of trance, like yesterday at the Sunset Café. Only this seemed worse. "Barbara?"

His senses responded to her gentle fragrance even as he wondered how to help her. Didn't she say her friend was a doctor? He hurried into the kitchen and began digging through her drawers, seeking her personal phone directory.

The doorbell interrupted his search. He hastened to answer it. A woman with short blond hair stood there. She looked him up and down, then tilted her head. "You must be Chad Ryker. I'm Dr. Edie Harcourt."

"Thank God." Relief sloughed through Chad.

"Why, has something happened to Jane?"

"Yes, I was just trying to reach you. We were talking and she sort of lost it. She's on the couch."

Edie went right to her, checked her pulse and lifted her eyelids. "Jane, Jane, can you hear me?"

"It's Barbara," Chad said.

Edie looked up at him sadly and nodded as if she were having trouble assimilating the sudden changes that were occurring in her friend.

"Barbara." Edie gripped her firmly. "Barbara!"

Barbara opened her eyes with the look of someone coming out of a trance at the snap of a hypnotist's fingers. She blinked at Edie, then at Chad. "What happened?"

"You zoned out," Chad told her.

"And you called Edie?" Confusion tripped through her. "How long was I out?"

"A few minutes." Chad squatted.

"No one called me, hon," Edie said. "I heard about the attempted break-in on the news and came over to make certain that you were really okay."

"Oh, Edie, I'm sorry. I meant to tell you about that when I called this morning. But we—"

"Had other things to talk about." Edie's eyes were red-rimmed and Barbara recalled that her friend had been crying earlier.

She shoved herself into a sitting position. "The intruder was the scar-faced man who locked us in the cellar the other day."

Edie scooted back into one of the two chairs across from the sofa, her eyes widening. "What was he doing here?"

"We think he planned on abducting Missy." Chad joined Barbara on the sofa.

Edie's eyes widened in alarm. "Dear God, no."

"Maybe we can be certain once I've remembered something important." Barbara glanced at Chad. "You were going to tell me what your assistant discovered about my past."

Edie scowled. "As much as I want to protect Missy, I must caution you against rushing your memory."

"I appreciate your concern, Edie." She smiled reassuringly at her friend. "But Kayleen's husband seems to be at the root of our running away in the first place and Chad has offered to help me find out why."

"I'm all for that, but the memory will return on its own—when it's ready," Edie protested.

"I can't wait until it's ready. Marshall Emerson is breathing down my neck and I need some defense against him." She addressed Chad again. "Did your assistant find out my husband's name?"

Chad swallowed uncomfortably. "There's no record of your ever being married."

"No husband?" Unexpectedly, relief surged through Barbara. "So I had Missy on my own. Didn't I name someone as the father on her birth certificate?"

"Really, both of you, I'm not sure this is wise," Edie protested again, twin dots of color on her cheeks.

"I have to know." Barbara glanced at Chad. "Please, answer my question."

"No, no name," Chad said.

Edie closed her eyes as if she couldn't bear to hear what was coming next.

Barbara frowned, and got up from the couch. Anxiety clamored through every vein, every nerve. "I don't understand."

Chad cleared his throat and stood, too. "There is no record of your ever having a baby."

Her frown deepened. This made less and less sense. "Someone destroyed the record?"

He looked more uncomfortable. "Several people who knew you just before you 'died' claim you weren't pregnant."

Barbara laughed, a high-pitched sound that rang with disbelief instead of mirth. "Then they didn't know me very well."

Edie lurched to her feet. "I really must insist that you stop this now."

Barbara glared at her friend. "Tell him, Edie. Tell him he's wrong."

Edie was as white as a ghost. She twisted her hands in front of her. "I—I wish I could tell him he was wrong, Barbara."

"What are you saying?" Her voice rose even as her

N IMPORTANT MESSAGE ROM
HE EDITORS OF HARLEQUIN®

ear Reader,

ecause you've chosen to read one of our ine romance novels, we'd like to say thank you"! And, as a **special** way to hank you, we've selected <u>four more</u> of the ooks you love so well, **and** a beautiful herub Magnet to send you absolutely *FREE!*

lease enjoy them with our compliments...

Candy Lee   Editor,
Intrigue

?.S. And <u>because</u> we value our ustomers, we've attached something extra inside ...

EDITOR'S
FREE
GIFT
SEAL
THANK YOU

PEEL OFF SEAL AND
PLACE INSIDE

THE EDITOR'S "THANK YOU"
FREE GIFTS INCLUDE:

- ▶ Four BRAND-NEW romance novels
- ▶ A beautiful Cherub Magnet

PLACE
FREE GIFT
SEAL
HERE

YES! I have placed my Editor's "thank you" seal
in the space provided above. Please send me 4 free
books and a lovely Cherub Magnet. I understand I am
under no obligation to purchase any books, as explained
on the back and on the opposite page.

181 CIH CCLF (U-H-I-10/97)

_____

NAME

_____

ADDRESS   APT.

_____

CITY   STATE   ZIP

Thank you!

DETACH AND MAIL CARD TODAY!

THE HARLEQUIN READER SERVICE®: HERE'S HOW IT WORKS

Accepting free books places you under no obligation to buy anything. You may keep the books and gift and return the shipping statement marked "cancel". If you do not cancel, about a month later we will send you 4 additional novels, and bill you just $3.12 each plus 25¢ delivery per book and applicable sales tax, if any*. That's the complete price, and—compared to cover prices of $3.75 each—quite a bargain! You may cancel at any time, but if you choose to continue, every month we'll send you 4 more books, which you may either purchase at the discount price…or return to us and cancel your subscription.

*Terms and prices subject to change without notice. Sales tax applicable in N.Y.

If offer card is missing write to: Harlequin Reader Service, 3010 Walden Ave., P.O. Box 1867, Buffalo, NY 14240-1867

BUSINESS REPLY MAIL
FIRST-CLASS MAIL   PERMIT NO. 717   BUFFALO, NY

POSTAGE WILL BE PAID BY ADDRESSEE

HARLEQUIN READER SERVICE
3010 WALDEN AVE
PO BOX 1867
BUFFALO NY 14240-9952

NO POSTAGE
NECESSARY
IF MAILED
IN THE
UNITED STATES

heart plummeted. She clutched her stomach, her arms crossed protectively over the womb that had carried her child for nine months. "You've examined me."

"Yes." Edie's eyes glazed as though she were looking back in time at something too sad to view. "That first pelvic."

"Yes." Barbara nodded, encouraging her to remember. "That's right! The one the year after the accident."

Edie pressed her hand to her chest and tears welled in her eyes. "I discovered then...that you'd never been pregnant."

Barbara couldn't believe what she was hearing. Chad was lying, Edie was wrong. "No. You would have told me. My best friend would have told me."

Tears streamed down Edie's cheeks. "How could I tell you that? You and Missy—" A shuddery sob spilled from her. "I'd give anything to have a child—one to love as you love Missy. But fate stole my three babies and there wasn't a thing I could do to help myself. Well, I could help you. And I did. I wasn't about to let the system snatch Missy from you. God forgive me, but I'd do it again if I had to."

Barbara felt as if a train were rushing toward her and she couldn't get off the tracks. She dropped back onto the sofa. "If she isn't mine...then whose little girl is Missy?"

But, in her heart she knew. Had known since last night. Missy was Kayleen's daughter. Her niece. Barbara's vision blurred and pain rallied at her temples, her stomach churned and a clammy sweat swept her body; but this time none of it could hold the memories at bay.

Slowly, steadily, like water leaking from a cracked glass, she began recalling the minutes right before the accident.

Chapter Ten

Chad was seated beside her again, Edie back in the chair opposite them, looking as if her world had also come apart at the seams. Barbara glanced from one to the other through unshed tears. She'd pulled her knees to her chest, but still her insides trembled.

"We were on the bus. Kayleen and Mom were sitting near the front," she started, reporting the tale as if she had only heard it and not lived it, her voice devoid of emotion—dull, flat, even to her own ears. "I'd taken Missy to the back, where the swaying seemed to quiet her. She'd been terribly fussy that day, as if she knew the awful mission we'd undertaken.

"Kayleen claimed she had colic. I thought the baby was picking up on *her* anxiety." How odd that she could now recall clearly that which yesterday—even this morning—had been beyond her grasp, her knowledge. Her shoulders slumped forward and a tiny sigh slipped out. "My sister had always been high-strung. When we were little, Mom used to call her Nervous Nelly because she constantly fussed or fidgeted. As an adult, that nervousness became an internal force, underlying every motive, every word, every action. Do you remember her that way, Chad?"

"When I first met her, I wondered if she was a little

hyper. But as I got to know her—'' he spoke softly, reverently, as though in deference to a once-cherished friend ''—I realized she was just one of those people with the kind of relentless energy that attracted you and repelled you at the same time. Just sharing space with her could wear you out.''

Edie nodded as though she had known someone like Kayleen. Her eyes were sad and damp, her expression melancholy, wistful. ''Babies are sensitive to their mother's moods.''

''I think Missy was.'' Barbara clutched her knees tighter, locking her hands over her arms, a curious numbness spreading through her limbs. ''And Kayleen was at her worst. I mean, I'd never seen her so anxious. Whenever she picked up the baby, Missy fussed. But the minute Missy was in my arms, she'd settle right down.''

Even this memory failed to stir emotion in her. ''From the first moment I held her, I felt such a connection with her.'' Barbara stared at the toes of her boots, absently thinking they needed polishing. ''The last thing I remember is stroking Missy's cheek and whispering to her that I wished she was my daughter. Then someone shrieked and I looked up to see a semi-truck coming through the middle of the bus.''

Barbara heard Chad curse quietly. She drew a shuddery breath and closed her eyes. Her pulse roared in her ears. She could still hear the screech of metal smashing metal, still feel the whoosh of air as the bus ripped apart, still hear the screams, still smell the acrid smoke. Why couldn't she feel anything? And why were there still gaps surrounding the accident—chunks of time, events she couldn't recall?

She glanced at Edie. ''I don't remember getting out of the bus or how I got to the hospital.''

A wan smile touched Edie's lips. "Probably, you never will. It's symptomatic of the amnesia."

That was the only good piece of news Barbara had had in the past few days. She shifted on the sofa and glanced at Chad as she felt a weird fissure in her chest and realized it was her heart, splitting in two. "You were right. Missy is Marshall Emerson's daughter."

He raked his hand through his hair. "Believe me, that doesn't give me any pleasure."

The two halves of her heart began falling away from each other. "I don't have any legal right to her."

Edie sniffled.

Chad grasped Barbara's hands, dismayed at how cold they were. "The courts will have to take into consideration that you're the only parent she's known for five years."

"Will they? You're a reporter, Chad." Her voice was devoid of the pain that he knew was ripping her apart inside. "The news has been full of natural parents' rights versus adoptive parents' rights lately. The natural parents seem to win every time. And I haven't even adopted Missy."

She fell silent with that, pulling free of his grasp and hugging herself as if the rest of her were as cold as her hands.

Utter helplessness descended on Chad. She'd nailed the problem dead on, he thought, hating that a ready solution eluded him. If only there was something he could do or say—a few words of solace he could offer this woman who every minute meant more to him than he would have thought possible.

He couldn't bear the look on her face. If only she would cry or scream or something. Anything but this weird calm. He'd covered a hurricane once and he'd seen its destructive force, had spent a good part of the afternoon wonder-

ing what it would be like to be at the center of that storm—
where calm prevailed while all around it the world
shattered and blew apart like confetti in a wind tunnel.
"Barbara, I won't let Marshall Emerson take Missy from
you."

She raised her eyebrows. "But you're the one who ad-
vocated that he should have his daughter."

"I said Missy deserved to know her father. I didn't say
she should live with—" The doorbell interrupted his feeble attempt to explain. All three of them jerked toward the
foyer. Barbara lifted herself to her feet. Chad caught her
arm. "Ignore it."

"No. It might be the police again. Or Missy's baby-
sitter."

He stood and handed her the clean handkerchief from
his pants pocket. "Then let me get it."

Realizing she must look a mess, she agreed, then daubed
beneath her eyes and dried her cheeks with the handkerchief, gently wiping her nose last.

As Chad reached the door, the bell rang again; the high-
pitched sound grated across his tensed nerves. He pulled
the door open, blocking the view into the living room with
his body. *Elvis and Marshall Emerson.* His stomach hit
the floor.

As a rule, Chad prided himself on his quick wits. He'd
wriggled his way out of lots of tight spots, and getting rid
of unexpected visitors with bad timing should have been
a piece of cake. Would have been if the visitors had been
anyone other than these two men.

"Does a Jane Dolan live here?" There was a flicker of
recognition in Elvis's bleached-blue eyes.

Chad scrambled for something to say, but his acumen
seemed to have deserted him. Was it because he was per-

sonally involved in this? He shifted his weight to his other foot. "She's unavailable."

Elvis puffed up his considerable chest. "Well, when will she *be* available?"

"Maybe tomorrow."

Marshall leaned forward. "Look, Mr....?"

"Ryker," Chad said.

"Mr. Ryker, I'm Marshall Emerson. Ms. Daw—Dolan is my former sister-in-law."

"I know who you are, Dr. Emerson."

Marshall frowned. "Sorry, I don't—"

"You know my boss, Victor Lansing."

Disquiet darted through Marshall's green eyes. "You're a reporter for the *Courier?*"

"Yes."

Marshall looked uncomfortable. "What are you doing here?"

"He's a friend of mine, Marsh." Barbara appeared beside Chad, her hair freshly brushed, lipstick freshly applied, her nose freshly powdered.

Chad could hardly tell she'd been crying and doubted either of these men would pick up on it. Hoped neither would.

"Hi, B.J." Elvis grinned at her lasciviously.

She eyed him as if seeing him for the first time. "Why, you're the man I bumped into in Cle Elum yesterday."

Chad watched her with disbelief clattering inside him. Barbara was too calm again. But he decided he would follow her lead and back her up wherever she was going with this. She invited the men inside.

He stepped aside, and they all went to the living room. Edie wasn't there. Since the apartment had no back way out, Chad assumed she was in one of the bedrooms or the bathroom.

Elvis patted his hair with his hand, his gaze sweeping the tidy room. Landing on Chad's travel bag.

Marshall's eyes never left Barbara. "You can imagine how I felt when Elvis said he'd run into you in Cle Elum. Why, I couldn't believe it was true. I had to come and see for myself."

Slick, Chad thought. Just the right amount of concern in his voice. Good-looking, poised, self-assured. The man not only looked like an actor, he was one. It probably explained why smart men were taken in by him. But a scratch across the glossy public surface and they would soon realize Marshall Emerson was all facade.

Barbara said, "I'm sure it's a shock to discover that I'm alive, but believe me, you're not the only one finding it difficult to believe. You see, I didn't recognize Elvis yesterday because—"

"She's been suffering from amnesia." Edie entered, her own hair and makeup showing signs of repair. "In fact, she still is. I'm her doctor. Edie Harcourt." Edie shook hands with Marsh as Barbara made the introductions.

Two cool cucumbers when the chips were down, Chad thought. If he didn't know they were both going through hell inside, he would never have guessed. His only fear was that they couldn't carry it off for long. He wanted the Emersons out of here as fast as possible. But how?

"Amnesia?" Elvis grinned. "So that's why you acted like you didn't know me in the bar last night. I thought you were putting me on."

"No, I don't play those kinds of games." A rosy hue touched Barbara's cheeks. Chad wondered if Elvis realized she didn't like him.

Even Marshall seemed offended by his brother's redneck manners. Marshall cleared his throat. "Melissa?"

The sudden silence in the room was thick enough to

slice. Marshall frowned, a wary glint coming into his eyes. "Is she alive?"

"You can't have her!" Edie snapped, startling everyone. She had stepped in front of Barbara like a human shield.

"Hey!" Elvis whooped. Grinning, he slapped his brother's shoulder. "She's alive, bro."

Marshall swallowed so hard his Adam's apple bobbed. When he spoke again, his voice rasped. "Was she injured in the accident?"

"No." Barbara shook her head. "She escaped completely."

"It was a miracle those who survived did," Edie interjected, still angled between Marshall and Barbara, a miniature force field. "And that a few escaped with nothing more than minor burns or contusions."

Marshall glanced down at her. "Is she a healthy child?"

Chad had the distinct impression that he wouldn't want Missy if she weren't perfect. After the one evening he himself had spent with the little girl he couldn't imagine not wanting her, no matter what imperfection she might have.

"She's perfect." Edie's hands were on her hips, her chin high in indignation.

"May I see her now?" Marshall directed his gaze at Barbara.

She stiffened. "She's at school."

"Then, I'll go there." Marshall nodded to Elvis. "Where is it located?"

"Please, don't." Chad stepped forward. He'd had enough and was pretty certain Barbara and Edie had, too. It was just like Marshall Emerson to think the whole world would bend to his outrageous ego. But he had to make him see reason. "If you love your daughter—let Barbara explain this to her first. She won't understand who you are and is likely to be terrified if you show up at the school claiming you're her father.''

"Claiming?" Elvis stepped toward Chad, looking as though he would like an excuse to punch him. "He is her father.''

"No one is disputing that," Chad said, deliberately keeping his voice calm. "But this is a hell of a mess. Barbara has only just discovered she isn't Missy's mother. Imagine what the child will have to deal with. I'm only asking that you wait a—''

"Like hell, we'll wait!" Elvis retorted angrily. "He's already waited five years.''

Marshall raised his hand, signaling for his brother to back off. "It's all right, El. Mr. Ryker has a point. A five-year-old needs time to adjust.''

"Thank you," Barbara said.

Chad couldn't believe the man was giving up this easily. Doubted he would.

Marshall glanced at Barbara again. "I'll give you tonight to tell her. I'm staying at the Thunderbird Ho—'' He broke off, his gaze catching on a photo of Missy displayed on the far end table. "Is that her?''

"Yes." Barbara hugged herself.

Chad wanted to hold her up, steady her, reassure her that he was going to stay and see her through this. But he knew if he reached for her now, she would fall apart. He sensed it was important to her that she not do so in front of these two men.

He watched Marshall cross to the end table and lift the gilded frame. The doctor's expression altered, softened. His hand trembled as he touched the photo, one finger gently tracing the line of Missy's mouth, the shape of her hair, the curve of her nose. He was looking at her much the way Chad's father might have gazed upon a childhood photo of him—had Tom Ryker ever been sent such a photograph.

Chad's loyalties wavered. Kayleen had wanted Marshall and his money more than anything Chad could offer. She'd tossed away his love as though it didn't matter. He'd been hurt, bewildered, and angry. Especially when he learned she'd gotten pregnant right away to reestablish her union with Marshall. He'd never understood nor forgiven her for running off with the baby. It had hit too close to the bone.

Then, out of the blue, Kayleen had called, claiming the reason she'd run was because she feared Marshall would kill her. Before Chad could find out why, she'd been murdered. He'd naturally suspected Marshall. Had set out to prove it.

But the truth was, the police had a suspect in custody whose fingerprints were all over the weapon. Chad shoved his hands into his pockets. Had Marshall hired someone to kill Kayleen and Betty? Or did he just want that to be the case, so that Barbara wouldn't lose Missy?

Marshall's green eyes glistened. "She resembles Kayleen."

"Yes," Barbara said. The word sounded choked. "The likeness is even more striking in person."

Chad saw Marshall flinch, and his own throat constricted. Did Missy's resemblance to her mother bother the good doctor? What kind of man was he? The decent guy Chad's boss thought him? Or the monster Kayleen had hinted at? If he had anything to do with Kayleen's murder, wouldn't the little girl be a constant reminder? A thorn in his side?

The thought sent a chill through Chad's stomach. Somehow, he had to find out why Kayleen had feared her husband would kill her. And he had to do it before the little girl spent one minute in her father's custody.

Marshall set the photo back on the table and pinned Barbara with a hard stare. "Tomorrow."

CHAD SHUT THE DOOR on the Emersons and returned to the living room, his face scrunched in fury. "Tomorrow. You'd think the jerk would realize you need more time than that."

"He's only asked to *see* Missy tomorrow." Edie was using her best "voice of reason" tone. "He hasn't said he's going to take any further steps."

"Yet." Barbara scrambled to stave off the sorrow that threatened to weigh her down. Missy needed her to be strong. She needed to be strong for herself, as well. "You don't know him as Chad and I do, Edie. He'll stretch that inch into a mile in a heartbeat."

"This has been an awful day." Edie's feeble attempt at stoicism crumbled, and she looked on the verge of tears again. "Maybe you should lie down...try and get some sleep."

She should be offering herself this advice, Barbara thought. "I couldn't sleep, Edie."

"I could give you a sedative."

"No, thanks." She'd lived in an amnesia fog for five years. Now that it was clearing, she didn't want a drug-induced one taking its place. "I'll get through the rest of this day by tackling one problem at a time, and the first thing, Chad, is the signing of our statements at police headquarters. I'd really like that behind me."

"Sure." Looking as though he wasn't at all certain she was up to going anywhere, he gathered his coat and car keys. Handed Barbara her parka.

"I'd say that was my cue to take off." Edie donned her

own coat. She squeezed Barbara's hand. "Call if you need me."

Barbara nodded. Those words had brought her comfort over the past five years, knowing Edie was only a phone call away, should the need for a friend arise. It had arisen more often than she could count.

She thought now of what Edie had done for her—letting her believe she'd given birth to Missy. She'd held a terrible secret, but by doing so, Edie had saved her sanity. She could never hope to repay this woman for her friendship.

"Thank you...*for everything.*" Barbara hugged Edie tightly, whispering in her ear. "Don't you even think about finding a new best friend—you're stuck with me for life, lady."

Edie hugged her back, then pulled away. She nodded in silent agreement. Tears stood in her eyes again—tears of compassion and relief. But distress also radiated from her.

Barbara's nerves ached. She feared she knew why Edie was worried. And it had nothing to do with Missy.

"WHAT AM I GOING TO tell Missy?" Barbara asked Chad as they returned from signing their statements. "How will I explain this to her?"

Chad pulled his car to the curb in front of her apartment building, then turned in the seat. He brushed her hair from her cheek, his cool fingers touching her flushed skin. "Yesterday you told me that you'd tell her the truth."

"But she's only five years old. Will she even understand this mess I've made of her life?"

He feathered a lock of her hair between his finger and thumb as though testing the texture and finding it to his liking, but he kept his gaze fixed on hers. Tenderness, kindness shone from his compelling eyes. "She's old enough to understand that people sometimes get sick and then get well. Just explain it that way.''

Mulling over his suggestion, Barbara got out of the car and walked beside him to the building. Purposely, she avoided looking at the smashed snowman and the police tape surrounding it. "For a man without children, you seem to have some great insights into parenthood.''

Chad opened the door. "I've covered a lot of tragic stories—with children at the center of some of them. It's never easy, but in that experience I've made one solid observation: Kids deal better with the truth than lies.''

They started up the stairs, neither talking, his shoulder colliding with hers. The intermittent touch both comforted Barbara and disconcerted her. With her memory basically restored, she realized the last man she'd relied on for comfort was her dad. He'd died the day before her sixteenth birthday, and his death had stirred in her a rebellious streak that had lasted until she'd ridden that fateful bus.

But never had a man disturbed her as Chad Ryker had. Did she really want him in her life? Or was he merely arousing long-dormant urges?

On the second floor, they strode the long hallway toward her apartment. The moment she unlocked the door and stepped inside, a sense of dread descended on her. But she wasn't alone. Chad was here, she reminded herself, finding strength in the thought.

He stood behind her, his hot breath delicious on her neck as he helped her out of her coat. "What did you tell Missy the first time she asked about her dad?''

Barbara sighed and spun to face him. "You know, I nearly followed the same path as your mother and pretended he was dead.''

Chad made a noise that sounded like a grunt, but the warmth in his eyes, although tinged with cold memories, lacked reproach of any kind. She admired his self-restraint. It was a subject that had to twist his guts into knots.

She watched him hang her parka on the coatrack, then start to shrug off his jacket. She didn't know why his mother had told him his father had died, and she wouldn't judge the woman without all the facts, but Chad's bitterness made her glad she hadn't chosen that route. "It would have been easier. For me. But not for her. Besides, I always feared I'd regain my memory and regret the lie."

Chad stepped toward her, standing so near she was certain he could hear her crazily beating heart. He lifted his hands and grazed them down her arms. "What did you tell her?"

She swallowed hard. "I stuck as close to the truth as I could."

She had the sense that he expected she would have done this. Approval radiated from him. He kissed her cheek lightly, and whispered, "Then do the same now and you'll be fine."

His advice quieted her churning stomach. She smiled. "I think you're a good influence on me."

"You definitely have the opposite effect on me." Chad dragged her into his arms and captured her mouth with his.

His kiss sugared through her, melting her insides like so much heated caramel, stealing her breath, stirring her desire. She was free to make love to this man and right now, she wanted that badly.

But Chad pulled away. "Isn't it time to pick up Missy?"

Trepidation chilled her sexual ardor. She started to shake. Chad hugged her again. "Look, I'll go with you to get her, then I'll fix us all dinner while you talk to Missy.

If she takes the news badly and you want me to leave, I'm gone.''

"Okay."

MISSY AND SHE SAT in the middle of the sofa. She took the little girl's hands in hers, caressing them as if she would never get to hold them again. The aroma of toasted cheese sandwiches and tomato soup issued from the kitchen.

Missy's huge aqua eyes were turned up at her. Barbara swallowed hard and began. "Remember how I always told you that Daddy had gone away when you were just a baby?"

"Uh-huh." Missy nodded. "You looked and looked, but couldn't find him anywhere."

"That's right."

"You said he's always thinking about me and sad and missing me."

Her throat tightened at the earnestness in her daughter's voice.

"And one day you'll find him and we'll go visit him." Her eyes brightened. "Did you find him, Mommy?"

Barbara drew a shaky breath. "Well, first I need to explain some other things to you. It wasn't Daddy who got lost, it was me. I got a really bad bump on my head and forgot everything—even my real name. The only things I remembered were your name and that I loved you very much. I couldn't find your daddy because I didn't remember where to look."

Missy listened with a serious expression, asking the occasional question as Barbara explained about the interstate accident and as much of its aftermath as was pertinent. Always bright, Missy seemed to be understanding more than Barbara had thought she would.

"My name isn't Jane Dolan. It's Barbara Jo Dawson."

A thoughtful frown creased the little girl's brow. "Is my name Missy Dawson?"

"No, sweet pea, it's Missy Emerson."

Her frown deepened, then cleared. "Tommy Leber's mommy has a different name from his 'cause she got divorced. Is that how come my last name is different from yours? Did you and Daddy get divorced?"

Barbara blanched. She glanced up to find Chad hovering in the archway. A wayward urge to rush straight into his arms for a dose of courage swept her. He nodded, his expression reassuring her that she was doing okay. She smiled gratefully and felt the butterflies in her stomach settle.

She gave Missy a quick hug. "I have to tell you something that might be really hard for you to understand."

"I'm not a baby, Mommy."

After reassuring her that she didn't ever consider her "a baby" anymore, Barbara told Missy all about her real mother and her grandmother, including the fact that they were both dead. At first the child didn't seem to realize it was a true tale about her own life.

But as Barbara finished the story, tears filled Missy's eyes, clinging to her thick blond lashes like plump raindrops, and her bow-shaped mouth puckered with sadness. "Are they in Heaven with God, now?"

"Yes." Barbara's throat constricted with unshed tears of her own. She wasn't certain how much Missy really comprehended about death and Heaven. Or how she might deal with this news. It was overwhelming to Barbara and she'd lived it.

"This belonged to my mom. Your grandmother." Barbara caught hold of the locket and clicked it open. "This is me and this is Kayleen, your real mommy."

Missy wiped at her damp eyes with the backs of her hands and peered closely at the photographs. After a long minute, she gazed up at Barbara with a look of awe in her eyes. "She looks like me." Missy touched the photograph, then gazed up at Barbara again, a sorrowful expression capturing her precious face. "Did she die in the accident?"

"No. But she didn't know that we had lived, and I couldn't remember who she was because of the bump on my head."

"When we go to Heaven can we see them again?" She released the locket and snuggled against Barbara's side.

Barbara hugged her, gently pressing her cheek to the top of Missy's head. "You betcha."

Missy lifted her face and gazed at her with fear in her eyes. "Can you still be my mommy?" Her voice quavered.

Barbara pulled her close and hugged her again. "I'll always be your mommy, Missy."

But would she? What legal claim did she have on this child? And what of Marsh? Under the circumstances, would he consider his daughter's welfare first? Or exact his revenge against Kayleen on her, Barbara?

Her gaze collided with Chad's, and she knew that she couldn't control Marshall. She could only be responsible for her own conduct, and she would make this as easy on Missy as she could. She pulled back and stroked the child's silken white-blond hair. "Your daddy wants to meet you tomorrow."

Missy sniffled and nodded thoughtfully. "Okay."

"I hope you two are hungry, 'cause dinner is served." Chad grinned at them.

Barbara tapped Missy on the bottom. "Go wash your hands, sweet pea."

The second Missy was gone, she glanced at Chad. Her insides trembled. "I'm so afraid I'm going to lose her."

He opened his arms, and she slipped willingly into his embrace. He kissed the top of her head. "Marshall Emerson will only take her away from you over my dead body."

Anxiety wove through Barbara. Would Chad be so eager to help her once he discovered what Edie and she had done?

Chapter Eleven

"Mommy, look. It stopped snowing." Missy stood on the kitchen stool, where she'd been helping dry the dinner dishes. She leaned over the sink and wiped the towel across the steam-misted window. "And the moon is shining bright as day."

Barbara pressed her own face against the chilly glass and gazed out at the night. A full moon spilled across a fresh blanket of snow—which had started falling when they'd picked Missy up from school. Like a pale sun, the moon gave the world outside the appearance of cleanliness, as if the pristine white flakes had banded together in a cloak of chastity that could purify all the evil in life simply by covering it.

If only it could, she thought, pulling back and smiling at Missy. "It is pretty, isn't it?"

"We're all done with the dishes. Can we go out and make a new snowman?"

Being reminded of what had happened to the other snowman sent a shiver scurrying down Barbara's spine. "I don't know, sweetie, it's getting very near your bedti—"

"Oh, please, Mommy, please," Chad piped in, his expression so endearingly pathetic, Barbara laughed.

"How could I resist two such earnest pleas." Besides,

she mused, she would rather have a happy image to associate with snowmen, than the one now lodged in her brain. She hung the dish towel on the refrigerator, deciding she would also welcome the diversion—any distraction, on this night of uncertainty, when she didn't know what tomorrow would hold for her daughter and her. "Okay, one snowman. Then you're taking a warm bath and getting to bed."

"Yippee!" Missy whooped.

But Chad crooked his head at Barbara, his eyes gleaming sexily as if the reference to bed were meant for him and not the child. Her body gave a silent, honeyed response and her cheeks warmed. She pulled her gaze from his and glanced at Missy. "Let's get your snow pants and boots."

Missy rushed from the room.

Shaking her head at Chad, Barbara brushed past him. "I'm not sure which one of you is the bigger child."

"I'll show you the difference any time you say," he offered, his voice full of raspy promise.

Ten minutes later the three of them were outside. One deep breath of the crisp clean air convinced Barbara of the merit of this outing. "It seems warmer than it was this afternoon."

Chad nodded. "And quieter."

"That's what I love about snow—it mutes all the rude sounds of civilization."

He grinned down at her. "Ah, but without the rudeness of mankind, there would be no news. And without news, I wouldn't have a job."

"Be glad you only have to write about those vulgar aspects of life and humanity. I've worked with them."

"Really?" He tipped his head. "What did you do before you...became a bartender?"

"Five years ago, I was very idealistic. A mere college sophomore, I intended to make my mark on the world by becoming a social worker. Every chance I got, I volunteered at a homeless shelter."

He raised his eyebrows.

"But five years in a bar developed my cynical si—"

"Mommy!" Missy shouted. "Aren't you guys coming?"

Barbara turned to see the little girl had ducked under the police tape and darted to the spot where the snowman she'd built with Mrs. Ferguson once stood. Now nothing more than a misshapen series of bumps beneath the new cover of snow, nothing more than a bad memory, it was newly surrounded by Missy's myriad footprints.

Barbara drew a sharp breath. Despite her best intentions not to think of the intruder, her mind conjured his scarred face. Her insides quivered. Who was he? What had he wanted in her home?

"Missy, come back here," Chad called softly. "No one is allowed inside the taped-off area."

Noticing the yellow tape as though for the first time, Missy pivoted in a complete circle, then stared at her mother. "How come it's taped?"

Barbara's chest tightened. Perhaps this hadn't been such a great idea after all. "Come here and I'll explain."

She flicked a worried glance at Chad. How could she explain and yet not frighten Missy?

The child crunched through the snow, scattering more evidence of her presence across an even greater area. As she reached Barbara she asked again about the tape. "What is it?"

Missy could read, but Barbara doubted she understood the meaning of the words. "The police put it there."

"Why?"

"I—"

"We don't know, sweetheart. But we aren't going to let it ruin our fun, are we?" Chad scooped his hands full of soft snow and tossed it at Missy.

She giggled and chased after him. He led her to the opposite side of the building. Apparently lying to children was okay with Chad Ryker in selected instances, Barbara surmised, following.

She caught up with them as Chad let Missy overtake him. He pretended to trip and pulled the little girl to the ground with him, both of them laughing, their glee bouncing off the silent night and straight into Barbara's heart.

It struck her that someone looking out at them might mistake them for any normal family, and the wayward notion saddened her. Chad's mother had soured him on marriage. He might never have a family of his own. And soon even she and Missy would no longer be a family unit— not as they had been.

Barbara shoved that thought away. Why waste this night imagining the future without Missy? There would be time enough to grieve once Marsh asserted his parental rights. Too much time, then. She bent down and gathered a scoop of snow between her hands. "Hey, you two, do I have to build Frosty all by myself?"

The snow, just wet enough to be of excellent packing consistency, was quickly rolled from a small ball into one of giant proportions. Grunting and groaning, she and Chad made a great game of lifting the middle onto the bottom portion. Then he and Missy shaped the head, sculpting a nose and mouth, while she packed snow between the three sections, cementing them together.

"She needs eyes," Missy declared.

"She?" Chad questioned.

"Yeah, she looks like Mrs. Ferguson."

Barbara and Chad laughed, then began searching their pockets for something to use as eyes. Chad came up with two black cough drops. He unwrapped them and lifted Missy so she could poke them into place, then lowered her to her feet.

Beaming, Missy stepped back to admire their creation. "She's perfect."

Chad bowed at the waist. "Nice to meet you, Mrs. F."

Missy was still giggling over his antics when they returned to the apartment for hot chocolate, and Barbara realized the little girl's laugh reminded her of Kayleen. The unexpected memory both jarred and warmed her.

After her bath, Missy fell asleep halfway through her story. Barbara kissed her on the forehead, double-checked the window lock, and left the room.

Missy's resemblance to Kayleen continued to haunt her. She supposed it was because it was only sinking in that she'd lost her mother and sister forever. She'd spent five years not knowing whether she had family. But always, hope had blazed in her heart. With that snuffed out, grief hovered at the edges of her mind, held at bay by sheer willpower...and the conviction that, once unleashed, that grief would stymie her emotionally.

She couldn't afford to dwell on her loss. But one look at Chad's face told her he wanted to discuss that very subject.

"I REFILLED OUR CUPS." Chad handed a mug of cocoa to Barbara as she entered the kitchen. She looked ready to fold. It had been a hell of a day. But she'd come through it like a trouper. He suspected she was running on pure adrenaline at this point. He'd done that often enough— covering some intense story or other that had kept him wide-awake and pumping on all cylinders for hours past the endurance of most mortals.

He also knew what it was like to crash after such an experience. She held the cup between both hands as if the heat of the ceramic could warm her. She ought to be in bed. Trying to sleep. He should insist on that, but right now, they needed to talk. He pulled out a chair for her. "Sit and drink."

She set the cup on the table, dropped onto the seat and lifted her hair off her neck, letting it fall enticingly around her face. He longed to reach across and stroke those silken tresses. Instead, he sat next to her, determined to keep his mind on the problem at hand. "I know you're beat. And I'd let this go for another time, if I could."

"Let what go?" She curled her fingers around the mug again and stared blankly at its contents.

Chad wanted to take her in his arms and warm her from the inside out. He settled for stroking a finger across her knuckles. She lifted her gaze to his questioningly. He licked his lips. "I didn't want to ask you in front of Edie, or discuss this before you had your talk with Missy. One problem at a time, you said."

"Another problem?" She sounded as though one more complication would be laughable at this point.

"No. The same old problem." He took a sip of his hot chocolate. "Something set you and your family on the run from Marshall Emerson. Have you remembered what it was?"

She blew out a breath and rolled her neck. "Actually, right before I saw Elvis and Marshall on the street today, I had a vivid memory. Kayleen, Missy, Mom and I were at my mother's house in Bellevue. In the library."

She seemed to realize she was giving him unnecessary details, stopped, took a long swallow from her cup, then continued. "Kayleen had discovered something in an old journal of Marshall's that she claimed would get her a healthy divorce settlement, while stripping Marsh of his medical license and maybe landing him in jail for life."

"Good God." Here it was, finally. The story he'd come looking for. Chad leaned toward her. "What did he do? When did he do it?"

Barbara shook her head. "She wouldn't tell us."

He couldn't believe it. Would every lead be a dead end? "Why not?"

"She said the less we knew, the less threat we'd be to Marshall."

"But as long as he *thought* you knew something, you were just as much a threat."

"Exactly. That's what terrified us. That's why Mom and I went along with Kayleen, why we allowed ourselves to be swept into her hysteria. That and Dad's being killed by that carjacker. Murder had touched our lives once and we truly believed it could again." She realized with a jolt, that it *had* touched her life again. Her stomach ached as though filled with ice.

Chad lurched back against the chair. "Why didn't you just go to the authorities? Why run away?"

She played with her hair again, distracting him. "Because Kayleen feared Marshall would kill us all before the police could commence an investigation."

"And you believed that?"

"They never caught the man who killed my dad. Our distrust of the local police, right or wrong, was founded on how they mishandled that case from the get-go. We had to protect ourselves before launching an attack on Marshall."

"But how could you ensure he wouldn't find you?" Chad sipped the cocoa.

"We couldn't. But we could cover our tracks and hope he didn't find some way to pick them up. We went to the airport and bought tickets on Kayleen's credit card for three different destinations, then caught that fateful bus."

Her expression sobered. "The bus was supposed to take us as far as Billings, where we were picking up a car from an old friend of my dad's. Then we were going to drive to a small town in Idaho, where this friend of Dad's knew a lawyer. Kayleen was going to turn over the journal pages to him, and we would stay in hiding until Marshall was safely behind bars."

"Damn," Chad swore under his breath. "If only she'd confided in someone before you left town."

"She did."

That took him by surprise. His eyes widened and hope leaped inside his chest. "Who?"

"Unfortunately, I don't know. She said she'd sent a copy of the pages to a girlfriend. Someone who would forward them to a male friend, should anything happen to us, and that man would see to it that Marshall was investigated."

Chad wondered if *he* was the man Kayleen had intended would investigate Marshall. If so, why hadn't she contacted him before she'd run? His conscience nudged him. All right, he could guess why she hadn't. Then again, maybe she'd met someone else—someone she meant to marry as soon as she received her healthy divorce settlement.

Surprisingly, that prospect didn't bother him as it might have a while back—didn't bother him at all. "So, we don't know what was in the journal and we don't know who the mystery lady was who didn't do anything about those pages."

"That's about the size of it." She looked as dejected as he felt.

He covered her hand with his own. "If we just had an idea when the journal was written, maybe—"

"I do know that." Barbara tilted her head. "It was a college journal."

Chad grinned. "It's not much, but it gives us a starting point. I'll have Bonze check into the paper's morgue and see if there were any scandals at the university at or around the time Marshall attended college."

"He won't be happy if you find something. All he really cares about is his career. Not that he strove to be a *good* doctor. Just a wealthy and powerful one."

Chad twitched. Barbara's opinion of her former brother-in-law sounded like a duplicate of Kayleen's description of the man, and a mirror of his own assessment: shallow and ambitious. But it seemed Kayleen hadn't disliked her husband's money as much as she'd claimed. It dawned on Chad that he hadn't known her as well as he'd thought.

And what of Marshall Emerson? Kayleen had feared he would murder her. But had he? Chad had been so certain two days ago. Now he wasn't so sure. Being shallow and ambitious didn't make a man a killer—especially a man who'd taken an oath to save lives. Still, he supposed Marshall could have hired Dean Ray Staples to do the dirty deed. But how would he have known where to send the man?

Chad shook his head. He had to be certain. The more he was around Missy, the more fond of her he became. She needed a father who cherished her. If Marshall Emerson was that kind of person, as well as an innocent man, then he deserved a chance with his daughter.

But what about Barbara? In every respect, she *was* Missy's mother.

Barbara touched him between the eyebrows. "I thought this lead would please you, but you're scowling."

"I was thinking about Missy and you. I know it's irrational, but I feel somehow responsible for this awful mess with Emerson."

She narrowed her eyes at him. "I'd say that sounds more egotistical than irrational. I had already begun remembering when we met, Chad. The truth was already bearing down on me."

His cocoa no longer tasted sweet on his tongue, but bitter. "Maybe I should have let you run away the other night."

"What?" She gaped at him. "Why are you waffling on an issue that you believe in with all your heart?"

He shrugged. But he knew it was because he also believed in Barbara and Missy with all his heart. Believed they belonged together. "This situation is impossible. I can't stand you and Missy getting hurt."

She reached out and stroked his cheek. "You can't prevent it, either, Chad. But you've made it a little easier to bear."

He kissed her palm, then her wrist, lifted his gaze to hers, his hand reaching up to touch her hair, graze her cheek. Need pooled hot and quick in his groin. "You've had a hell of a day. Maybe you should call it a night."

"No. I don't want to go to bed." Hunger gleamed in her eyes. "Not alone. Not tonight."

Chad groaned. "Don't say that unless you mean it. I can barely keep my distance from you now."

"No one's asking you to," she crooned in throaty invitation.

"Are you sure?" His own voice sounded gravelly.

She grinned wickedly at him. "I can honestly say for the first time in five years, I'm positive."

A smile tugged at his mouth and seemed to sweep the length of him, warming every cell in his body. He rose and pulled her out of the chair and into his arms, need spiraling hard inside him as her lush curves pressed against the length of him. At first it was enough just to hold her, his hands skimming over her back, her bottom; but soon he ached with need, his hunger for her obvious to them both.

She lifted her face to his, her glorious aqua eyes full of trusting, yearning. He cupped her cheeks in his hands, then brushed his lips over hers gently, again and again, with the tender thoroughness of a honeybee gathering nectar from a budding orchid, savoring the flavor of her as she opened to him, welcoming his tongue inside her, thrusting her tongue into his mouth.

Impatience swept him and he reached for the hem of her sweater. She pulled back. "Not here. Missy…"

Still kissing, they moved awkwardly into her bedroom and closed the door. A burning candle sat on the nightstand, its single glow filling the room with the softest of lights and the gentlest of rosy scents, like the dusk of a summer evening in a secret lovers' garden. Somewhere intimate. Inaccessible. Locked away from the world and its cares.

Chad reached for her again, resuming his sensual assault on her mouth, freely stroking the curve of her waist, her ripe firm buttocks, and pulling her hips against his, torturing them both with need.

Her fingers curled through his hair as she deepened the kiss, urging him on, encouraging his exploring caresses until passion sang through his veins, heating his blood, speeding his pulse, stealing his very breath.

His conscience nudged him anew. This wasn't right. There were things he should tell Barbara. She said she was sure she wanted him, but would she if she knew everything about Kayleen and him? He angled away from her a couple of inches.

She blinked, breathless and frowning. "What?"

"Before we go any further, there's something I need to tell you about Kayleen and—"

"I don't want to talk about Kayleen anymore tonight." She pulled his head to hers, her lips as sweet as sugared candy, her kisses distracting, mind-robbing bandits stripping him of his good intentions.

He moaned against her mouth. "But I—"

"Not now," she whispered, her breath a feathered wisp against his flesh. His pulse shivered in response, his blood surging through his veins like charged ions, scattering every thought in his head but those of Barbara, beautiful, precious, wonderful Barbara, and his need for her.

He carried her to the bed, then stepped back and peeled off his sweater, enjoying the delight that danced in her eyes as she stared at his naked chest, her gaze lowering to the waist of his jeans as he worked the top button free.

"I'm not sure—" she said.

He watched, mesmerized, as she ran her tongue over her bottom lip, ached to taste her mouth again, to feel her tongue on his bare flesh.

She rose up on her elbows. "I mean, I don't want to disappoint you."

He closed his eyes, swallowing his impatience, thanking God that he'd found this giving treasure, praying that he would make her grateful she'd waited to share this moment with him. "You aren't going to disappoint me."

"But it's been so long since I—"

He laughed softly, a warm rumble in his throat. "You know what they say about riding a bike—you don't forget."

"Oh, I know *how*." Her smile darkened her eyes to the hue of a mountain pool. "I just don't know that I was ever—"

He silenced her fears with his mouth, savoring again the heady taste she evoked as his tongue twined with hers; this union, a prelude to the greater one ahead, caused exquisite tremblings throughout his body, straining his patience. He wanted to go slow, but could he?

Yes, because more than his own need, he wanted her pleasure. He dug a condom from his pocket, and leaving his jeans on, he joined her on the bed.

Soon her sweater was on the floor beside his, and he reached for her bra, a lacy pink wisp of fabric that unhooked in the front with one flick of his experienced fingers; but for all that experience, his hand trembled as though he were a virgin and this the first woman he'd ever desired, ever made love to, ever loved.

Achingly slowly, he whisked aside the silken cloth, exposing the most beautiful breasts he'd ever seen. He drew a sharp breath but couldn't swallow, or think—only respond. He brushed his knuckles across one dark tip, hesitantly, gingerly, gathering the taut nipple between his fingers.

Impatience swept him again with the force of a released floodgate. He closed his eyes, schooling his need, striving for forbearance, taking deep breaths until control returned, then once more feasting his eyes on her incredible beauty. "God, you're perfect."

"So are you." Barbara sighed, joy cascading through her. She tilted her breast toward his mouth, inviting his attention, and the second his wet tongue flicked across the distended bud, tingles exploded through her, eliciting mind-boggling heat waves in every intimate depth of her.

Her breath rushed and passion crashed through her like

breakers on a shore, thundering unrelentingly, driving her greed for him higher and higher with an urgency she had never experienced until this moment, with this man.

She feathered her fingertips down his rock-hard stomach, stroking the trace of soft blond hair there, until she came to the open waistband of his jeans. Chad groaned, a sound rich and potent, full of pleasure and need, that spurred her on to tug open the second button of his fly. Then the third. The fourth.

She slipped her hand inside his shorts, through the nest of thick hair and touched him, tentatively, shyly, with fascination rippling through her at the feel of him, the size of him. He moaned, and she watched his eyes glaze with desire as she grew gradually bolder.

He murmured her name and pulled her to him, kissing her mouth with yet more abandon as he squirmed out of his pants and reached for hers, swiftly undoing the zipper and dragging her panties down her legs with her jeans.

He paused then, gazing at her with awe in his eyes as if he'd never seen a naked woman before, skimming his knuckles over her tummy as if she might melt at his touch, dipping his fingertips into the cleft between her legs as if she belonged to him.

And at that moment she wanted nothing less. She arched to meet his delving fingers, marveled that they seemed to know exactly where and how to touch her, wallowed in the delicious sensations he evoked—sensations that quickly spiraled out of control and lifted her into the clouds above. Closing her eyes, she moaned, her whole being responding to Chad as though she were a four-stringed musical instrument and he a master violinist playing her to perfection, filling her with such rapture that it racked her body from head to toe, dampening his fingertips.

She opened her eyes to his smiling face. In the golden candlelight his magnificent body glistened, tanned and muscled. Lean and hard, throbbing with desire—as her body ached for him. "Oh, Chad, I've waited for you for so long. Don't make me wait any longer."

Slowly he found her mouth again and kissed her with unleashed passion as he slipped on the condom. Then he rose above her, settling between her parted legs, his thrust gentle, demanding, their joining smooth, hard, thrilling.

Barbara cried out his name in sheer ecstasy as with every thrust of their hips, her pulse hummed higher and higher, faster and faster. Exquisite sensations coiled inside her, then erupted in a burst of pure pleasure, sending sparkles of light dancing before her eyes and through her mind.

Chad cried out her name as he reached his own climax and collapsed against her. A moment later he rolled onto his side and pulled her with him. In the tender silence that followed, Barbara pondered what had just happened between them. Sex had never been like this for her, ever. Was this what they called "making love"? How had she gotten so lucky to experience this most precious of gifts with a man she actually could love?

She propped herself on one elbow and gazed down at Chad, her heart still hammering, her breathing still ragged. "You were definitely worth the five-year wait, Chad Ryker."

His mouth crooked in a teasing grin. "I could see to it that you give up celibacy for good, if you like."

"I like." She trailed her fingertips through the tawny hair on his chest, then stroked down his stomach and reached for him again, not wholly surprised to find him ready and eager.

Half an hour later, Barbara fell asleep in his arms. Chad gazed down on her face. She seemed as innocent as Missy at this moment. But "uninformed" would be a more apt description. She thought he was a great guy; he felt like a dog. He should have told her about Kayleen. Should have insisted she listen. Before they'd made love.

To tell her now would clear his conscience, but he would be doing it to make himself feel better. It would only hurt Barbara. God willing, she would never need to know the whole truth.

Chapter Twelve

Chad woke around 6:00 a.m. to find himself alone in Barbara's bed. He stretched, lazily, happily, thinking she must be in the bathroom, expecting her to return at any moment. After five minutes, he started wondering where she was. After ten minutes, he threw off the covers and dressed.

Muted voices filtered to him from the kitchen. He paused in the living room. Barbara and Edie sat huddled together at the table, deep in conversation, both of their expressions anxious, grim. His chest squeezed with worry. What was going on?

"Oh, Edie, be serious," Barbara said, lifting her hair off her nape in a gesture that he was starting to love. "Marshall is going to demand to have his daughter returned to him."

"Even so, surely he'll be open to some sort of joint custody—for Missy's sake, if nothing else." Edie's eyes were underscored with dark purple hues as though she hadn't slept in days, and she sounded as if she were the one in danger of losing Missy.

Chad remembered how fiercely she'd defended Barbara's rights yesterday and it occurred to him that Edie probably did feel as though Missy were part of her own family. His heart ached at this awful situation.

"Joint custody? Oh, God, Edie." Barbara's voice held no hope. "That isn't possible and we both know it."

"No one needs to know about—" Edie caught sight of Chad and broke off. Her eyes widened in warning to Barbara.

He strode to the coffeemaker. "Good morning, ladies."

"Good morning." Barbara's greeting came out in a quavery voice. Chad wished he could attribute her dismay to his presence in her kitchen the morning after a night of lovemaking. But he feared it was because he'd overheard something he shouldn't have.

"Good morning, Mr. Ryker." Edie's reception was as stiff as her back.

"Please, call me Chad." He filled a mug with coffee, then turned and faced both women. "There's no point in my pretending I didn't overhear some of your conversation. Would one of you please explain what it is you're trying to cover up?"

Edie chuckled, a short sarcastic chirp. "The last thing I'd tell an investigative reporter is a secret that I wanted kept."

"I promise, I'm not here as a reporter. Anything you tell me will be strictly off the record. Private."

Edie rolled her eyes.

Chad steadied his gaze on Barbara. "I think I proved yesterday whose side I'm on."

Her cheeks reddened. But the fear in her lovely eyes roused his concern, fed his curiosity. She shook her head. "Chad, I—"

"No," Edie interrupted. "He doesn't need to know."

Barbara sighed. "I don't think Chad would willingly do anything to hurt Missy or me."

The doctor blew out a long breath through pursed lips,

her tired blue eyes suddenly even more weary with resignation. "Is that true, Mr. Ryker?"

"Chad. Yes, it's true."

"Then maybe it would be better if I did this." Edie motioned him to the chair between them. "Sit."

"Edie," Barbara protested. "I can't let you—"

"You aren't letting me do anything. I've already done It. I did it willingly. I've always known I'd have to accept the consequences one day."

"I don't like the sound of this, ladies. What the hell have you done?"

"The only thing I could think of to help a terrified young woman and her child." Edie took a long sip of coffee, then set the cup down gently and raised her gaze to his. There was no apology there. Whatever she'd done, she didn't regret.

Barbara said, "Edie filled out a 'live' birth certificate so that we could establish Missy's ID."

"Why?" Chad asked. "Why would a doctor do that?"

Edie blew out a breath and sat straighter. "My reasons were personal, but suffice it to say, Ja—er—Barbara and Missy entered my life at a time when I was vulnerable to their plight. Not as a doctor, but as a woman. Despite every professional ethic I hold dear, I just *had* to do whatever it took to help them."

Chad's gaze steadied on her. "What else did it take?"

Edie swallowed hard. "I also secured the documents of one of my deceased patients for Barbara. To establish an identity for her."

Chad studied the doctor for a moment. "The patient's name was Jane Dolan?"

Edie nodded. "She was a drifter, around the same age as Barbara. No family. She died of blood poisoning a week after the interstate accident." Edie ran her hands through her mussed blond hair. "It seemed somehow...providential. I was responsible for the death certificate, so I altered one or two of the statistics. Since there was no family to collect her personal effects, I volunteered to dispose of them."

"And gave Jane's birth certificate and social-security card to me," Barbara concluded for her friend.

"What about the police?" Chad glanced between the two women. "Didn't they question either of you?"

"Not me." Barbara shook her head. "I checked us out of the hospital and into a motel the day after the accident."

Edie said, "I told the police she'd paid her bill in cash and walked away without leaving a forwarding address. She had that right. She wasn't under arrest or anything."

"But why?" Chad frowned, shaking his head.

Barbara's eyes pleaded for his understanding. "I needed to have identification in order to get a driver's license, a job. Missy and I needed a place to live, money for food."

"That's not what I meant. There are legal ways to establish a new identity. Why didn't you do it legally?"

The color fell from her face and she grew somber. "Because that would have involved courts, judges, lawyers and reporters. I was terrified of something that I couldn't remember. How could I risk unleashing God-knew-what kind of horror on Missy and me?"

Chad whistled. This mess just kept getting worse. He reached out and covered Barbara's hand with his. He was, he realized, starting to care for this woman on levels he'd never even tapped into before.

"I'm worried that Marshall will discover what we've done and use it against us," Barbara continued. "I might never get to see Missy again and Edie could lose her medical license."

"Would lose it." Edie's voice was flat. "The hospital

can't have staff doctors engaging in illegal activities of this sort.''

Chad touched Edie's arm. "Then we'll do our damnedest to keep this secret under wraps and hope Emerson doesn't stumble on it." He doubted it would be easy. Or possible. But neither woman needed to hear that right now. "Meanwhile I'll have my assistant check into the matter. See what he can learn about the legal ramifications. Surely there's some provision for amnesia victims."

"That won't hold any water with Marshall."

Or with the hospital board, Chad thought, unable to look Edie in the eye.

Barbara lifted her hair off her neck again. The moment of truth was nearing and she looked ready to collapse beneath the weight of heartache she would have to face this day.

"Mommy?"

Barbara started as though she'd been pinched. She jerked around. Missy stood in the archway to the kitchen, her hair tangled, her cheeks rosy. She clutched Mr. Bear to her chest with one hand and rubbed at her aqua eyes, which reminded Chad of Barbara's, with the other.

The little girl frowned. "Did Aunt Edie and Chad come over for breakfast?"

Barbara blushed, and Edie looked as though she'd been caught doing something else illegal.

Chad said, "Would you like it if we did?"

Missy gazed at him shyly and nodded.

Barbara scraped her chair back and stood, smiling at her daughter. "We thought we'd have a breakfast party for this special day."

"'Cause my daddy's coming to see me?"

"Yeah." Barbara moved to Missy's side and squatted, tucking a strand of the little girl's hair behind her ear in a gentle gesture of love. "But he won't be here until much later. So we'll have this party with just us friends. Okay?"

"Okay."

"Good. Now, I'd say a special party like this calls for some Mickey Mouse waffles."

"Yea!" Missy said.

Barbara straightened and bent at the waist. "Why don't you talk Aunt Edie into helping you get your bathrobe and slippers on."

Edie rose immediately, obviously functioning better when she had something to do.

The moment they were alone, Barbara turned to Chad. "I should have told you sooner—about what Edie and I did—but the time never seemed right." And she'd been afraid he would think less of her. Was scared of that still, but she couldn't bring herself to admit it out loud.

Something dark passed through his eyes—a sign that he hadn't told her everything about himself, either. But there was no reproach in those gray-blue orbs, only concern for her. "It doesn't change anything between us. I won't desert you."

He opened his arms and she rushed into them. They stood that way for a moment, then heard Missy and Edie returning and broke apart. Barbara got the waffle maker out of the cupboard and gave everyone a chore.

Later, as they ate, Missy regaled them with the tale of a schoolmate who'd used her art scissors to snip a chunk of cloth from the shirt collar of a boy who'd been particularly annoying.

Chad bit back a chuckle. Edie hid her grin behind her napkin.

Barbara struggled to keep from smiling. "Missy, that's awful. She shouldn't have cut his shirt. I don't ever want you to do something like that if someone is annoying y—"

The doorbell interrupted her. The few bites of food she'd managed to swallow churned in her stomach. She flicked a frightened glance at Chad.

He touched her hand. "Do you want me to get it?"

"No, that's all right." Barbara lurched to her feet. "It's probably Mrs. Ferguson. She and Missy were supposed to make cookies this morning. I completely forgot to cancel. Missy, you go get dressed, sweetie. Your clothes are laid out on your bed."

"I'll help her," Edie volunteered, rising.

"I'll start the cleanup." Chad began stacking dirty plates.

As Missy hurried with Edie into her room, Barbara strode to the foyer. She had told Mrs. Ferguson nothing about her amnesia and certainly didn't want to broach the subject with her now. The older woman would likely smother her with caring and concern. Trying to think quickly of some excuse for canceling Missy's visit with her today, she flung open the door.

It wasn't the baby-sitter. Marshall and Elvis Emerson and a woman whom Barbara recognized as Marsh's clinic nurse, Joy Jamison, stood outside her door. A dozen reproaches sprang to her tongue—from *What are you doing here so early?* to *I thought you'd at least wait until I called you before coming over.* But all were confrontational, and that was not the tone she wanted for this meeting.

Stifling her annoyance, she invited them into the living room. The sound of dishes being washed echoed from the kitchen. "We just finished eating."

Realizing they could probably guess that for themselves, what with the smell of hot syrup and fried bacon in the air, Barbara warned herself to calm down. She forced a smile. "May I take your coats?"

Marsh slipped off his overcoat and handed it to her. She

accepted it, along with Elvis's ski jacket and Joy's fur parka, carried the coats to the foyer and hung them on the rack beside her own coat. When she returned to the living room, she found Marshall and Joy on the sofa and Elvis in one of her armchairs.

Tension reigned. Silently, she willed Chad to abandon the dishes and come and see who the guests were.

"Missy is dressing. She's at that age where she likes to choose her own clothes, and even though she doesn't always make the best decisions, I let her and she very much likes dressing herself." Barbara could hear herself babbling, but couldn't seem to stop. Why had her composure deserted her now, when she needed it most?

"Is Mrs. Ferguson here, Mom—" Missy stopped in her tracks at the sight of the strangers, looking like a startled fawn caught in highway traffic, not knowing which way to run.

Barbara opened her arms. "Come here, Missy. These are some people who want to meet you."

Missy shook herself and scurried to Barbara.

Barbara pointed to Elvis. "This is your Uncle Elvis."

Elvis Emerson grinned. "Nice to meet you, Missy. You're sure a looker."

"Oh, Marsh, she's beautiful. She has your mouth," Joy gushed.

The awe in her voice sent a shiver down Barbara's spine. Why had Marsh brought this woman with him? She started to ask, and saw the look of pure delight in Marshall's eyes as they fixed on Missy. Her stomach churned anew. She steeled herself.

"And," he said, "I'm your daddy, Melissa."

"I know. Mommy told me."

Joy gave Barbara a scathing look.

Marsh pointed to the woman beside him, taking her hand in his. "This is my wife, Joy."

"Your wife?" Edie exclaimed.

Barbara started. She hadn't seen her friend enter the room. In fact it was only now that she noticed the huge diamond on Joy's left ring finger. Well, she mused, some things never changed. Kayleen had been Marsh's clinic nurse before they were married. But her sister had never had anything as nice as that fur parka or that hefty diamond. What had Marsh done? Won the state lottery?

Marsh's gaze was focused on Missy, as though they were the only two people in the room. "Joy is going to be your new mommy."

Edie drew a sharp breath.

Barbara's chest squeezed and tears stung the backs of her eyes. Missy hugged her around the legs. "This is my mommy."

Barbara looked up to find Chad coming in from the kitchen carrying a tray of filled coffee cups. "No one's in a real rush right now, are we, Dr. Emerson? Let's all have some coffee and you can spend some time with Missy and get to know her and give her a chance to know you."

Marshall scowled at Chad, but the look of fright on Missy's face and the fierce way she clung to Barbara finally had him nodding. "I like cream in mine."

Chad set the tray on the coffee table and the guests helped themselves. Barbara alone abstained. She feared she would wear more of the coffee than she would drink in her agitated state. "Missy, why don't you show your daddy your room and some of your toys?"

Missy reluctantly agreed, leading the Emersons to her room. Barbara walked to the living-room window and pulled the blinds open. A dull sun peeked through the gray clouds and wind blew-dried snow along the street. She felt cold inside, as though the wind were blowing through her heart.

Chad stepped close behind her. "How are you holding up?"

Barbara sighed. "What do you think?"

"You've had more fun during a root canal?"

She nodded.

"This is outrageous." Edie sidled up to them. Her whisper held scathing disapproval. "How dare that pompous jerk waltz in here and announce that—that raven-haired witch will be Missy's new mother. As if she didn't already have one. I can't believe he fathered our darling Missy."

"It does seem incredible. But it's true," Barbara assured her.

"He's the kind of doctor that gives my profession a bad name. More interested in money than patients, if you ask me." She leaned closer to them conspiratorially. "Did you get a look at the *rock* that wife of his is wearing?"

Barbara glanced at Chad. "And I'd swear his overcoat was cashmere, Joy's parka mink. Did Marsh suddenly strike it rich?"

"Guess you could say that." Chad stroked his crooked pinkie finger. "A wealthy uncle left him a bundle. Did you know the uncle's daughter, Suzanne? Seems she disappeared about three years or so before Kayleen and you left town."

"I didn't know her." Barbara frowned. "But I do remember the search for her was intense. The police feared she was the victim of a local serial killer and that her body might never be found. This theory brought on her father's fatal stroke."

"But just before he died, he altered his will," Chad said.

Barbara nodded. "That's right. Kayleen mentioned the

new clause. If Suzanne didn't turn up in seven years, the estate would go to Marshall.''

"Yep. He collected last month."

Barbara's heart clutched. "If he has that kind of money at his disposal, how will I ever fight him for Missy?''

"You won't need money." Chad touched her cheek. He wanted to hold her, to haul her back to bed and make love to her until all her pain was forgotten. "You have Missy's love on your side."

Edie patted her arm. "We'll find a way through this, Barbara. I promise you.''

Barbara gave them both a wobbly smile. What had she ever done to inspire such loyalty? She decided not to question her good fortune; just to appreciate it. "Thanks. Both of you. I don't think I could get through this without you.''

"Daddy's going to read my new library book," Missy announced as she and the three Emersons reentered the living room. Marsh settled beside her on the sofa, and Joy perched daintily on the coffee table, staring with covetous eyes at the little girl. Elvis, looking as out of place in this family setting as a giant gnome, nevertheless returned to the armchair and listened to his brother read one of the Berenstain Bears' adventures.

Barbara, Chad and Edie retreated to the kitchen. Ten minutes later, Marshall appeared in the archway. "I'd like a word in private with you, Barbara.''

She braced her back against the kitchen counter and clasped the locket tightly, dreading what was coming. "Whatever you have to say to me, you can say in front of my friends."

"Yes, but not in front of the child."

"The child?" Edie chirped. "What kind of loving father calls his daughter, 'the child?'"

Marshall ignored Edie as though she hadn't spoken. But

Barbara didn't miss the crimson climbing her friend's throat. She barely contained her own temper. "What do you want me to do with her?"

"I thought you might let Joy or Elvis take her out into the hall for a few minu—"

For the second time that morning the doorbell interrupted. Barbara blew out a frustrated breath, but was secretly glad of the diversion. "Excuse me."

She brushed past Marsh and hurried to answer.

"Good morning, dear." Mrs. Ferguson, a spitting image of Opie Taylor's Aunt Bee, looked startled at the way Barbara had flung open the door. She straightened her apron. "Is Missy ready for our cookie bake-off?"

Oh, no. She'd forgotten again to call and cancel after the Emersons had arrived. What could she say now?

Missy ran to the door. "Hi, Mrs. Ferguson. Did you come to meet my daddy?"

"What?" Frances Ferguson's hazel eyes widened.

"Er." Barbara felt her cheeks flame. "Missy's long-lost daddy has shown up. It's a really complicated story, Frances. Could I tell it to you at another time?"

"Of course, my dear." Curiosity flared in her hazel eyes. She turned to Missy. "We can bake cookies another day."

Barbara stopped her. "No, wait. Actually, I think baking cookies right now would be a good idea. I need to talk to Missy's daddy and I'd rather she was at your apartment."

"Oh, certainly." Mrs. Ferguson nodded in understanding.

Barbara glanced down at Missy. "Sweet pea, I want you to go with Mrs. Ferguson and I'll come and get you in a little while. Okay?"

"Will my daddy still be here?"

"Yes." Unfortunately, she thought, he probably would be.

She returned to the kitchen and found the whole group had gathered there. She explained where Missy was.

Elvis said, "Good. Now give it to her, bro."

Marshall scowled at Elvis and Barbara wondered if Elvis knew how much of an embarrassment he was to the doctor.

"Give me what?" she asked.

Marshall dug into his suit pocket and handed her an official-looking envelope.

She took it with a trembling hand. "What is this?"

"It's perfectly legal," Elvis chimed in.

Edie moved to Barbara's side as though readying for battle. She peered at the envelope. "It's from some lawyer's office."

Marshall said, "In layman's terms, this document gives me full and immediate custody of my daughter. I'm taking her home with me today. Now. As soon as you've packed her belongings."

"No!" Edie leaped at Marshall as though she could stab him in the chest with her fists. "You can't."

"He can." Elvis grabbed her by the wrists.

Joy's hands were on her hips. "Melissa is *our* daughter."

Chad wrenched Edie's arm out of Elvis's grasp. "Keep your hands off her."

The room exploded with colliding voices.

"Everyone!" Barbara shouted with every ounce of the fury and fear that possessed her. She would have liked to throttle this clan of interlopers, go after Marshall harder and longer than Edie, but she needed leverage. Needed to retain her senses, to watch her step, or she would lose

Missy forever. She forced her hands outward in a gesture meant to defuse the situation. "Please. Calm down."

Edie's face was crimson and tears stood in her eyes. Elvis's face was equally red, his pale eyes narrowed in fury. Chad returned to Barbara's side and settled a hand at the back of her neck, possessively, reassuringly. Her muscles knotted tighter.

She said, "Marshall, please be reasonable."

He laughed bitterly. "I've been reasonable for five years. Your bitch of a sister robbed me of the first five years of my child's life. If you don't turn her over to me now, I'll have you prosecuted for kidnapping."

Fear skittered through Barbara as cold and icy as the day. Kidnapping? No. It was just a threat. A bluff. Even if he tried it, chances were it would never stick.

But the fact that he would use whatever he could to legally keep her away from Missy scared the hell out of her. She wouldn't have a leg to stand on if it came out that she and Edie had created fraudulent papers to prove Barbara had given birth to Missy. She'd chosen the illegal way out because she'd been afraid of this man. But she had no proof of that. A judge would likely say she'd been afraid he would find her and take his child back home.

Chad stepped between Marshall and Barbara. "Hold your threats, Doctor. Or so help me, God, I'll go to every tabloid in the country and turn this into another 'Baby Richard,' with you as the heavy. The media will have a field day with the fact that the newest board member on the Fred Hutchinson Cancer Center is a bigamist. Not to mention how your bedside manner will be trashed by your unsympathetic attitude toward an amnesia victim, and your callous unconcern for your poor daughter."

Marshall's face was beet red. "You wouldn't dare."

Chad laughed, but there was no mirth in it. "I *promise*

you I will do it...unless you back off and let Barbara handle getting Missy ready to accept the changes in her life.''

"This is ludicrous." Joy flicked her black hair across her shoulders. "It's blackmail. Our lawyer will make mincemeat out of you."

"Let him try." Chad smirked at her. "By then it will be too late. The stories will be in circulation, the press camped on your doorstep."

"Marshall, tell him he can't do this," Joy protested.

"Why, I ought to..." Elvis stepped toward Chad, tension issuing like smog from his huge body.

"Don't, El," Marshall warned.

Elvis backed down. "You're right. No need to lose our heads over this. The law's on our side."

"Exactly." Marshall glanced at Barbara again. His expression was that of the one thing he wasn't—a kindly country doctor. "What would you consider a 'reasonable' time to prepare Missy for this change?"

Forever! Barbara's mind screamed. But she knew that was out of the question. She clutched the locket. "I'm not sure...."

Marshall arched a brow at her. "I won't allow this to linger on indefinitely."

"I realize that." But what kind of time frame could she give herself for losing her daughter?

"I'm a fair man. Make me a fair offer."

She swallowed hard. "Two weeks?"

"I see." He studied her for a moment, then withdrew a business card from his pants pocket and handed it to her. "I'll expect you to bring Missy to this address." He paused. "In two days."

Barbara stared at the card as if it were the worst bit of garbage she had ever had the misfortune of touching.

Chapter Thirteen

The old brick building loomed out of the darkness. Barbara stood still, silent, the ground beneath her feet solid. The sounds of heavy traffic along the viaduct filled her ears. The air reeked of harbor smells, creosote and salt water. It was a place she knew: the homeless shelter on the Seattle waterfront.

The door of the building opened, beckoning her. Fear sliced through Barbara. This time she knew what awaited her inside. Her pulse skittered and her eyes blurred. She wanted to run in the opposite direction, but her legs disobeyed her pleas, propelling her forward and across the threshold.

A thick haze enveloped the interior. She could see nothing. The rank odors of unwashed bodies and soiled clothing rushed her. Repulsed, she stumbled back. The haze lightened and through the semi-fog, she saw the room was filled with cots, lined up like headstones in a graveyard. Every cot was occupied. Even though she now knew these people were not dead, only needy, she shrank farther back into the doorway. Was she frightened by their collective neediness?

Or by the neediness of only one of them?

With growing horror, she watched a lone figure rise

from a cot and step toward her. The woman's ripe smell burned Barbara's nasal passages. She moved ever closer. Her tattered coat of indiscriminate color hung open over a stained, garish-pink sweater and orange-striped wool skirt. Grungy men's slacks peeked from beneath the skirt like cuffed bloomers, grazing the tops of her army boots.

Barbara knew her as Saucy Sue, a homeless woman who had earned her nickname from her penchant for foraging in Italian-restaurant Dumpsters for any sauce-smeared scraps of food.

She stretched a bony finger toward Barbara and spoke in an eerie voice. "I can't rest, B.J. Help me. Only you can help me."

Barbara shook her head, her heart clambering against her chest, bile climbing into her throat. "I can't. I don't know how."

"You do." Saucy Sue's toothless mouth twisted and she clasped a skeletal hand around Barbara's wrist. "You know he killed me."

Barbara let out a startled scream and jerked awake. The room was shadowed in filtered light and it took her a pulse-sputtering moment to realize she was in her own bedroom. Her chest heaved. Her breath came in taut spurts. How long had she been asleep?

Emotionally drained, she'd lain down in her room shortly after the Emersons and Edie had left. Chad, anxious to initiate his investigation into Marshall's college days, had remained at her apartment, spending most of the time on the telephone, calling and receiving calls from his assistant.

"Barbara?" His knock rattled her door.

"Come in."

"Are you okay?" His handsome face showed lines of

stress around his firm mouth and his wonderful eyes. His tawny hair was rumpled. "I thought I heard a scream."

She blushed. She'd never been a screamer, but then she'd never had bad dreams until the interstate accident, either. This, however, was different. And confusing.

"I had a nightmare." She hunkered against the headboard and hugged her knees. "Where's Missy?"

"Still at Mrs. Ferguson's. She said she'd keep her busy. She's a pretty neat old gal."

"Yes." Barbara nodded. Her insides trembled. "We've been lucky to have good people surrounding us...these five years."

Chad moved to the bed and pulled her close. "Hey, hey, it's okay. It was just a bad dream."

It seemed as if her whole life had become an endless bad dream. Starting with Marshall and his two-day deadline. Even the warmth of Chad's embrace couldn't ease the chill this time. "I've had this nightmare before. This woman from the homeless shelter keeps asking me for help. She insists only I can help her."

And she'd said something else that lingered at the edges of awareness, something that Barbara could not quite grasp.

Chad leaned back and gazed down at her. "Maybe it's some residual confusion from your save-the-world phase."

She considered that, then shook her head. "I don't think so. Her plea is...compelling. Haunting. She said something that scared me awake, but when I woke, it snapped out of my mind."

He lifted her hair from her cheek. "Maybe you can visit the shelter when you're in Seattle. Talk to the woman."

"No." She shook her head, and a shiver shuddered through her. "Sh-she's dead."

"What's the matter?" Chad traced his knuckles along

the side of her face, his touch as gentle as the compassion in his eyes. "Did her death somehow involve your volunteering at the shelter?"

She rocked back against the headboard, frowning as the fragment of her dream flickered through her mind, then vanished. "No." What *had* the woman said to her? "She caught a cold and died...of complications."

Chad frowned, his tawny brows furrowing intriguingly. "Then why are you dreaming about her?"

"It feels like more than a dream. It's frightening. And somehow very real. If only I could remember what she said to me in my dream."

"Tell me about her."

Barbara closed her eyes and conjured the long-ago memory with such ease it seemed impossible that she couldn't have done so last week.

She opened her eyes, lifted her gaze to Chad's. "It was a bleak December day, early evening, actually. I had collected some flannel shirts and cast-off coats from classmates and some of my mom's neighbors, and was anxious to deliver them to the shelter. On the way, thoughts plagued me of those poor souls who would spend the night outside without enough protection against the falling temperatures.

"People were beginning to filter into the shelter as I arrived. I carried my load to the director, Empala Jones, a large African American woman with a no-nonsense haircut—much like mine." She grinned, remembering the short, platinum buzz cut she'd favored in those rebellious days. She lifted her long mahogany hair away from her face, and saw Chad's eyes darken with desire.

She tamped down her own sensuous response. "Empala was thrilled by my donation. I told her I'd take some of those poor folks home with me...if I could. Giving them cast-off clothing seemed like too small a thing to do, you know?''

"Yeah."

Barbara heaved a sigh. "Anyway, Empala laughed and said I had more heart than sense. But her bleak expression disquieted me. I insisted she tell me why she looked so worried."

"And?"

"Her concern was for the woman in my dream. Saucy Sue." Barbara explained how Sue had acquired her nickname. "Empala said Sue was ill with a bad chest cold. Apparently the county nurse had advised Sue to go to Harborview's emergency room and Sue had started screaming something about hospitals, then run off. Ritzy, another homeless woman and constant companion of Sue's, went after her, but Empala hadn't seen either of them since."

Chad tipped his head to the side. "Did she die on the street?"

"No. As we were handing out the clothes I'd brought, Ritzy staggered in, all but carrying Sue. Empala and I got Sue settled on a cot, but she was burning up. I offered to drive her to the emergency room, but she grasped my hand and croaked, 'No, no hospitals.'"

Barbara shuddered. "I can still feel the clammy touch of her bony hand, still hear the heat of hysteria in her voice. I promised her no hospitals, but knew she needed a doctor. I decided to call Marshall.

"I wasn't sure he'd lower himself to come to the shelter and help a person he considered the dregs of the earth. But I was young and idealistic. I believed I could talk anyone into anything if I was determined enough. And I was determined about this. I caught him at home and pleaded my case. It took some doing, but eventually I wore him down.

He probably just wanted to shut me up, but he agreed to come and that was all that mattered.''

"Real dedicated doctor." Chad's voice rang with sarcasm. "The man might be Missy's father, but from what I've seen of him, he's a first-class jerk.''

"I think you're prejudiced." She offered a weak smile. "Marshall showed up an hour later. He seemed so out of place in his designer sweats, and he made no bones about being bothered by the smell, the general lack of hygiene among the people in the shelter—especially Sue and her friend Ritzy, who hovered nearby. He shooed Ritzy to one side, but she stood like a sentinel, watching him with something like wild-eyed distrust.

"Marshall donned rubber gloves, then, as gingerly as possible, began his examination of Sue, acting as though he could barely stand to touch her. And suddenly, Saucy opened her eyes and stared at him." Barbara sat straighter. "Then she did the oddest thing.''

"What?"

"She said, 'Hello, Marshmallow.'''

"'Marshmallow?'''

"Yes. I just figured she'd heard me call him Marsh and had concluded, in her childlike mind, that it was short for marshmallow. But Marshall drew a sharp breath and his face went as pale as...well—'' she grinned ''—as a marshmallow.''

Chad lovingly flicked her nose. "Why did he react so sharply?''

"That's what I wondered. I mentioned it to Kayleen later and she said Marshall's nickname as a child had been—''

"Marshmallow," Chad concluded.

"Bingo.''

"What happened next?''

"Nothing." She frowned. "I mean, Marsh gave Saucy a shot of some antibiotic or other, then promised he'd be back in the morning before rounds to check on her again."

"That's surprising."

"Why?"

"His distaste for the chore, for one thing."

"Good point."

"Did he come back?"

"Empala told me he did. I wasn't there. I had classes that next morning."

"And was Saucy Sue dead when he arrived?"

"No, Empala thought she was better. Marshall gave her another shot. But it didn't work. She died that night of complications."

Chad frowned, and they both grew quiet. Barbara asked, "Why do I keep dreaming about her? Why does she keep asking for help—if she's dead?" Suddenly, she remembered the lost snatch of dream. "Oh, my God. Sue said, *'He killed me.'* Do you suppose...?"

"Who killed her?" Chad's eyes widened. "Marshall?"

"Who else could she have meant?"

Chad's chest rose and fell and his vision turned inward. She could almost hear the cogs of his mind spinning. "Do you think Marshall knew the woman—in some previous existence?"

"You mean the way she said, 'Hello, Marshmallow?'" She pictured his reaction anew. "His whole attitude took a ninety-degree turn right afterward."

Chad rubbed his crooked pinkie over his jaw. "Was an autopsy done on Saucy Sue's body?"

"No, she was under Marshall's care. He signed the death certificate, listing the cause of death as pneumonia." Barbara blew out a weighty breath. "Chad, what difference would it make if he had known this woman? Why would he kill her? What kind of threat could she be to him?''

''Maybe not a threat. Maybe Saucy Sue was something more to him than a stranger who lived on the street. Maybe she was one of the people who'd called him Marshmallow as a child. Maybe Sue was the Emersons' missing cousin, Suzanne.''

A startled cry climbed her throat. She clamped her hand over her mouth. ''If you're right—''

''Then Marshall killed her for the inheritance.''

They stared at each other for several seconds, letting this idea take root. Barbara drew a deep breath and released it slowly. ''Do you suppose *that* was what he'd written about in the journal that could land him in jail for the rest of his life?''

''It would explain Kayleen's conviction that he'd commit murder to keep the journal pages from reaching the police.''

''Somehow, we have to find out whether or not Saucy Sue was the missing Suzanne Emerson.''

''And we have to do it before the courts give Marshall custody of Missy.'' Chad stood, pulling her to her feet with him. ''We need to go to Seattle and dig into this.''

''When?'' Anxiety heated her blood.

''Now.'' He kissed her, delicately. ''As soon as you get Missy and yourself packed.''

''But we can't drag Missy all over that area of Seattle investigating this.''

''No, but she does have to go to Seattle with us and she can stay with my dad and stepmom while we're checking into the Saucy Sue/Suzanne Emerson theory. We're also going to get a lawyer or two involved in your rights versus Marshall's.''

Barbara stepped into his arms. "Oh, Chad. I haven't been this frightened since we left Seattle five years ago."

As THE LAST OF THE snowy landscape gave way to solid green and driving rain, Barbara's nerves tightened. She hadn't ventured west across Snoqualmie Pass since the day she'd boarded that fated eastbound bus five years earlier. She wouldn't be here now, if it weren't for Missy.

Missy, safely buckled in the back seat, had fallen asleep. Barbara and Chad had refrained from talking about the subject that she knew had to be consuming his every thought as it was hers. Were Suzanne Emerson and Saucy Sue one and the same? Would they be able to prove it? Prove that Marshall killed her?

The sluice of the tires on the wet pavement echoed inside the car, punctuating the silence between them. Barbara twisted her hands in her lap. Dusk was rapidly darkening the sky, obscuring the passing terrain, blackening her mood. She made out myriad lights, their bright colors blurry through the wet windshield. "I can't believe how this area has grown."

"Five years can make a big difference." Chad glanced at her and then back at the road, his face illuminated by the light of passing cars.

"But we only have two days, Chad. Is it enough time?"

"It's going to have to be."

"Where will we start? The shelter?"

"Yes. According to Bonze it's still in operation and still run by one Empala Jones."

Barbara felt the first stirring of hope. "It saddens me that I feel glad the shelter is still operating. I hate that there's a need for such places. But maybe Empala will know something that can help us."

"Would you be able to tell from a photograph whether or not Saucy Sue was Suzanne Emerson?"

Barbara considered. Saucy Sue's face sprang clearly into her mind. "You know, I think I've just discovered the only benefit to having amnesia. Things that happened five years ago are as fresh as if they happened last week. I recall Saucy Sue quite clearly."

But she'd never met Suzanne before she'd disappeared. What if she couldn't be certain they were one and the same by looking at a photograph or two? At the time of her disappearance, Suzanne would have been a refined young woman, but the ravages of street life and her mental illness would have taken their toll. The identification might prove impossible. "All I can do is try."

"I have Bonze checking the *Courier* morgue for photographs that accompanied any articles written at the time of her disappearance."

Barbara leaned back against the seat. Exhaustion settled over her. It had been a long day of questions and explanations. Edie, who'd been the rock in her life, had all but fallen apart after Marshall and company had left that morning. Mrs. Ferguson, the one she could count on to react to distress with smothering compassion, had been stoic and supportive after hearing the whole story.

Barbara hadn't had time to explain everything to Vesta, but her kindhearted boss offered to cover her shifts until she returned. Would she be returning without Missy? Clutching the locket, she closed her eyes on the pain. If only they could find some solid proof of Marshall's guilt. She glanced at Chad. "I wonder who Kayleen gave those journal pages to."

He blew out a slow breath, then glanced at her. "Can't you remember any of her friends?"

Barbara considered for a long moment. "She was tight

with one or two women during her nurse's training. But I didn't pay much attention to the names. Losing my dad put me into a real tailspin. And like most teenagers, I was pretty self-involved. But I do remember one woman. Believe it or not, she *thought* Joy Jamison, Marshall's new wife, was her friend.''

Chad's head jerked toward her. "You're kidding."

"No. Joy and she took courses together at the U, and after Kayleen married Marsh and gave up her position as his clinic nurse, she recommended Joy for the job.''

"Did Joy have designs on Marsh from the start?"

"I suppose it's possible, but I know Kayleen still considered her a friend at the time we left Seattle.''

"Well, if Joy ever had those journal pages, we can bet she destroyed them.''

Barbara fell silent as he left I-90 and drove onto Highway 18. "What about Kayleen's copy?''

"Burned in the crash," Chad said with conviction. "Otherwise she would have used those pages sometime in the ensuing years, would have offered them to me when she called.''

Frustration wound through Barbara, much as the car wound through the twists and turns of the poorly lit road. She hugged herself. "Do you really think we stand a chance of proving any of this?''

"We're sure gonna try." He reached over and touched her knee, the warmth of his hand penetrating her jeans, sending reassuring heat through her chilled limbs. Even in the dark, she could tell he was looking at her. "Together we've got a better chance.''

Together. The word gathered like a fuzzy shawl around her heart, as though she were understanding its true definition for the very first time. Again, her hand stole to the golden locket nestled between her breasts, its weight and cool finish reassuring—as though a piece of her mother were with her at all times.

But it didn't ease the loneliness the way Chad did.

Despite having friends, during the past five years she'd often felt alone. Then Chad Ryker had forced his way into her life. Had made her need him. Rely on him. Trust him. Together, they would search for the truth about Marshall.

She placed her hand over Chad's, and in that instant, she realized she was falling in love with him. That knowledge snatched the fuzzy warmth from her heart. Scared her as much as contemplating their upcoming investigation.

"Here we are." Chad pulled the car to a stop before a closed garage door.

His house, nestled in a suburb on East Hill in Kent, was surrounded by dozens of similar two-story single-family dwellings, each indistinguishable from its neighbor. And yet, as Barbara stared at it through the rain-slicked windshield, she felt the difference. This was *his* house. The home of the man who was slowly stealing her heart.

She should have insisted on staying in a motel. She reached for the seat-belt buckle. Moving in, even for two days, was only encouraging heartache. His house would reveal intimacies of Chad's life, things he hadn't told her or shared with her, things that would make her feel closer to him.

More connected to him.

She didn't want to feel connected to him. What would happen when their investigation of Marshall was over? Her throat tightened. She knew exactly what would happen. Chad Ryker would walk back out of her life.

Hell, he'd run.

Chapter Fourteen

Lightning split the darkness and the resounding thunder-clap that followed an instant later shattered Barbara's dark musing. She swallowed hard, jarred by a second booming crash, then a third. In the next moment, rain hit the roof of Chad's car in a torrent that sounded like bullets dropping from the sky.

"Whew." He laughed. "We'd better park inside."

The garage door slid open, illuminating an unfinished interior large enough for two vehicles; except for a push lawn mower and a broom, however, it was empty. Chad angled his car into the center of the garage. The rumble of the door closing behind them quickly muffled the downpour.

"I'll turn on the heat and a few lights, then come back and carry Missy upstairs."

He returned a moment later. Missy, still asleep, snuggled against him as he lifted her from the back seat. It struck Barbara that the little girl was becoming as attached to Chad as she was. She prayed they wouldn't both have their hearts broken by him. She could handle it. Missy could not. Hefting their bag from the floor of the car, she followed. She had only packed enough clothes for both of them for two days, and the bag weighed next to nothing.

The garage led into a kitchen-and-family-room combination. Barbara had the impression of lots of oak and tile, everything pale and pristine. A leather sofa and end table looked new, unused; barstools and a dinette set seemed functional without being stylish, the big-screen television nothing more than a black box. The only personal touch was the array of framed photographs on the fireplace mantel, none of which she could make out now.

Later, she promised herself, hurrying after Chad into a formal foyer and up a curving staircase to the second floor. The carpet was forest green, as deep and plush as a path in the woods. For some reason she'd pictured him living amid the gray blues she favored—though why she'd decided that, she couldn't imagine...unless, perhaps, because he'd seemed so at ease in her apartment.

So far, the one thing she'd guessed right about his house was that he kept it tidy. Maybe too tidy. What she'd seen lacked a feeling of occupancy, as though Chad visited his home instead of lived in it.

The rain was louder upstairs, pummeling the roof like the hooves of some wild creature seeking entrance. Barbara shivered inside her parka.

"We'll put her here." Chad shoved open a door. The room was small, barely accommodating the queen-size bed and six-drawer dresser squared off against each other on opposing walls. Bare, white walls. The comforter and matching drapes were ecru with a forest green pinstripe. The result was cool, reserved, as though Chad didn't want his guests making themselves too comfortable, as though he were saying, *Visit, but don't stay too long. Don't get too close.*

She'd already gotten too close.

"Mommy?" Missy squirmed and rubbed at her eyes. "Where are we?"

"We're at Chad's house, sweet pea."

"In my guest room." Chad stepped back. "Why don't I leave you to get her settled? I want to check my phone messages and make a couple of calls."

"Sure."

"Night, Missy."

"Night, Chad." Missy struggled to her elbow and looked around the room.

Barbara set the bag down on the foot of the bed, unzipped it and pulled a stuffed toy free. "Here's Mr. Bear. I'll help you get your jammies on and then tuck you in and read you a story. I brought *The Big Red Kite*."

"Okay," Missy said on a yawn.

Barbara began helping the child out of her clothes, but her mind was on Chad. She realized he didn't intend for her to share this room with Missy. Was she crazy to feel delighted by that? Certifiable, no doubt. But her life the past five years had held little joy and less self-indulgence. Zero spontaneity.

Besides, she'd known the thrills and the risks when she'd bought her ticket and climbed on this roller coaster. Heartache was inevitable. But she might as well enjoy the ride until it was time to get off. Wind howled against the window, a stark reminder of how brutal the future might be. When this was over, she would need every warm memory just to get through the long lonely nights.

HEAVY BURGUNDY VELVET drapes covered the French doors in Chad's office, but the wind howled against the glass like a disembodied voice, sending a shiver through him. He strode to his wide mahogany desk—an antique of French design, a gift from his dad and his most prized possession. The office, a room the builder had intended as a formal dining area, looked as though the wind had swept through it.

It was the one room in the house where he actually worked and lived. Papers, files, books were everywhere, but he knew where everything was. He laid his laptop on the desk and began connecting cords to ports. He glanced at his answering machine. The red light blinked a dozen times, then repeated the count.

He pushed the button. Several of the messages were from his boss, Vic Lansing. He decided he'd better call him, but first he wanted to talk to a lawyer and find out what Barbara was facing.

Adam de Wolfe, a highly respected Seattle attorney, played golf every week with Chad's dad. Chad and he had gotten friendly on those occasions when Chad had filled in for one or the other of the weekly foursome. Adam was in his late thirties and knew the law forward and backward.

"Hello." Adam's deep bass stirred images of television courtroom dramas. He might have been a stage actor or a radio personalty with that rich voice. But his clever mind would never have been satisfied living by other people's scripts.

"Adam, sorry to bother you at home." Chad settled down in his chair and reached for a pencil and pad. He began stating the problems facing Barbara.

"Criminal impersonation in the first degree is a gross misdemeanor," Adam said. "She could be fined and prosecuted. A judge might take pity on her because of the amnesia. You never know."

Chad prayed the judge would be lenient. Especially if they could find proof that she had reason to fear Marshall Emerson finding her.

"As to the other matter, she is definitely guilty of custodial interference," Adam continued. "All the father has to do is call the police and have the child picked up. He doesn't have to allow your friend one minute with his daughter ever again, if he's so inclined. As for what criminal charges she might be facing in that area, I'll do some checking in the morning and get back to you.''

"Thanks, Adam.'' With a sinking heart, Chad hung up. What lay ahead for Barbara? Why did he feel the need to stick by her, no matter what? When had she stolen past his self-protective defenses? Gotten under his skin? Into his heart? He could almost picture her, innocently tucking Missy into bed, a child that wasn't hers, a child that would remain in her custody only as long as Marshall Emerson dictated.

Why was life so unfair? Why were the wrong people parents?

He shoved the tablet aside. He had better call Vic. It wouldn't do to keep putting off talking to him. It was after nine, but he decided to try the paper first, and wasn't surprised to find the conscientious editor at his desk. "Vic, this is Ryker.''

"It's about bloody time,'' his boss's crusty voice grumbled down the line. "Where the hell have you been?''

Chad's hackles rose. He was in no mood for a dressing-down. "You're the one who insisted I take vacation days to go after the Kayleen Emerson story—which by the way put me on scene for that crash of those three semi-trucks the other night on Interstate 90. I was obliged to cover the story—on my own time—and I expect to be paid handsomely for it.''

"Just turn in the voucher,'' Vic snapped. "Now, when are you getting back to work?''

"I'm already back. I'm following a new lead.''

"A new lead? What happened to the original one?''

"Kayleen Emerson was murdered before I could talk to her." *And find out what she had on the good doctor.*

Vic drew a sharp breath. "Why didn't I hear about it?"

"No one knows who she really was...yet."

Silence greeted this statement. Then Vic coughed. "We've got an exclusive?"

"Yes, but I'm still doing some investigating before I have the full story. Meanwhile, it would be wise to keep this under wraps."

"What exactly are you investigating, Ryker?"

Chad rolled the pencil between his finger and thumb. "Marshall Emerson's background."

Vic made a noise that sounded like a growl. "I really resent your going after my friend."

"I'm sorry, Vic." Chad kept his voice even, deliberately tempering the next words. "But you might need to come up with a new criterion for picking your friends."

"What is that supposed to mean?"

Chad hesitated, tapping the pencil on the edge of his desk. "I think it's highly possible that Dr. Emerson killed his missing cousin for the fortune he recently inherited."

"Whoa! *That* is absurd."

"No. It's not." Chad tapped the pencil harder. "We have proof that the cousin was a homeless woman at the Sunshine Shelter on the waterfront."

"That doesn't mean—"

"Marshall was brought to the aid of this homeless woman when she collapsed at the shelter. While he was examining her, she called him a nickname only those who knew him as a child would have known. Although she greeted the next day showing signs of recovery, she died shortly after Emerson's second visit to her. I'm checking it out first thing in the morning."

"Forget it. Or I'll tell Marsh that you're still after him."

"Still?" The nerves in Chad's neck tensed. He stopped tapping the pencil. "When did you tell him I was after him?"

"I called Marshall before you took off for Cle Elum."

"What!" Chad rocked up and out of his chair. "You did what?"

"You're talking about the man who saved my life in Vietnam. I owed him. I called and told him you'd located his ex-wife outside of Cle Elum."

"Vic, how could you?" The pencil snapped in Chad's grip. "That was unethical. Unprofessional."

"I won't be lectured by the likes of you on ethics or professionalism. Last time I looked, I was *your* boss, Ryker."

"Well, 'boss.'" Chad's voice shook with his rage. "Did you also go through my desk and give him the name she was hiding under?"

Vic had the decency to hesitate, then said with an edge of self-righteousness in his voice, "How else was he going to contact her?"

The bottom dropped out of Chad's stomach, dragging him back into his chair as the implications of Vic Lansing's deed weighed him down. "How could yo—?"

"I'm not going to defend my actions to you, Ryker. Marsh Emerson is my friend. I did what any friend would have done under the circumstances."

Lightning flashed outside. The phone crackled and went dead. Chad sat clutching the receiver as though he were frozen.

BARBARA TUCKED THE covers up to Missy's chin and turned down the bedside light. She stepped out into the hallway and pulled the door nearly closed, then pressed farther down the hallway until she came to the master bedroom. She stepped inside. She expected to find a king-size bed, but was surprised.

A brass bed, no larger than the queen-size one Missy slept in, dominated the room. The spread was simple— velvet, a soft green shades lighter than the forest green carpet. On the chest of drawers were photographs—all framed in brass. Barbara moved closer. The first one was of an older man and woman. Several pictures were of Chad and the same older man. She could see the resemblance and supposed this man was his father, guessed the woman was his stepmom.

There were also framed snapshots of Chad with a diverse collection of world leaders, his age and the year discernible by the varying length of his hair. She moved slowly from photograph to photograph, studying each, gaining respect for Chad and the work he did. He'd led an exciting life. Traveled the world. Met famous people. Made others famous with his stories. All of those experiences had shaped his life and his attitudes and resulted in the man he was today.

Thunder crashed across the roof, then turned into a low rumbling like the grumbling belly of some huge, starving beast. Barbara trembled, feeling as though she'd been chastized for snooping into some private corner of Chad's life. But now that she'd started, she couldn't get enough. It was dangerous, she warned herself. Dangerous to let his essence seep into her soul and take root.

She returned to the hall and headed for the stairs. The lights flickered, then burned bright again. Alarmed by the idea of the power failing and thrusting her into total darkness, she quickened her steps, hurried down the stairs and searched through the house for him.

She found him in his office, replacing the telephone receiver. "Oh, I should call Edie and let her know we made it here without any trouble."

"Sorry." He grimaced. "The storm just blew out the phone."

"Really?" Her concerns about the power failing leaped to the forefront of her mind again. "Does that happen often?"

"Almost never." Chad shoved out of his chair and stood. "There was a big burst of lightning a split second before it died. Must have hit something. You could use my cell phone, but the battery is charging. Too low right now. If the power stays on, it should be charged by morning."

"Do you have any candles?"

He smiled at her, as though recalling the scented candle that had burned during their lovemaking. "Nothing fancy like you have."

A warm glow swirled through her belly. "We may need them just the same."

She followed him into the utility room. Two six-inch white tapers, standing in brass holders, rested on a cupboard shelf. He carried them into the kitchen and began digging in a drawer for matches. The lights flickered again.

Barbara glanced uneasily at the windows, then back at Chad. Worry lines etched the corners of his eyes, held his firm lips taut. She doubted his anxiety stemmed from the possibility of losing the electricity. "What's the matter, Chad? You seem edgy."

Rain slammed the windows. Wind screamed against the house. He shrugged. "Just the storm."

She didn't believe him. "You aren't the type of man who's bothered by bad weather. What's going on?"

He abandoned the search for matches, crossed to her and folded her into his arms. The gesture was meant to comfort; it only increased her concern. "Chad, please, you're scaring me."

He released her and leaned against the counter. "My boss told Marshall about Kayleen's call to me."

Her eyes widened. "What?"

Chad released a heaving breath. "Vic told Marshall where she was and the alias she was using."

"Oh, my God, no!" Barbara slapped a hand over her mouth as shock and horror shot through her, slamming the full meaning of this home. "We eliminated him as a suspect in Mom's and Kayleen's murders because he couldn't have known those names or their whereabouts."

Chad nodded. "The reason I suspected him in the first place was because I thought it was possible that he or someone he knew had seen Kayleen in Cle Elum, recognized her and was following her. She had sounded like she was afraid someone would catch her talking to me on the phone."

"Maybe *she'd* seen Marshall."

"Or Elvis," Chad suggested.

"Or maybe she was just scared." A sour sensation swam through Barbara's stomach.

Chad narrowed his eyes, recalling something else. "When he came to your apartment yesterday, Marshall acted as if he hadn't heard of me. It was a lie. He knew exactly who I was the moment I told him my name. And he knew what I was doing with you."

She raised her eyes to Chad's. "Did he hire Dean Ray Staples to murder Kayleen and Mom?"

"He had means, motive and opportunity. And he had a head start on me. It's real damned likely."

Barbara bit her trembling lower lip. "What if we can't prove it? What if he gets away with this? What if he takes Missy and I never get to see her again?"

"We just won't let that happen." But Chad feared that was exactly what would happen. And soon. He moved toward Barbara and pulled her close again. "There's nothing we can do about any of this tonight. Tomorrow is another matter. We need to get some sleep."

The thought of being held by Chad throughout the night eased Barbara's jitters. "Yes, I'm beat."

But the need for sleep seemed to disappear the moment they slipped naked beneath his bedcovers. They had lit the candles and placed them on the chest of drawers across from the bed. The room was bathed in a creamy glow.

Chad opened his arms, and Barbara slipped into his embrace, her lips welcoming his gentle kiss. Her insides fluttered with anticipation. Eagerly, she nestled against Chad's warmth, his desire. Encouraging him with her mouth, her hands, she deepened the kiss, twining her tongue with his, running her fingers through his dense hair.

Soon glorious sensation washed through her, turning her blood to sweet hot liquid as slow-moving as candied sugar. "Make love to me, Chad, until I can't feel anything but you."

He groaned, a silken growl that carried her myriad cares away like feathers floating on a summer breeze. His fingers skimmed across her back, smoothing down the sensitive flesh to cup her buttocks in both hands. He pulled her to him, his hard need feverish and rigid against her belly.

Desire coiled in her, quickening as Chad trailed kisses down her neck to the mound of one breast, his tongue laving the taut nipple, his demanding mouth suckling, sparking exquisite tingles that reached to the tips of her toes. All the while, his hands moved lower, grazing her stomach, stroking the tangle of tight curls at the vee of her thighs.

Gently, she pushed him onto his back and trailed her

own kisses down his neck, across his chest, over his flat belly, stroking his need, tasting him. He moaned, murmured her name, the word raspy. Ragged. Urgent. "I want you now."

"Me, too." She began kissing her way back to his mouth. He placed a condom in her hand and a moment later, she straddled his body with hers, lowering herself onto him slowly, savoring their joining, prolonging the rapturous bliss.

Chad's eyes glazed with pure joy and she felt certain he was seeing the same in her eyes. She smiled at him, lifting her hips, then plunging downward again and again, gradually increasing the speed of each thrust as the euphoria built to a frenzied pitch.

Delirium hummed through her, careening her higher into the realm of total pleasure, total joy carrying her over the peak of ecstasy in one exploding release that shuddered through her every limb.

She felt Chad tighten inside her a second later, his shattering climax bringing her yet another.

Languid and replete, she collapsed on him, and within minutes was asleep.

SOMETIME LATER, SHE awoke to find Chad gone. The room was dark, the candles doused. But a thin band of light peeked beneath the bedroom door. She got up and dragged her sleep shirt over her naked body, then went to the window and peered out. A streetlight burned down the way and she could see that the storm had subsided. The rain had diminished to a soft pattering on the sidewalk below.

With all that she faced in the next few days, she felt nonetheless an odd inner peace. Perhaps it was strength of purpose. Marshall Emerson might have the deck stacked in his favor, but she would do her best to bring down that house of cards. She could barely contain her impatience to talk to Empala Jones.

Cool air stole over her. She considered climbing back into bed, decided she would rather not be there without Chad, and set out in search of him. She trekked down the hall and peeked in on Missy. The little girl was fast asleep, but had kicked free of the blankets. Barbara smiled, strode to the bed and re-covered her. She stood gazing down at her for a long moment, then kissed her cheek and headed downstairs.

Voices reached her from the family room. She hesitated. Straining to catch some inflection or word that would identify Chad's visitor, she realized she was hearing the television. Chad didn't turn as she approached, his attention stayed riveted to the set. The volume was low, but she saw the news report was about a fire.

She sauntered up to him, nuzzling his backside, wrapping her arms around his waist. "How come you couldn't sleep?"

He didn't answer, just stood gaping at the TV, his body so rigid. Fingers of anxiety clutched her heart. Something was horribly wrong.

She released him and stepped forward, flicking her gaze between Chad and the television. "What is it? What is that building?"

She stared at the screen, past the reporter, her gaze zeroing in on the flames shooting into the night sky. A chill rammed through her. "Oh, my God. It's the shelter."

Chapter Fifteen

Tom Ryker, an older, shorter, balder version of his son, grasped Barbara's hand in greeting and pumped it up and down. His mouth parted in a smile that twinkled in his blue eyes and dented each of his cheeks. "Come on in, ladies. You just call me Tom. No strangers in this house. Lynnie, we've got company. Come say hello to Chad's friends."

Tom's face lit up even brighter as a woman with soft brown hair, graying at the temples, appeared in the kitchen doorway wiping her hands on a terry-cloth apron that hung about her slender waist. The love Barbara felt issuing between these two middle-aged adults awed her.

"You must be Barbara." Lynn Ryker approached, proffering her hand in greeting. Her brown eyes were as warm as hot chocolate, her welcome enveloping and genuine. "And you must be Missy."

Missy nodded. "Chad said you're his mom. Are you?"

Lynn blushed, but she didn't hesitate. "Yes. And he told me that you like to bake cookies."

"I do."

"I'm glad to hear that, because I was going to make some cookies this morning and I could really use some help. Would you like to help me?"

Missy glanced at Barbara. "Can I?"

"You may." Barbara smiled gratefully at Lynn.

Within fifteen minutes, it seemed that Missy had known and liked Chad's parents all her life. Watching her, Barbara realized the little girl was more adaptable to new environs than she'd anticipated. On a selfish level, the realization broke her heart. But if she had to return her to Marshall, she could console herself that Missy would adjust quickly, and would inevitably survive this fiasco.

And it had turned into a major fiasco.

Chad had tried reassuring her about the shelter fire, but this morning, pessimism underscored Barbara's hopes of learning anything helpful there now. Still, they'd decided to pursue the lead. It was all they had at the moment. And anything was better than standing around waiting for Marshall to act.

After assuring Missy that they would be gone for only a short while, Chad and Barbara drove to the Seattle waterfront. News vehicles jammed every parking spot, and television personalities—talking to co-workers hoisting minicams—crowded as near the ruined building as possible.

They found a parking place two blocks over. The nearer they came to the site, the more the damp sea air stank of smoke and ash. Traffic rumbled along the viaduct, the noise muted this morning as though in respect or deference to those who'd lost their lives here last night.

Barbara's gaze lifted to the burned-out hulk beyond the knot of people ahead. There had been something surreal about watching the fire on a television newscast, but visiting the scene in person brought the horror home. Her heart clutched.

What had once been the Sunshine Shelter was now a lopsided pile of blackened bricks, gift-wrapped in yellow police tape. The image of the cabin in Ronald filled Barbara's mind. She clutched the locket and forced herself to take a deep breath. But the smoke in the air sickened her. The thought that this safe place had been turned into a death trap sickened her.

Chad caught her hand. His solid grip infused her with warmth, reassured her that he would be there—through whatever faced them now.

He stopped beside a portly man in a rumpled brown corduroy jacket and planted his free hand on the man's shoulder. "Hello, Brickman."

The man jumped and jerked around, his expression brightening at the sight of Chad. Barbara recognized this man. He was the reporter who had stopped by their table at the Sunset Café in Cle Elum a few days ago and told her Chad worked for the *Courier*.

"Hey, Ryker." Brickman beamed. "We've got to quit meeting like this. People will start talking."

Chad nodded toward the building, his eyes narrowed, bleak. He kept his voice low. "So, what's the story?"

The reporter's beetle brows lifted. He glanced around as though to see who might be listening. "Unofficially?"

Chad gazed down at him. "Sure."

"I've heard some whisperings about arson."

"Arson?" Barbara gaped at the fleshy-faced man. Her heart tripped. Her throat tightened. She'd heard that word once too often in the past week. "Does anyone kn-know what became of the director of the shelter?"

"Haven't heard." Brickman grimaced. "But all the survivors were taken to Harborview. You might check there."

"Thanks, Don," Chad said softly.

Brickman's eyebrows rose again at Chad's use of his first name. "Anytime."

On the drive to Harborview Medical Center, the horror

of the fire replayed through Barbara's mind like a scratched record stuck in one track. Her insides quivered. "What are the chances that Empala was among the five who died last night?"

"We're not going there." Chad's voice rang with optimism, accentuating her own discouragement. He smiled and squeezed her knee. "You keep the faith. We'll find the proof we need against Marshall."

Did he really believe that? Or was he trying to raise her spirits? Her hopes? She sighed, loving him for his efforts. But she knew the foolishness of depending on love in return. The armor around his heart was impenetrable. He would never look at her the way his father looked at Lynn, would never let himself love anyone wholeheartedly.

Besides, real troubles loomed ahead for her. Even if Chad would be willing to stand by her, she would never ask it of him. She could be facing a jail sentence.

Trying not to think of that, she watched the flow of pedestrian traffic cross in front of them as they waited for the light to change. "It sure seems fortunate for the Emersons that someone set fire to the shelter last night."

A chill swept Chad's heart. He doubted dumb luck had had anything to do with the fire. Anger and guilt twisted his gut. When he'd talked to Vic last night he'd mentioned the shelter by name...said they would be visiting it for information this morning. He would bet his next paycheck that his boss had passed that tidbit on to his friend Marsh.

If he had, and if Marshall Emerson was behind the arson, then Vic Lansing was as guilty of murder as if he'd struck the match himself. Chad considered calling Vic and asking him. It wouldn't be the kind of evidence the police required to bring charges, but it would confirm it for him. Then he would have to figure out some way to find legitimate proof.

He pulled into the hospital parking area. The thunder of helicopter rotors shredded the morning air and announced incoming work for Harborview's impressive trauma team. Chad and Barbara strode into the lobby, which bustled with the activity of a hotel in convention frenzy.

With her nerves aching, Barbara followed Chad to the information desk, then stood back clutching her hands together as he inquired about Empala Jones.

"Well, let's see, now." The woman behind the desk shoved her glasses up the length of her narrow nose, and peered at the computer screen to her right. "Jones, Jones. Hmm. James, Jennings, Johanson, Johnson... Ah, here we are. Jones. Empala Jones."

Relief flooded Barbara, and she said a silent prayer of thanks that the woman who'd done so much good for others had been spared an unthinkable death.

The woman abandoned the computer screen. Her gaze shifted to Chad's and she gave them the room number. "You'll have to check with the ward nurse as to whether or not she can have visitors."

THE WARD NURSE, a woman as round as she was tall, eyed the flowering plant they'd purchased in the gift shop, and nodded her head. "She'd probably love some company. Don't make her talk, though. Smoke inhalation. Her throat is real sore yet."

"But she'll be all right?" Barbara wanted reassurance.

"She's a fighter, that one. She saved a lot of lives last night." The nurse grinned. "I hear the mayor's gonna give her a medal."

Empala sat propped up in bed, her milk chocolate skin a pasty gray from her ordeal. Red veins tracked her startlingly amber eyes, and weariness etched her full mouth.

Her short black hair had streaks of gray now. Otherwise, five years had aged her little.

She gazed at them as one did strangers, and Barbara realized that she, herself, looked completely different than the last time Empala had seen her. "Hi, Empala. It's me, Barbara Dawson."

Empala shook her head as though the name meant nothing to her.

"When you knew me five years ago I had a bleached-blond crew cut." Barbara grimaced at the memory.

Empala studied her face and reached for her hair. Barbara laughed. "My natural color."

The woman's eyes grew serious as she studied Barbara's face, then suddenly widened. She croaked, "Thought you...dead!"

"Nope. Just missing in action for a while." Barbara tapped the side of her head. "Amnesia."

Sympathy filled Empala's eyes, followed by a questioning lift of her eyebrows.

"I'm fine now." Barbara smiled and set the plant on the windowsill, then turned toward her companion. "This is my friend, Chad Ryker, by the way."

"Nice to meet you, Ms. Jones." Chad stepped forward.

"We'd like to ask you a few questions if you're up to it." Barbara returned to the side of the bed.

Empala touched her throat.

"We know," Chad assured her. "We don't want to cause you any discomfort. Maybe you could just nod or shake your head?"

She nodded.

"We heard about the fire," Barbara said. "That it might be arson."

Empala nodded. "Smelled...gas... Splashed...on building.'' Her voice broke off and a pained expression crossed her face as she swallowed hard.

"The fire investigators will likely prove you're right." Chad raised his hand to silence her. "But please don't try talking."

Tears flowed down Empala's cheeks and she shook her head. "Couldn't save ev—"

"Hush, now. You did save lives last night," Barbara said, guessing that the woman was upset because she hadn't been able to prevent the five deaths. "No one would have survived without you."

Empala closed her eyes and they gave her a moment to gather her strength. Finally, Barbara asked, "Do you recall Saucy Sue?"

Empala opened her eyes, the amber as deep and clear and curious as a cat's eyes. She nodded her head slightly, frowning.

Barbara drew a steadying breath. "She always ran around with Ritzy."

Empala nodded, her frown deepening to a scowl.

"We think she may not have died from pneumonia," Chad said.

"There's some question about the doctor I brought in to help her," Barbara added, her heart heavy with guilt.

Utter confusion sprang to Empala's face.

"We were hoping you might have had some clue that could help us find the truth—like a memory of Dr. Emerson's second visit to the shelter."

Empala shook her head as though not certain what they wanted from her.

Barbara asked, "Can you recall that morning at all?"

She made a face that said, "Vaguely."

"Try and think back," Barbara pleaded, desperation

gnawing at her. "A little girl's life depends on this. My little girl."

Empala's eyebrows twitched. She drew a deep breath and closed her eyes again. Barbara couldn't tell whether the woman was trying to think or was just exhausted.

Chad whispered, "Maybe we should leave. Let her rest."

"No," Empala rasped. "Ask."

Hope stirred in Barbara. "Did Dr. Emerson's actions that day seem furtive or suspicious in any way?"

Empala considered for a long moment, then seemed to sag as she slowly shook her head, looking apologetic.

"A DEAD END," BARBARA said once they were back in the hall, her voice ringing with the frustration and despair tangling her insides. "I'm afraid he's covered his tracks so well there just isn't any evidence to find."

"How he acted isn't proof of anything anyway," Chad said, catching her by the arm and gently pulling her against his side. He gazed down at her with confidence gleaming in his eyes. "Bonze will have those newspaper photographs for us sometime today. If you can identify Suzanne Emerson as Saucy Sue, that should stimulate sufficient suspicion to interest the police."

They headed out of the hospital and back into the cold damp morning. Near the entrance to Emergency, a knot of people swelled and ebbed as they hurried in and out of the doors. Barbara assumed the activity had resulted from whatever accident the helicopters were responding to when they'd arrived.

Chad released her and they wove through the crush. Lost in thought, Barbara took long strides, moving too quickly for the foot traffic. She careened into someone, and reached out instinctively to steady the person, only then looking at whom she'd collided with, only then catching the stench of soiled clothing, an unwashed body.

"Don't," the woman insisted, her pale blue eyes burning accusingly into Barbara.

There was something eerily familiar about those pale blue eyes. Why? Shock slid through Barbara. "Ritzy?"

"Don't touch Ritzy." Ritzy knocked Barbara's hands aside. "Ritzy don't like being touched."

Barbara stepped back. Then forward again, fearful the woman would run off. She barely restrained the urge to grasp her arm again. "Ritzy, I have to speak to you. My name is Barbara. I used to know you from the shelter."

Ritzy shuddered. "The shelter burned. Fire-man burned the shelter."

Barbara realized it was pure insanity to think this woman would remember her. The person she'd been five years ago held no resemblance to the one standing here. Maybe she wouldn't even recall her constant companion. But she had to ask. "Ritzy, do you remember Saucy Sue?"

"Don't touch Ritzy. The fire-man tried to touch Ritzy. But Ritzy is too quick for him."

Chad appeared at her side. "What's going on?"

"Chad, this is Ritzy."

"Saucy Sue's buddy?"

Barbara nodded. "I asked her about Sue, but she doesn't seem to understand."

He glanced at the woman. "Ritzy, my name is Chad."

Ritzy lifted her pale blue eyes, then grinned at him, showing a surprising set of perfect teeth, yellowed from lack of hygiene, but even and straight. "You think Ritzy's beautiful?"

"Yes, Ritzy." Chad grinned and nervously rubbed his crooked pinkie finger. "You're absolutely gorgeous."

Barbara stepped back. Something about Chad had

caught the woman's interest, as that same something had caught hers. Ritzy was as taken with him as Barbara was. Maybe he could get something coherent out of her. Barbara nodded for him to go ahead and ask questions.

He leaned toward her. "Do you remember Saucy Sue?"

The woman tilted her head, a coquettish expression on her filthy face and in her eyes. "Saucy's not as beautiful as Ritzy."

"No, she's not."

"Sue knows you." Ritzy tipped her head back and forth and began chanting in a singsong voice. "You know Sue and Sue knows you."

"Saucy Sue is dead, Ritzy," Chad said softly.

"Sue knows you and you know Sue," she sang again. "Sue's dead. Sue's dead. Marshmallows, marshmallows, gonna roast some marshmallows. The fire-man can't touch Ritzy. Ritzy's too quick for him."

Chad and Barbara exchanged a hopeful glance at the mention of marshmallows, but none of his further efforts at conversation elicited more from Ritzy than her odd little song. He shook his head at Barbara.

Barbara sighed, and fell into step beside him. "I thought we had something when she mentioned marshmallows. You know, that weird song she was singing was the same little ditty she sang when Marshall was examining Saucy Sue, the night before she died. The night she called him 'Marshmallow.' But I'm afraid she's more disoriented than she was five years ago—talking about Sue and the fire as if they both happened yesterday."

"Let's go see if Bonze has those photographs." Chad also wanted to talk to Vic.

As they climbed into his car, Chad's cell phone rang. He pulled it from his briefcase. "Ryker, here."

"Son, thank God."

"Dad?" The strain in Tom Ryker's voice alarmed Chad. "What's wrong?"

"Billy Bonze called. He's been trying to track you down. He said he overheard Vic Lansing talking to Dr. Emerson this morning and he gathered from the conversation that Emerson is bringing the police here soon to pick up Missy."

"Dear God. Try and hold them off until we get there."

Barbara's face turned the color of snow as he told her what was happening.

"Can he do that?" Her voice was shaky. "Just take her?"

Chad nodded unhappily. "The attorney I consulted on your behalf last night told me this might happen and that Marshall was within his rights."

"Oh, Chad." She felt as if her heart were being wrenched from her chest. "We have to get to your parents' house ahead of Marshall. Somehow, I have to explain this to her."

"I'll even risk a ticket for Missy."

He started the engine and drove onto the freeway, weaving through traffic on the floating bridge at dangerous speeds that seemed too slow to Barbara. The ride was the longest she'd ever taken. There were no police cars parked in front of Tom and Lynn Ryker's house when they pulled up, but they weren't sure what that meant. They hurried up the walk. Barbara's stomach churned with dread.

As the door opened she heard a screech of tires and glanced back at the road. Two police cars pulled to the curb. Chad sent her into the house as he turned toward the new arrivals and watched Marshall Emerson emerge from the back of the lead vehicle.

Inside, Barbara dragged Missy to a bedroom and began telling her what was happening. Calming her fears.

Wishing she could calm her own fears.

She pulled the locket from around her neck and placed it around Missy's neck. "I want you to have this. So you can look at the pictures inside anytime you want." She showed her how to work the catch.

A knock sounded on the door, and Lynn stepped in. "The doctor wants to speak to you, Barbara."

Barbara's nerves twisted tighter. She glanced at Missy, then at Chad's stepmother.

Lynn seemed to read her mind. "Go ahead. I'll stay with Missy."

Barbara dug deep into herself and dredged up the courage to face Marshall with her shoulders squared and her head held high. She was determined he wouldn't see her buckle. He was in the living room with Tom and Chad. She could see the police officers on the sidewalk outside.

She shifted her attention to her former brother-in-law. "You wanted to talk to me?"

Marshall grinned at her with all the warmth of a reptile. Hostility oozed from him like a foul odor. "When I leave here with my daughter in a few minutes, you will not see her again. Ever. If you don't abide by this, I'll have you prosecuted for custodial interference."

As the color drained from Barbara's cheeks, white-hot anger shot through Chad. "This isn't over, Emerson—not by a long shot."

"Oh, yes, it is." Marshall smiled like someone about to reveal a nasty secret. "And for your part in this—well, let's say, my friend Vic is in need of a new investigative reporter."

Chad stiffened. Unbeknown to Vic Lansing, he'd already decided he would be submitting his resignation. "I'm challenging your right to Missy."

Marshall laughed nastily. "I have her birth certificate right here. This document is all the claim on her I need."

Chad's gut twisted. He glanced at Barbara, wishing he'd found the right moment to tell her this. If only there was some other way. But his choices had just run out. "Missy isn't your daughter, Emerson. She's mine."

Chapter Sixteen

Chad's announcement had the effect of an exploded bomb, startling everyone to sheer, wide-eyed silence. Barbara gaped at him as if she'd never seen him before. His father frowned, confusion and disbelief controlling his features.

An unhealthy red crawled up Marshall's neck. "What the hell are you saying?"

"Six years ago, Kayleen and I were lovers." Chad stared at Barbara, silently pleading for her understanding. But his heart sank, weighed down with the pain and betrayal he saw in her glorious eyes. Unable to bear her hurt, he shifted toward Emerson, all the anger inside him issuing from his hard gaze. "I fathered Missy."

Bright spots of color stood out on the doctor's face. "That's preposterous."

But it seemed to Chad that Marshall wasn't nearly as sure as he sounded. Good. His uncertainty could buy them the time they needed to prove he was a murderer. "I don't need to tell you that a DNA test will settle the matter."

"Legally, Melissa is my child." Marshall shook the birth certificate at him. "I don't have to submit to any blood tests or subject my daughter to them, either."

"Even if I sue you for custody of her?"

Marshall's green eyes narrowed. "Bring the child to me now. We're leaving."

"Please, Marshall, we'll need to make arrangements for her clothing and toys." Barbara stepped toward him. The icy fury in his eyes sent her back a step.

He pointed a finger at her. "I'll buy my daughter toys and clothes. I don't care what you do with those rags you've furnished her with—burn them, give them to charity."

Marshall strode to the door and called a police officer inside and minutes later, he was ready to leave with Missy.

Tears dampened the little girl's lashes. "Mommy, will you come and see me at my daddy's house today? And bring me Mr. Bear. I left him at Chad's house."

Barbara inhaled a shaky breath and glanced questioningly at Marshall. "She sleeps with the bear."

Marshall huffed impatiently. "I suppose."

She gave him a grateful smile, then squatted beside Missy. "We'll be by later, after you've had a chance to get settled, but before bedtime. Now, kiss me goodbye."

Missy clung to her, weeping. Barbara hugged her back, then swallowed hard and pulled the little girl's arms from around her neck, kissed her cheek, and held Missy's hand toward Marshall's. Her heart cracked into a million pieces.

"At long last, Melissa, we're going home." Marshall led his daughter out of the house.

Barbara stood at the window, hugging herself, holding back tears, watching the cars pull away. She sniffled once, swiped at her eyes once.

Chad had never felt more helpless, more of a cad.

"Is it true, son?" His father's voice broke the tense silence. "Is that beautiful little girl my granddaughter?"

Barbara turned toward Chad, the same question bold in her eyes. She looked as though a rock wall had fallen on her. Chad knew he was responsible for some of the stones. He resisted the urge to go to her, to pull her into his arms, to kiss away the pain, to reassure her. Right now, he doubted she would ever want him to touch her again. The realization grated his heart to shreds. But he understood and would respect the unspoken request.

Feeling his parents' eyes on his back, he lurched around. "The chances of that are a million to one. I always use protection. Always."

"Then you did have...an affair with Dr. Emerson's wife?" His stepmother's words weren't judgmental. Lynn seemed only to be trying to understand.

"Not an affair. One week. She and Emerson were separated. I thought she was filing for divorce. And I thought I'd found my true love. I wanted Kayleen to be your daughter-in-law."

"Why didn't you tell me?" Barbara asked, her voice so low he almost hadn't heard her.

Lynn caught Tom by the arm. "I could use your help in the kitchen."

Chad stood staring at Barbara, saying nothing until his parents left the room. "I tried to tell you the other night, but you... I..." He trailed off. What excuse did he have? Nothing that would change the fact that he hadn't told her. "I regret more than you know that you learned of it like this."

"So do I." Barbara realized the emotion dominating her at the moment was pure anger. She clung to it for strength. "Why didn't Kayleen leave Marshall for you?"

"She didn't love me." Bitterness edged his words, and Barbara realized with an unpleasant jolt that her sister had been the woman in Chad's life after his mother, who'd destroyed what little remaining trust he'd had in the feminine sex. Her heart ached for him. And for herself.

If this weren't so personally devastating, she would laugh at the irony of Kayleen reaching out from the grave to punish her for stealing Missy. "And then Kayleen committed the ultimate sin in your eyes. She ran away with her child."

"Put like that, it sounds petty." He laughed, a miserable sound that rang with self-deprecation. "But, yes, that's about the size of it."

"And now you've challenged Marshall's paternity. Why?"

"To throw him off our investigation into Saucy Sue's death." Chad didn't mention how desperate he was to find that proof. Without it, Barbara faced an array of charges, a possible jail sentence. He would go down fighting to prevent that. "I wanted to occupy Emerson's mind with other matters. Plus, I couldn't let his right to Missy go unchallenged. I think she's better off with you."

Barbara didn't know whether to hate him or love him. Too much hurt layered her heart. She couldn't dwell on it, either. Not right now. But if she didn't do something, she would collapse with grief. "Do you think your assistant has those photographs yet?"

"I'll check my messages and call him, but first I want Adam de Wolfe to draw up papers and serve them on Marshall for custody of Missy."

"Won't that take days?"

"Normally, but if there's some way to speed up the process, de Wolfe will know it."

One of the messages was from Edie. Barbara dialed her beeper. Edie phoned minutes later. Barbara took the call in the master bedroom. She sat on the upholstered chair next to the bed. Absently glancing about the room, noting that like the rest of the house, this area was also done in shades of pink and mauve with heavy splashes of gray blue. Like Chad's eyes.

"Barbara?" Edie sounded as if she was speaking from her car phone—likely on her way to the hospital.

"The worst has happened." Barbara took a bracing breath and struggled to keep her voice even. "Marshall has Missy and wants me out of her life forever."

Edie gasped. "Then we'll just have to take her back."

"He's threatened me with prosecution if I try."

"That no-good—" Edie blew out a heavy breath. "He can't get away with that, can he?"

"Probably. I'd chance it, though, if I were the only one at risk. But I can't drag you any further into this mess."

A derisive laugh spilled along the line. "Marshall J. Emerson doesn't scare me. Hypocrites like him are all bark. It's my bite he should fear."

Brave words, Barbara thought, smiling. "I'm angry, too, Edie. Don't worry. Chad and I aren't about to be counted out yet. We're checking into something that may well land Marshall in jail for life."

"That would be too good for him."

"I agree. But it would go a long way toward my getting Missy back. Permanently. Legally."

"Then I'll wish you and Chad the best of luck. And if I can help in any way, let me know."

Barbara promised she would and hung up, then sat there staring at the phone. Tears stung the backs of her eyes, tightened her throat. She'd put on a brave facade for Edie—more courageous than she felt. In reality, she was near collapse. But what good would self-pity do? What good would it do Missy?

She shook herself and shoved out of the chair. No matter the outcome of this, Barbara realized she had to keep her emotions together. It was the only way she could go on. And she had to go on.

For Missy's sake.

Chad peeked his head into the room. His smile was easy, assured. Her heart tripped a beat faster.

He said, "Good news. Adam is going to try and have the papers ready around six o'clock today. He says we should plan our visit to Missy accordingly—so that the papers can be served on Marshall around the time we're leaving."

Chapter Seventeen

If Billy Bonze were any thinner, in Barbara's estimation, the storm brewing outside would blow him away. He seemed wound tight, with the energy of three people, and smelled strongly of the hair oil slathered over his wavy black mop. His best feature was his hazel eyes, round and thick-lashed, accentuated by plain-rimmed glasses.

He set a beige folder on Chad's kitchen counter. "There were only two stories about Suzanne Emerson that carried accompanying photos."

He opened a file folder and spread the copied pages out. The photographs were black-and-white and had lost some of their clarity in the photocopying process. Barbara leaned over them, taking in the full-faced, healthy teenager depicted there. Suzanne Emerson looked young, about sixteen—the age Barbara had been when her father was killed—but according to the article she was actually three years older at the time of her disappearance.

Chad moved close to her, close enough to touch her, but he refrained from doing so, kept the distance that seemed to widen between them by the minute. His minty breath grazed her cheek. "Is that Saucy Sue?"

She glanced at him. The tiny lines at the corners of his eyes had gained depth and length since this afternoon. She resisted the urge to touch them, to soothe away the tension that held his handsome features captive. "There is something familiar about the woman."

But Barbara realized it might be nothing more than her resemblance to the Emerson clan. She closed her eyes, conjuring Saucy Sue's image. The face that had so readily filled her nightmares seemed elusive now, hard to distinguish from a dozen others, as faded and unclear as a Polaroid left out in the sun.

A beeper went off, startling Barbara. Her eyes snapped open.

"It's me," Bonze said, yanking his pager from inside his pants pocket. He frowned as he read it. "It's the paper. Can I use the phone in your office?"

Chad laughed. "Help yourself, but I wouldn't tell Vic where you are if you want to keep your job."

"We need to talk about that later." Bonze pointed his finger at Chad as if it were a pretend gun, then left the kitchen.

Chad turned back to Barbara, his guard up, his feelings hidden. His smile was polite, as if they were newly introduced. Strangers. She wondered if he'd purposely not told her about Kayleen and him so that he could use the old relationship as an excuse to end whatever it was that had been happening between herself and him.

"What do you think?" he asked. "Is it her?"

Glad for any diversion from this heartache, she again glanced at the photocopies. "I thought I'd be able to tell instantly. But this is really difficult. If Saucy Sue was Suzanne Emerson, her face had aged beyond her years. I wish I could say positively, but I can't."

"Damn." Chad rubbed his crooked pinkie finger.

Bonze hurried into the kitchen. "I have to get to police headquarters. There's some new lead on the shelter fire."

Barbara felt an immediate rush of adrenaline.

"What?" Excitement stood out in Chad's eyes.

"Not sure." Bonze jabbed his arms into his baseball jacket. "Someone may have gotten a license-plate number. I'll call you when I have something positive."

"See that you do," Chad said, following him to the front door. He'd just returned to the kitchen when the doorbell rang. He pivoted again. "Bonze must have forgotten something."

Barbara stayed in the kitchen, studying Suzanne Emerson's picture. Voices issued from the foyer, but she couldn't make out what was being said and really didn't care.

Chad appeared a moment later, holding a large manila envelope. Excitement darkened his eyes from gray blue to slate.

"That was the messenger from de Wolfe's office with my copy of the papers that are being served on Marshall tonight." He held the envelope high. "We can take Mr. Bear to Missy whenever you're ready."

Barbara's throat constricted. "I'm ready."

BARBARA STOWED HER suitcase in the back seat of Chad's car, then settled in front, with Mr. Bear clutched to her churning stomach. She'd waited for and dreaded this visit all day, dying to see Missy and yet knowing it might be the last time she would spend with her child for years to come.

Chad opened the garage door and backed the car out into a steady, drizzly downpour. The night was as black and miserable as Barbara's shriveling heart. Her hands were wet, her mouth dry. Sitting beside the man she loved, she felt more alone than she'd felt in her whole life; now, when she most needed comfort and reassurance, he had withdrawn into himself, shutting her out.

Wind bent trees, stripping leaves from branches and slinging them through the air to slam against the windshield. Deep pools of standing water sprayed against the car with loud, unnerving regularity. Chad drove cautiously. Her anxiety increased with every passing mile.

She glanced at the envelope on the seat. It separated them like a wall, as solid and impenetrable as the stony silence in the car. If only she were more versed in love relationships. But her lack of experience limited her skills in that area. She didn't have the first idea how to make him open up and talk about a woman who had obviously hurt him deeply. She didn't know how to help him heal.

The journey seemed endless, but finally, Chad nosed the car through a pair of massive white masonry arches and along the Tarmac that fronted the Emersons' Mercer Island home.

A huge, two-story house, of Art Deco design, it overlooked Lake Washington. The drive curved past the front door. A new Jeep Cherokee claimed the spot nearest the porch steps. Barbara muttered, "New house. New car."

"Yeah," Chad said. "All bought with blood money."

She shivered at the thought.

Chad parked behind the Jeep. Barbara zipped Mr. Bear inside her jacket, then darted through the downpour beside Chad, up the concrete steps, and across the wide porch. Wind blew the rain against their backsides. Barbara hunched into the collar of her coat, and although the teddy bear was in no danger of slipping, cupped her hands under it.

The second Chad's knuckles connected with the door, it moved inward as though on a spring. He stepped back, startled, and laughed nervously. "That's appropriately creepy for a night like this."

"The last person in," she suggested, "probably didn't realize they hadn't shut the door tightly."

"Emerson," Chad called. "Hello. Dr. Emerson?"

No one answered. Chad glanced down at Barbara. "The lights are all on."

"Hello!" she cried. "Is anyone here?"

Still no answer. Uneasiness skittered through her.

"Maybe we should just go in." Chad shook rain from his shoulders. "We're getting soaked."

"I don't kno—"

"What was that?" He jerked his head toward the hallway.

"I didn't hear anything."

"Shush. Listen."

She heard it this time. A low groan.

Chad hastened inside with Barbara on his heels. Elvis Emerson lay sprawled on the floor of the entrance hall, clutching his stomach and writhing, obviously in pain.

"Check on him," Chad ordered, continuing on into the house as Barbara dropped to the fallen man's side and gripped his shoulder. "Elvis, Elvis, what happened?"

His pale blue eyes fluttered open. His gaze locked on her face. He groaned, "B.J."

Unbidden, the image of other pale blue eyes assailed her. She swallowed hard against the sudden shock of knowledge.

He groaned again. "Poison."

Fear shot through Barbara. "Where's Missy?"

But Elvis's eyes glazed, rolled back and shut.

"Barbara!" Chad called from the next room.

She lurched to her feet and ran to him, stopping abruptly

at the sight of Marshall lying on the floor near a glass-brick fireplace.

Chad was checking Marshall's neck for a pulse. "Looks like he tripped over the coffee table or something." He nodded toward the huge square that seemed to be made of white granite. "Has a hell of a bruise on his right temple."

Barbara's heart climbed into her throat. "Call 911, Chad. I have to find Missy."

She bolted for the stairs. Restrained by a terror she couldn't cite, she bit back the urge to scream the little girl's name. The thick blue carpet swallowed her footfalls. She raced up the geometrically shaped staircase and into a long, wide hallway lined with half-a-dozen doors.

Her chest heaved with fear. The only light shone from the last room on the left. Instinctively sensing she would find her child there, she headed for it.

As she neared the room, she heard a voice. A woman's voice. "It's all right, my darling Missy. Mommy didn't really die. And now I'm going to take you far away from all these bad people."

Chapter Eighteen

With her heart leaping against her ribs, Barbara stepped into the room. An overhead light glared brightly after the relative darkness of the hall. Blinking, she scanned the scene before her. Two women and Missy were in the room. Barbara's gaze shot to the little girl.

Fully dressed, she lay on the single bed that was centered beneath the window. She appeared to be asleep. Barbara's pulse skipped erratically. She suppressed the urge to run to her child and scoop her up.

"Mommy will be ready to leave in a moment, Missy," said the woman, bending over Joy Emerson's inert body.

Barbara's heart dropped through her like an elevator falling sixty floors. "Oh, my God, Edie? What is this? What are you doing?"

Edie jerked around, syringe in hand. Alarm widened her eyes, but her mouth was tight with purpose. "You can't have her. She's mine."

"Wh-what?" Horrified disbelief slammed through Barbara. This couldn't be. Not Edie. Edie, who'd been her friend from the moment they'd met, who'd shared her innermost secrets, her soul-wrenching fears. Who'd risked everything to protect Missy and her.

"Why are you doing this?" Barbara edged closer to the bed.

"I'm taking my daughter far away from you and all the others who think you can come between us."

"No, I—" Barbara broke off. This wasn't Edie her friend. This woman was deranged. No amount of logic would penetrate her psychosis.

Barbara took another step into the room, her gaze riveted on her child. A discarded cloth lay crumpled near Missy's face. Terror gnawed her. She wanted to run to her, but feared any sudden movement might startle Edie, might feed her instability. "What have you given Missy?"

"A little ether. It won't harm her. I'd never harm her."

"Why?" Barbara asked, hoping to distract Edie until she could reach Missy. "Why are you doing this?"

"I told you. She's mine." Edie ran a hand through her unkempt blond hair. "I deserve her after everything I've done."

Apprehension grabbed Barbara's nerve endings. She inched closer to the bed. "What have you done?"

Edie threw her head back and laughed. "God, what haven't I done?"

The crazed look in her eyes chilled Barbara. "What does that mean?" But she was starting to fear she knew what it meant. All those miscarriages. Edie's immediate willingness to help her after the accident. She'd wanted Missy from the first.

"Don't tell me you haven't remembered about Kayleen and me?"

Barbara shook her head. "You knew Kayleen?"

"We met at the UW. Became fast friends."

Barbara gaped at her, stunned.

"You really didn't know?"

"Kayleen's friends didn't interest me. I was only sixteen."

"Well, she chattered up a storm about you. Barbie, this, Barbie, that. Even had your picture in her room. You and your bleached-blond buzz cut. Downright unique." Edie shook her head. "And I was so worried you were going to remember and then figure out that *I* was the one she'd sent Marshall's journal pages to."

Barbara's stomach made a sickening lurch, stopping her cold. "Then you knew from the beginning who I was? Who Missy was?"

"Why do you think I helped you with the false ID? I wouldn't have risked my career for anyone—except that sweet baby. I'd planned on killing you, too, but then I couldn't figure out how I'd explain to Dirk, or anyone else, where I'd gotten Missy from. So, I did the next best thing and became her aunt."

"You knew Marshall would be looking for Missy." Barbara took another step toward her child.

"I didn't want him to find her any more than you did." A smug look crossed Edie's face. "Of course, that necessitated poor Jane Dolan departing this world a little ahead of God's schedule."

Revulsion flared inside Barbara. "You...?"

"I just put her out of her misery a little early." Edie was refilling the syringe from a vial.

Barbara took another step toward the bed.

"Then Kayleen saw me in Cle Elum two weeks ago," Edie continued.

Barbara stiffened. Until that fateful day last week, she'd avoided going to Cle Elum. Driving that stretch of freeway was too much for her. She gingerly touched the end of the bed.

"I really thought she'd perished in the accident. The

officials had found her ring, declared her dead, and she wasn't among the victims brought to Ellensburg.'' Edie raised her heated gaze and her face grew stony. "She was furious that I hadn't given the journal pages to Chad Ryker.''

Barbara scooted another step toward Missy. But she couldn't understand her sister's actions. "Wh-why didn't she try contacting you for five years?"

"You know, that's what I asked her.'' Edie squatted beside Joy and positioned the vial to appear as if it had rolled from the unconscious woman's limp hand. "She claimed she was so devastated by the loss of Missy and you that she spiraled into a deep depression. Your mother had to work to support her for all that time. She was finally coming out of it when she spotted me that day.''

Barbara could touch Missy's feet now. "I suppose she wanted you to give the journal pages to her?"

"Oh, yes. She went on and on about what she wanted. But did she care about the babies that *I'd* lost? Did she care about my hysterectomy?"

"Hysterectomy? Wh-when did you have a hysterectomy?"

"After the last miscarriage six weeks ago. It was the final straw for Dirk. He walked out.''

Barbara reeled inside. She hadn't even guessed. Had taken Edie's word that her marriage was on the mend. That she and Dirk were going to try again to have a baby. Edie must have been devastated. Maybe, if she'd shared her pain and heartache… "Why didn't you tell me?"

"Because all you care about is yourself. And what you want. Just like Kayleen. She only cared about what she wanted. And if she found out that Missy was alive, then there would be no question what she'd want then. I couldn't let her take the only child I'd ever have. I had to kill her."

Barbara's knees buckled. She dropped onto the bed. "You killed my mother and Kayleen?"

"Well, not me, personally. Although I'm quite accomplished with a gun, bullets aren't my method of choice. I had a friend, Willie Breen, hire Dean Ray Staples for the job."

Barbara's eyebrows rose. "But Staples will tell the police—he'll give them your name in exchange for a lighter sentence."

"He doesn't know my name." She moved closer. "I just told you that Willie Breen hired him."

"And you trust this Willie Breen to keep quiet?"

"Willie. Poor, stupid Willie. I wouldn't be here now, if he'd managed to get into your apartment and take Missy for me the other night."

"*Scarface* was Willie Breen?"

"Sad, but true." Edie waved the needle at her. "That wound to his face brought us together. He'd been slashed during an attempted robbery. Willie was terrified of going back to prison. So I didn't tell the police. He was very grateful."

A chill swept through Barbara. "You meant him to murder me that night."

Edie stepped toward her with purpose now. Barbara stared at the syringe as if it were a poisonous snake about to strike. Edie lifted her other hand. She held a gun. "Don't move. Like I said, I wouldn't like to shoot you, but I will."

Instinctively Barbara sucked in her stomach muscles. "Edie, you can't get away with this. Chad is with me. He's downstairs. He's called the police."

Edie stopped, her eyes wild as this sank in. In the distance came the sound of approaching sirens.

"No-o-o-o." Edie lunged for Barbara, and drove the syringe into her stomach.

A heartbeat passed before Barbara realized she felt no pain. *Mr. Bear!* She shoved Edie by the arms. The doctor fell back, pulling the needle free. Chad charged into the room. He tackled Edie.

Barbara scrambled toward Missy.

Chad and Edie hit the floor with a resounding crash.

The gun went off.

Barbara covered Missy's body with her own. The loud report rang in her ears. Her heart thudded against her ribs.

She lifted her head. Chad had Edie pinned to the floor. Barbara drew a shaky breath. He wrenched the gun from Edie's hand, then staggered to his feet. Keeping his eyes and the gun trained on the doctor, he asked, "Is Missy okay?"

The little girl moaned and her eyes opened.

"She was knocked out with ether," Barbara said. "But she's waking up now."

"And you?"

"I'm all right. Chad, she killed Kayleen and my mother."

"I heard." His voice was filled with sympathy and she knew he understood and cared about the pain she was feeling, even if he could no longer tell her.

"Mommy?" Missy struggled up. Barbara hugged her, shielding her from the sight of Joy's inert body and of Chad with the gun trained on Edie.

"Drop the syringe." He took a step closer to Edie, cocking the gun. "I'm serious, Doctor."

Edie grinned at him, a crazed gleam in her eyes. She

held the needle out toward him, then jammed it into her chest. Into her heart.

And pressed the plunger.

Chapter Nineteen

For Barbara, the next hour passed in a kaleidoscope of commotion. It seemed to her that police and paramedics were everywhere. A medic pronounced Missy wide-awake and suffering no ill aftereffects from her ether-induced sleep.

Elvis, Marshall and Joy were rushed to the hospital— along with the spent syringe—so an antidote could be found for whatever "poison" Edie had injected them with.

It was too late for Edie.

Barbara and Chad moved Missy to a different upstairs room to keep her away from the chaos. A uniformed policewoman found them there a few minutes later. "Detective Quinn would like to speak to you now. He's in the dining room. I'll stay with Missy until you return."

At the bottom of the stairs, they encountered Billy Bonze. "Hey, Ryker."

Chad strode toward his assistant. "How'd you get wind of this so fast?"

"I didn't. I was still following the shelter-fire lead."

A spark of hope flicked through Barbara. "And that brought you here?"

"Yep. They're going to nail Emerson for it."

"Marshall?" She gasped.

"No, Elvis."

Chad's eyes narrowed. "It was his license reported in the anonymous tip?"

"Yep. They searched his trunk and found a bunch of empty gas cans. The idiot hadn't disposed of the evidence yet."

"What about Marshall?" Barbara's hands landed on her hips. "Surely they know he's behind this?"

Bonze shrugged, then turned back to Chad. "Apparently that new Jeep out there belongs to the dead woman, but it's registered under a different name than you gave the police. They found false ID in the glove box and a suitcase full of children's clothes and toys on the back seat. What's going on here, anyway?"

"That's what I'd like them to tell me," a brusque male voice interrupted. "I'm Detective Quinn. I'd appreciate it if you two would come into the dining room. Now."

Barbara turned toward the detective and gazed up. He had an athlete's body that suited his well-cut street clothes, tanned skin and trim gray hair, which he wore a little longer than was fashionable. His shrewd brown eyes swept over her. She swallowed over a twinge of discomfort.

She and Chad followed him into the dining room, which was elegant in its simplicity and sparsity of accessories. Fresh-cut roses scented the air. Quinn walked to the head of the table. "Please, sit down anywhere."

Barbara and Chad sat on either side of the detective and another officer took a chair at the opposite end of the table. Quinn steepled his hands. "I'd appreciate it if one or the other of you would tell me exactly what went on here tonight."

She and Chad took turns explaining how they'd come to be here and what they'd found when they arrived. The officer at the end of the table took notes.

"May I join this group?"

Chad shifted around, recognizing the deep bass voice instantly. He smiled and half rose from his chair. "Adam. I was wondering what happened to you."

"It's a nasty night for driving," Adam replied, removing a damp raincoat. He was medium height with a commanding presence and a voice that demanded respect. He approached them with an air of confidence that told Barbara he expected Quinn to acquiesce to his request to join them.

Feeling Chad's gaze on her, Barbara glanced at him questioningly. "Barbara, this is Adam de Wolfe."

The attorney. The knot in her stomach eased slightly. "It's nice to meet you, Mr. de Wolfe."

"I called him right after I called the police," Chad explained.

"I'm acting as Mr. Ryker's and Ms. Dawson's counsel," Adam informed Detective Quinn.

"No problem. Take a seat," the police officer said. "And let's get on with this. I'm sure we'd all like to go home sometime tonight."

With Adam's approval, Barbara briefly explained her history with Edie. Both Chad and she related Edie's confession and that she'd taken her own life.

"I guess that covers my questions for now." Quinn started to stand.

"Wait." Chad stopped him. "That's not all. Ms. Dawson and I are certain Marshall Emerson killed a homeless woman named Saucy Sue five years ago and that that murder is directly connected to the Sunshine Shelter fire last night."

Quinn looked skeptical. "Why would the doctor have killed a homeless woman?"

Chad leaned forward. "For the inheritance that he recently collected."

Barbara nodded. "You see, Detective Quinn, Marshall thought Saucy Sue was his missing cousin—the wealthy Suzanne Emerson."

"'Thought'?" Chad questioned.

"He was wrong." Barbara grinned. "Marshall may have killed Saucy Sue, but she wasn't Suzanne Emerson. His cousin is still alive, calling herself Ritzy."

"What?" Chad gaped at her.

"I realized it when I saw Elvis tonight. Ritzy and he have the same pale blue eyes. Emerson eyes."

"What sweet justice." Chad laughed and spread his arms out to encompass the elegant room. "All of this actually belongs to that dotty woman we spoke with today at Harborview."

Barbara sat straighter. "Detective, when we spoke with Ritzy today, she was confused, but she kept saying the 'fire-man' couldn't catch her. I think she saw Elvis setting fire to the shelter and recognized him. I'm not sure what kind of witness she'd be. But she and Saucy Sue were good pals and it's very likely Ritzy recognized Marshall and told Saucy Sue his name—the name she'd called him as a child."

"That's some kind of tale, but I wouldn't smear Dr. Emerson's good reputation on the word of a woman who's kept his child from him for five years."

"Then maybe this will help convince you that Marshall isn't the upstanding citizen he appears to be." Chad stood and handed some folded papers to the detective. "Those pages were taken from a journal Marshall kept years ago. It should be easy to prove the handwriting is his. They document quite clearly how he cheated on his board exam in order to get his medical license."

It was Barbara's turn to be surprised. Chad hadn't told her he'd found the journal pages, but she realized he must have searched Edie before the police arrived. Edie had probably used them to gain entry into the house this evening. She inhaled a quavery breath.

Quinn looked the papers over for a long moment, then nodded. "I think it might be worth the county's expense to exhume Saucy Sue's remains and have the ME look for evidence of murder."

He glanced at a uniformed officer standing near the door. "Go to the hospital and check on the Emersons. I want both of the men brought in for questioning as soon as they're released."

"Is there anything else, Detective?" de Wolfe asked.

"Not for now." Quinn stood and left.

"I think that went well. Very well." Adam reached for his coat.

Barbara rose on unsteady legs. "Mr. de Wolfe, if Marshall goes to jail, could I petition to adopt Missy?"

"Certainly. I'd even handle it for you...if you'd like."

"Yes, please." She beamed, the ice inside her beginning to melt. But the lawyer's grim expression stopped a complete thaw. "What? Aren't my chances any good?"

"I'd say they were very good, but meanwhile, Missy will have to be remanded over to Child Protective Services and will be placed with a foster family until the issue is decided."

"How soon would she have to go?" Chad asked.

"Right away, I'm afraid."

Barbara's emotions bounced between sorrow and relief as Chad and she returned to the room where Missy waited. They sent the policewoman away. Chad sank to the floor in front of Missy, and Barbara joined her on the bed.

The little girl huddled against Barbara, holding a teddy

bear that the police had exchanged for the heroic Mr. Bear, who'd been bagged as evidence. Missy lifted sad eyes to her. "Auntie Edie scared me. She had a gun and a big needle and she put something stinky on my nose."

Barbara kissed Missy's head, caressed her temple. "Aunt Edie was sick, sweetie. We didn't know it, but she was confused in her mind."

Missy made a face. "Is that why she said she was my mommy?"

"Yes." The answer seemed to satisfy Missy. Barbara wasn't sure it would ever satisfy her. Everything she'd ever known about Edie—from the first moment she'd walked into the emergency-room cubicle and introduced herself—had been a lie. All the trust and friendship was a lie.

"Can we go home now?" Missy asked.

A knock at the door startled Barbara. Chad stood, uneasiness in his eyes. "Come in."

A young woman, with dark hair hanging loose around her kind face, entered the room. "I'm Mrs. Graves, with Child Protective Services."

She produced identification, which Chad inspected carefully, then returned to her. She nodded toward Missy. "Is she ready?"

Barbara's heart sank to her toes. Her gaze flicked between Chad and the woman.

He frowned at Mrs. Graves. "We were telling her now."

Missy looked frightened. Chad hurried to her side. "Hey, princess, this is nothing to be sad about. But you can't go home just yet."

Barbara hugged the child. "Remember this afternoon when I told you the judge said you had to live with your daddy full-time?"

Missy nodded. "But I don't like it here. I want to go home with you."

"Good. Because I've got a lawyer who's going to see if we can't get the judge to change his mind and let you come back and live with me."

Her lip trembled. "Now?"

"No, sweetheart." Chad held her hand. "First you have to go with Mrs. Graves…but just until the judge decides."

"No, I—"

"You must, Missy." Barbara pleaded for the little girl to understand, even though she knew it was beyond a five-year-old's comprehension. "If we cooperate with Mrs. Graves, she'll tell the judge that we deserve to be together."

Missy peered at Mrs. Graves with wet eyes. "Will you?"

Mrs. Graves nodded.

"Can you come and visit me, Mommy?"

"Not for a while, sweetie. But soon, I promise. And you've got the locket."

Missy nodded and sniffled.

For the second time that day, Barbara kissed her little girl goodbye and watched helplessly as she was led away.

Chad looked as devastated as she felt. And guilty. So guilty she couldn't bear gazing into his beloved eyes. He made no move toward her, no offer of a comforting embrace. The ice that had been melting around her heart froze into a solid layer, chilling her. Numbing her.

Where could she go? Whom could she stay with? She no longer knew anyone in Seattle well enough to call and intrude on. Her gut wrenched. All she really wanted to do was go home to her haven—her little apartment in Ellensburg where every memory she had of Missy lived.

Once they were in Chad's car, she insisted he take her

to the nearest motel. As much as she hated spending this night alone, it was better than sharing small talk with him, being frozen out by his pity, his guilt, his inability to give them a chance.

He carried her bag into her room, then looked reluctant to leave. He stood by the door, so damned handsome and needy it ripped her heart to shreds.

He rubbed his crooked pinkie finger. "I can't..."

She nodded. "I know."

Again he hesitated. "Do you have to go back to Ellensburg?"

"Yes. Vesta needs me at work. And I need the diversion."

"How will you get there?"

"It's not your concern." She closed the door and leaned against it, shuddering.

Tomorrow, just like five years ago, she would be heading east on a bus. Only this time she was going without family or friend.

Epilogue

The noon crowd at the Buckin' Bronc had kept Barbara and Vesta hopping for three hours, but was now down to one couple in the back booth. Wynonna Judd's latest single, a slow, soulful tune about love and betrayal, played in the background, the words painfully stroking Barbara's wounded heart.

She slammed the phone down and swore under her breath.

Vesta looked up from putting glasses in the dishwasher. "Hey, what's wrong?"

"I tried reaching my attorney, but he's out of town."

Swishing a strand of her fiery red hair out of her eyes, Vesta shifted her weight to her other leg. "He called you when the prosecutor's office decided not to press charges against you. He called when Marshall was arrested for Saucy Sue's murder. And he'll call you when there's something to report about Missy."

The examination of Saucy Sue's exhumed body proved she'd been poisoned with the very drug Marshall bragged about in the journal pages that Edie had so accommodatingly provided for the investigation.

Barbara swiped a bar rag across the counter. "I know,

but I just hate Missy having to stay in that foster home another day.''

Sympathy entered Vesta eyes. ''Are you sure you don't want time off to go to Seattle?''

''What good would that do? They won't let me visit her.''

''Maybe you could visit Chad.''

At the mention of his name, Barbara's heart skipped. She missed him as badly as she missed her little girl. She'd thought it impossible that she would ever love a man as much as she loved Missy, but she did. Trouble was, he couldn't return her love. She shook her head. ''That's not a good idea.''

''Really, Barb.'' Vesta blew out an impatient breath. ''I don't know why you don't call that man. At least, meet and talk to him.''

''I can't.''

''Why not?'' Her auburn brows cocked and her green eyes softened. ''Does it bother you that he had a fling with your sister long before either of you knew the other existed?''

Barbara lifted her hair off her neck. ''I don't give a hoot about that. But he does. Kayleen convinced him that marriage and commitment were four-letter words.''

''Humph! I can't believe you'd let him go on believing that.''

''If he loved me he would have called me sometime in the past five weeks. He hasn't. Not once.''

Her gaze was pointed. ''Have you called him?''

''Well, no, I...''

''Then do it.'' Vesta pressed the phone into her hand. ''Now.''

Shaking her head and fighting the jitters in her stomach, Barbara dialed the number she'd almost dialed ten times a day, every day since she'd arrived home. His number. After four rings the answering machine picked up. "This is Ryker. Leave me a message."

She listened to the long beep, but could think of nothing to say, and hung up. Vesta was staring at her. Barbara drew a shaky breath. "He's not there."

Vesta pressed her lips together sympathetically. Barbara dropped the bar rag into the sink, ran water through it, then wrung it tight, twisting it with all her pent-up frustration.

Vesta let out a soft whistle. "Now that is one fine-lookin' cowboy. He could park those shiny loafers under my bed any time."

Barbara's head jerked up. Adam de Wolfe was strolling toward her. Her stomach crashed to the floor. "That's my lawyer."

"If you'd told me he was this fine, I'd have offered to go to Seattle with you." Vesta raised her voice. "What do you suppose he's doing here?"

"That's what I'm wondering." But Barbara was sure it was bad news. He wouldn't have driven all the way from Seattle for good news. "Hello, Adam."

"Barbara." His rich voice should have soothed her. Instead, it terrified her.

"Aren't you going to introduce us?" Vesta nudged Barbara gently.

"Of course." She made the introductions, dropping the bar rag and drying her hands.

"Could we speak?" Adam asked. "Somewhere alone?"

"Use the dining room," Vesta offered. "It's between lunch and dinner and you'll have the place to yourselves."

Barbara led the way. They chose a corner table and sat across from each other. She couldn't have stood if she'd wanted to. Nor could she bear wading through a lot of small talk and pleasantries. "Are you here because of my petition to adopt Missy?"

"Yes. Partially."

"Please, don't keep me in suspense."

His eyes revealed nothing, but the firm set of his mouth confirmed her first impression that the news was bad. He replied, "Full custody of Missy has been granted to her father."

"But he's in jail." Barbara's mouth dropped open and her spirits sank to their lowest point ever. She hadn't felt this bereft since she'd arrived home to her apartment to find that Edie had used her spare key and removed every stitch of Missy's clothing, every one of her toys, rendering the once-loved home an empty shell. Now her heart felt the same.

"If you'll excuse me." Adam stood. "There's someone here to see you."

Barbara was too dumbfounded to object. Too shocked with disbelief. She glanced up at the man coming through the dining-room doorway. Chad. Despite the misery wrenching her heart, it leaped with joy at the sight of him.

He sat in the chair Adam had vacated. She gathered her pride around her like a coat of armor and gave him a haughty glare. "If you're here to try and console me, forget it, Ryker. I don't need your pity."

"Good, because pity is the one emotion I don't have for you."

Surprised, Barbara lost some of her bluster. What, exactly, was that supposed to mean? What emotions did he have for her? Any he could admit to? Live with? "What are you doing here, then?"

His gray-blue eyes seemed to devour her face. "I had to see for myself if you were as beautiful in person as you are in my dreams."

Discomfited, she blushed. ''Chad, I haven't heard from you in five weeks—''

''I've been busy. Thinking. Finding a new employer. Thinking.''

Something about the way he said this reached inside her and caressed her—a sensation so intimate and real he might have touched her. Her mouth dried. ''Thinking about…?''

''About us. About the way I treated you. I was a real jerk…about Kayleen.'' He winced as though his actions caused him physical pain.

She put her finger to his lips. ''I don't care about Kayleen and you.''

He leaned across the table, his expression so vulnerable, she knew she held his heart in her hands. The realization sent a zing of hope through her. He murmured, ''Do you care about me and *you?*''

Her throat constricted. ''What are you asking me, Chad?''

''I guess I'm doing this pretty clumsily. But it seems I've fallen head over heels in love with you. I've been one miserable man since I dropped you off at that motel room.''

She wanted to tell him she'd been miserable, too. But she feared she would break the moment and he wouldn't say what he'd come to say.

''My dad and I had some long heart-to-hearts. He told me he was afraid of commitment, too…after what my mother had put him through. Then he met Lynn. He said he thought I'd met 'my Lynn' in you. He didn't understand how or why I'd let you walk out of my life. God, he was so right.''

Chad shoved his hand through his thick tawny hair. ''I was a fool to let you leave without at least trying to find out if you felt the same way about me as I feel about you. I love you, Barbara. I want to spend the rest of my life with you. I want to make it legal."

She gaped at him. "Is this a marriage proposal?"

He pushed his hands across the table until his fingertips touched hers. A solitary diamond engagement ring was on his crooked pinkie finger. He pulled it off. Proffered it to her. "What do you say?"

How could her life have gone from devastating one moment to rapturous the next? "I guess I should ask where this new job is?"

He narrowed his eyes. "Is that a yes? Should I get down on one knee?"

"I love you, Chad." She laughed and extended her left hand for him to slide the ring onto her finger. "But I'd rather you stood and hugged me."

He leaped to his feet and held his arms open. She couldn't get up fast enough, couldn't feel his arms locking about her tight enough, couldn't breathe for the pure joy of it, and didn't even care.

"Mommy, Mommy!" Missy's unmistakable voice startled Barbara. She felt Chad's embrace ease and twisted in time to see the little girl come running toward her, followed by Tom and Lynn Ryker and Adam de Wolfe.

Happiness lifted her on wings of pure elation. Tears sprang to her eyes and spilled down her face as she scooped up the little girl, hugging her, crying and laughing with delight. Her gaze collided with Chad's. "What is this? How did you get her out of foster care?"

He tousled Missy's platinum hair, his eyes misty, but warm and as full of love as her soul. "The judge," he said, his voice cracking with emotion, "took pity on me, since I've been deprived of her for the first five and a half years of her life."

"What?" Barbara shook her head, knowing she was missing something.

"You were wrong, Mommy. My name's not Missy Emerson. It's Missy Ryker. The judge said so. Chad's my real daddy." Missy beamed. "And I even have a grandma and grandpa, too."

Surprise and shock sifted through Barbara's too-full heart. She set Missy down, but held tightly to her hand, her gaze locked with Chad's. "You said it was a one-in-a-million chance. Why did you have the DNA testing done?"

He grinned wryly, but his voice cracked with emotion. "Joy Emerson insisted on it. Even though Marshall will likely be locked up for a long time, she wanted to raise his daughter."

Missy tugged her hand. "We came to get you, Mommy, so we can get married and live together. Forever."

Laughing and crying at the same time, Barbara squeezed her daughter's hand and reached out for Chad's hand, too. A one-in-a-million chance that Chad could be Missy's father. A one-in-a-million chance that she could be her mother. She'd won the biggest lottery life offered, had gained riches beyond the dreams of kings and queens.

Chad kissed Barbara's hand and folded it against his chest, where she could feel his heart thundering with bliss, and in that moment, her chest swelled with a sensation so alien, so filling, she realized it had swallowed every ounce of despair that had once taken residence there. "You know, I have a hunch that my mother and sister are smiling down on us with approval."

"I think so, too," Chad said, his eyes alight with adoration. He crooked his pinkie finger around hers. "No more walls."

She nodded. "No more fears."

He squeezed his finger with hers. "Just love, trust, and—"

"Commitment," they said together.

Take 4 bestselling love stories FREE

Plus get a FREE surprise gift!

Special Limited-time Offer

Mail to Harlequin Reader Service®

3010 Walden Avenue
P.O. Box 1867
Buffalo, N.Y. 14240-1867

YES! Please send me 4 free Harlequin Intrigue® novels and my free surprise gift. Then send me 4 brand-new novels every month. Bill me at the low price of $2.94 each plus 25¢ delivery and applicable sales tax, if any.* That's the complete price and a savings of over 10% off the cover prices—quite a bargain! I understand that accepting the books and gift places me under no obligation ever to buy any books. I can always return a shipment and cancel at any time. Even if I never buy another book from Harlequin, the 4 free books and the surprise gift are mine to keep forever.

181 BPA A3UQ

Name	(PLEASE PRINT)	
Address	Apt. No.	
City	State	Zip

This offer is limited to one order per household and not valid to present Harlequin Intrigue® subscribers. *Terms and prices are subject to change without notice. Sales tax applicable in N.Y.

UINT-696

©1990 Harlequin Enterprises Limited

COMING NEXT MONTH

#441 HER HERO by Aimée Thurlo
Four Winds
Navajo healer Joshua Blackhorse was the one man who could help
Nydia Jim keep a promise to her son—and save a life. But when she
arrived in Four Winds she found Joshua accused of a terrible crime.

#442 HEART OF THE NIGHT by Gayle Wilson
Driven by a need she told herself was professional curiosity,
Kate August delved into the mystery of Thorne Barrington, the only
living victim of a serial bomber. But for what need did she follow him
into the darkness, determined to find the heart of the mystery…and
the man?

#443 A REAL ANGEL by Cassie Miles
Avenging Angels
It was Rafe Santini's job to stop an outbreak of a deadly virus.
Making love to his earthly assistant Jenna wasn't part of his duties. In
all his years as an Avenging Angel, Rafe had never been tempted by
the sins of the flesh. Why now, when so many lives were at stake?

#444 FAMILY TIES by Joanna Wayne
When Ashley's husband was nearly killed, she went into hiding,
taking with her the best part of Dillon Randolph—his baby. It took
three years for Dillon to find her and now he wanted her and his child
to come home to Texas. Surely now it'd be safe to be together
again…or was it?

AVAILABLE THIS MONTH:

#437 FATHER AND CHILD
Rebecca York

#438 LITTLE GIRL LOST
Adrianne Lee

#439 BEFORE THE FALL
Patricia Rosemoor

#440 ANGEL WITH AN ATTITUDE
Carly Bishop

Look us up on-line at: http://www.romance.net

Free Gift Offer

With a Free Gift proof-of-purchase
from any Harlequin® book, you can receive
a beautiful cubic zirconia pendant.

This stunning marquise-shaped stone is a genuine cubic
zirconia—accented by an 18" gold tone necklace.
(Approximate retail value $19.95)

Send for yours today...
compliments of ✦HARLEQUIN®

To receive your free gift, a cubic zirconia pendant, send us one original proof-of-purchase, photocopies not accepted, from the back of any Harlequin Romance®, Harlequin Presents®, Harlequin Temptation®, Harlequin Superromance®, Harlequin Intrigue®, Harlequin American Romance®, or Harlequin Historicals® title available at your favorite retail outlet, together with the Free Gift Certificate, plus a check or money order for $1.65 U.S./$2.15 CAN. (do not send cash) to cover postage and handling, payable to Harlequin Free Gift Offer. We will send you the specified gift. Allow 6 to 8 weeks for delivery. Offer good until December 31, 1997, or while quantities last. Offer valid in the U.S. and Canada only.

Free Gift Certificate

Name: _____

Address: _____

City: _____ State/Province: _____ Zip/Postal Code: _____

Mail this certificate, one proof-of-purchase and a check or money order for postage and handling to: HARLEQUIN FREE GIFT OFFER 1997. In the U.S.: 3010 Walden Avenue, P.O. Box 9071, Buffalo NY 14269-9057. In Canada: P.O. Box 604, Fort Erie, Ontario L2Z 5X3.

FREE GIFT OFFER   084-KEZ

ONE PROOF-OF-PURCHASE
To collect your fabulous FREE GIFT, a cubic zirconia pendant, you must include this
original proof-of-purchase for each gift with the properly completed Free Gift Certificate.

084-KEZR